SACRIFICIAL GROUND

Also by Thomas H. Cook

Blood Innocents
The Orchids
Tabernacle
Elena

SACRIFICIAL GROUND

THOMAS H. COOK

G. P. Putnam's Sons
New York

G. P. Putnam's Sons
Publishers Since 1838
200 Madison Avenue
New York, NY 10016

Library of Congress Cataloging-in-Publication Data

Cook, Thomas H.
Sacrificial Ground / Thomas H. Cook
p.   cm.
I. Title
PS3553.055465S2   1988
813'.54—dc 19
ISBN 0-399-13339-9

Printed in the United States of America
1   2   3   4   5   6   7   8   9   10

For Roux Sorden-Martin
Still crazy after all these years

After the first death, there is no other.

Dylan Thomas

1

He drained the last of the bourbon from the glass, then glanced over his shoulder toward the dance floor. The music had slowed, and the dancers were swaying languidly to the country drone of Waylon Jennings. Strings of yellow lights hung like a web above them, bathing them in a hard light. At other places, pink and blue coils of neon formed themselves into longhorn steers and cowboy hats.

Frank turned back to the bar and tapped his empty glass.

The bartender stepped up. He was dressed in a bright red western shirt with pearl-handled six-guns embroidered on the shoulders. "Another bourbon?" he asked.

Frank nodded.

The bartender filled the glass, and stepped away.

Frank took a drink, then swiveled around on the stool. The place was called The Bottom Rail, and it was not his favorite spot on earth, but the drinks were cheap, the music loud, and the smoke thick and engulfing. Across the dance floor, he could see a large bearded man in bib overalls smoking a Mississippi Crook. It was a zigzag-shaped, whiskey-soaked cigar, and he had not seen one since he'd left the piney woods of the Alabama north country eighteen years ago to come to Atlanta. He remembered a game he'd played with a few friends, something they called "smoke-out," which was nothing more than six people in a car in the summer and all of them smoking Mississippi Crooks until someone finally broke and ran gasping from the car. Summer had not seemed so terrible then. He'd had the high, cool streams and the shady pine breaks of the mountains. He shook his head slightly, remembering them. But in Atlanta, summer became a nightmare of thick, motionless heat which everything made worse, the steaming pavement and sweltering sidewalks, the glass towers baking in the sun.

They had found her in the summer, three years ago, his daughter, Sarah, just sixteen, her body blackened and bloated after only a few days in the woods. From the distance she had looked almost twice her size, a huge black doll in his daughter's dress. She'd parked her car by the river and wandered off for miles into the surrounding forest in search of the right place to die. Suicide. "You shouldn't see her," Alvin had said as they moved nearer to the spot. "You know what it's like." But he'd rushed ahead and found her there, a swollen mass decaying in the heat. Dropping to his knees, he'd noticed that some animal had already made a feast of her hands.

Frank stood up slowly, and felt the room shift around him, grabbed the barstool and steadied himself for a moment, then began to walk toward the tables at the other end of the bar. He could feel the whiskey sloshing onto his hand as he walked. He could almost feel its heavy warmth soaking up his blood. His legs were going. He knew that instantly. They weren't exactly numb, but they were getting there. Everything was getting there. Even the country-rock on the jukebox was slow and muffled, as if the needle were grinding to a halt.

He sat down and continued his surveillance. He could tell that they were the usual mixed group, everything from country boys washed in from La Grange, to junior stockbrokers who routinely reached for credit cards in places where everybody else reached for a knife. All the faces were familiar. There was a factory worker looking for a night's entertainment from some old lush who couldn't make it home alone, a skinny, blond-haired type who'd probably just taken it up the arm in a Cabbagetown flat, and across the room, sunk into a shadowy corner, a silent, sleepless drifter with an edge.

Frank shook his head groggily. "The Animal Kingdom," he muttered. His three-word phrase for life.

Still, though it wasn't the top of the world, it wasn't the bottom either. He still preferred hazy nights and honky-tonk bars to the milky squash of his brother Alvin's life, its flat, suburban stupor. For a moment he saw Alvin in his mind, balding, overweight, saddled with a dull, imperishable goodness. He had grown up a perfect flower in the garden of his father's righteousness. He had sat through those endless, screeching Holiness services without so much as a blink of disbelief. Frank could remember how sternly his own dissolution had been compared to Alvin's flawless rectitude, how all his life he had been made to play Cain to his brother's Abel. Alvin Jesus-jumped among the pews like a Shawnee brave, whooping and crying out in holy tongues while the congregation reeled in frenzy or slithered about on the church floor. The old man had renamed him Abednego, after one of the prophets who had walked unharmed through fire. Then he had turned to Frank and said, "You are Daniel, who tamed the lions." Daniel had been able to do that, Frank knew, but as for himself, he had never been able to tame anything, not one hungry lion, not the one in his belly, or the one in his heart.

He felt his head grow suddenly very heavy, and he allowed it to droop forward toward the table. The scrawled writing which had been carved into its scarred wooden surface swam into his view: names and initials, obscenities and crude limericks, the poetry of the pocketknife. Then he closed his eyes.

When he opened them again, he could tell almost instantly that the mood of the bar had changed. Only the rogues were left. People with homes were in them; people with lovers were with them. The rest were all around him, grim and sullen, their moods darkening with each passing second.

He wanted to leave, but he could tell that his legs had not quite returned to life. He closed his eyes for a moment, then opened them sharply. He did not want to pass out and get dragged out onto the sidewalk like a sack of empty bottles. That was the fate Alvin expected for him, and Sheila, his ex-wife, and countless other righteous souls.

Slowly, groggily, he raised himself to his feet and made his way to the bar. The bartender moved over to him. "We're closing," he said. "You want a cab?"

"No," Frank said.

"Okay." The bartender pulled him forward quickly, then guided him to the back door. "Take care of yourself," he said. Then he stepped back into the bar and closed the door.

Frank stood motionlessly at the center of the alley. In the distance, a single streetlamp threw a circle of graying light toward him, but its hard glare hurt his eyes, and so he turned in the opposite direction and stumbled forward down the darkening alleyway. He could hear the scuff of his shoes against the gravelly earth, and for what seemed many hours, this was all he heard.

But after that, a voice.

"Where you headed, buddy?"

Suddenly, he saw a face, very near to his own, and then another beside it, dark and bearded.

"I said, where you headed?"

Frank said nothing, and the voice, when he heard it again, seemed harder than before.

"Now, you didn't spend all your money on whiskey, did you, son?"

"Home," Frank said softly, answering the first question.

"What?"

He started to repeat it, but then he felt himself thrown backward with tremendous force, his body lifted first with one blow, then another, until he felt his back plunge against a wall. They were hitting him hard in the chest and belly, and he could hear the sounds of their fists as they rocked him left and right.

"Stand him up!"

He felt the grip of two enormous hands on his coat as they wrenched him up and slammed him once again against the wall.

"Check his pockets."

The fists released him, and his head fell forward as his body began slowly to slide down the wall toward the ground.

Another voice said, "Six fucking bucks."

"Pull him up."

He was sliding up the wall, his back scraping against the rough brick.

"Right there."

He knew that he was standing again, and that the fist was coming toward his face like a hard, white light. Beyond the lights, he could hear the whirr of the fist as it plunged through the air toward him, and the voices around, and the helpless, broken groan that came from inside him. He heard them over and over until something hit the ground as he slumped forward again, a piece of metal which clattered onto the street.

"Oh, Jesus Christ," someone said.

And instantly, he knew that they had gone, had left him sprawled out in the alley. He opened one eye, then another, and he could see what had frightened them, what had dropped from his pocket, and now shined toward him from the gutterwash. He squinted fiercely to keep it in his view, and realized that he could make out the details, but no longer the design: POLICE ATLANTA.

2

It was four in the morning when the phone rang, and Alvin Clemons did not move to answer it. It rang a second time, then a third, and finally his wife, Mildred, shifted over to the nightstand, flipped on the lamp and answered it herself.

"For you," she said, tapping the receiver lightly on her husband's shoulder.

Alvin turned over onto his back and took the phone. "Yeah?"

The voice on the other end belonged to Fred Pitman, a homicide lieutenant who was manning the graveyard shift at the headquarters on Somerset Terrace.

"It's Frank," Pitman said. "Again. Only this time somebody gave him a pretty bad beating."

Alvin sat up quickly. "Beating?"

"That's right," Pitman said. "Outside that place over on Glenwood, the Bottom Rail."

"Dear God," Alvin whispered. He glanced knowingly at Mildred, who shook her head despairingly.

"Two patrolmen are with him," Pitman continued, "rookies, more or less, but they know how to keep their mouths shut."

"Good," Alvin said, "you make sure they do. I'll be there in about twenty minutes."

He hung up and rolled himself out of the bed.

"Somebody beat him up, Alvin?" Mildred asked.

Alvin pulled a shirt from the doorknob of his closet. "Yeah."

"Sheila did the right thing letting him go," Mildred said.

"I guess," Alvin said. He buttoned the first button, then the second, hoping Mildred would just shut up about it.

"Someday you'll have to, Alvin," she said. "Let him go, I mean."

He buttoned the last button, then grabbed for his pants. "He's my brother, Mildred."

"And you've done everything you can for him," Mildred said. "Brought him to Atlanta, got him on the force. What else is expected? Huh? What else?"

"His daughter killed herself," Alvin said, suddenly looking his wife straight in the eye. "Who knows what I might do if Maryann did that."

"He was on his way already," Mildred said, almost disgustedly.

Alvin tightened his belt, grabbed his pistol from the top shelf of the closet and fled the room. "Get some sleep," he said as he closed the door. "I'll call you when I know the details."

Mildred waved her hand. "Don't bother."

The drive in from Decatur took longer than he expected, but the two patrolmen were still waiting when he got there. They were both standing idly in the alley, one of them smoking a cigarette, the other sipping at a can of Pepsi. They straightened themselves quickly as Alvin got out of the car and began walking toward them.

"How bad is he?" Alvin asked.

"He took a pounding," one of the officers said. "We've got him in the back of the car here."

Alvin bent over and peered into the rear of the patrol car. He could see Frank balled up in the seat, his arms folded around his midsection, his knees pulled up toward his chest.

"Dear God," Alvin said.

"He didn't want to be taken anywhere," one of the patrolmen said.

Alvin glanced at the identification tag on his uniform: Billings. "You been on the force long?" he asked him.

"No, sir," Billings said.

Alvin nodded. "Well, you did the right thing calling Homicide. We'll keep this an in-house operation."

Billings reached into the pocket of his uniform and pulled out a badge. "We found this on the street. That's what tipped us off."

Alvin took the badge and dropped it into his pants pocket. "Thanks. I'm much obliged to both of you." He opened the back door of the patrol car and pulled Frank out, bringing him ponderously to his feet. "Come on, little brother," he whispered. "Let's get you home."

It was almost dawn by the time Alvin finally managed to drag Frank up the stairs and deposit him on the stained green sofa that sat in the middle of the living room.

It was a dingy room, with unpainted walls and a linoleum-covered floor. There were no pictures on the walls, no curtains on the windows, just a set of venetian blinds which drooped to the left and rattled softly when the wind blew through the blades.

"You ought to dump this place, Frank," Alvin said as he brought a wet dishcloth in from the small kitchen and began gently daubing the bruises on his brother's face.

Frank brushed his hand away. "No more Good Samaritan shit, Alvin." He nodded toward the chair opposite the sofa. "Sit down. Relax. I'm all right."

"No, you're not," Alvin said. He dropped the cloth into Frank's lap. "Do it yourself, then."

Frank picked up the cloth and held it against one swollen eye. "Thanks for coming to get me," he said quietly.

Alvin nodded quickly. "What happened?"

Frank shrugged. "There were a few of them. I'll settle up."

Alvin leaned forward in his seat. "No, you won't, Frank. You either file a formal complaint and let the department handle it—I mean a formal complaint, the paperwork, everything—you either do that, or you forget it." He shook his head exasperatedly. "You can come into headquarters in the morning looking like you just got hit by a bus. That's fine, no questions asked. It's all been handled. But you go after those guys, that's it, Frank. You're hanging by a thread anyway, and I can tell you, the department'll slam-dunk you for the smallest thing. You might say, they're looking for a reason."

Frank glanced away wearily, his eyes staring at the naked bulb which hung in the small kitchen.

"You're a good man, Frank," Alvin said, with a sudden gentleness, "but you got bad weaknesses. Remember what Daddy used to say: 'The weakest thing in the world is a strong man who can't control himself.' "

Frank shifted his eyes over toward his brother, but said nothing.

"I mean, you got to pull it all back together somehow, Frank," Alvin continued. "You got to learn to finish things. You know what I mean? You went to college for three years, busted your butt in night school, then, after all that, dropped out." He shook his head. "Then you married Sheila." He squinted slightly. "How long you married to her, eighteen, nineteen years?"

"Twenty," Frank said.

"Then divorce, after all that time."

"I married her when I was nineteen and she was seventeen, Alvin," Frank said.

"So what? It's still the same problem," Alvin said. "You don't finish things."

Frank swabbed his neck with the dishcloth. It felt very cool against the morning heat that was beginning to rise all around him.

Alvin looked at Frank pointedly. "Sheila wasn't so bad," he said. "Okay, maybe you two weren't made for each other. Who is, Frank? Grow up." He glanced around the room, taking in its dishevelment. "At least she kept a clean house, had a hot meal on the table for you when you came home."

"That's not a marriage, Alvin."

"And this, the way you're living, you call this a life?"

"It'll do," Frank said quietly. He stood up, walked to the window and parted the blinds. "I'm on duty today at eight."

"I got the afternoon tour," Alvin said wearily.

Frank released the blinds and returned to the sofa. "How's Mildred these days?" he asked.

"She'll do," Alvin said. "Says maybe I should let you go, just like Sheila did."

Frank shrugged. "Well, maybe you should, Alvin. I mean, what the hell, right?" He cleared his throat roughly, then changed the subject. "How's Maryann?"

"Fine," Alvin said. "Dating a quarterback." He reached into his pocket, pulled out the badge and tossed it to Frank. "Patrolmen found this in the alley."

Frank placed the badge on the small table in front of the sofa. "I'll thank them."

"Where was your service revolver?" Alvin asked pointedly.

"I left it home."

"You're supposed to have it with you all the time."

"I don't think that's a good idea for me."

"Could have saved you a beating."

"Or got me something worse, like a manslaughter rap if I'd smoked one of those guys."

"Still regulations, Frank," Alvin said. "Next time, take it with you." He stood up. "I'm heading home now." He glanced at his watch. "Might be able to grab an hour of shut-eye."

The phone rang as Frank stood up to walk his brother to the door. He answered it immediately. It was Pitman at headquarters, making a last call before leaving duty.

"You fit for a tour?" Pitman asked.

"Yeah."

"We've got a body off Glenwood. Feel like checking it out?"

"Okay," Frank said. He reached for the small pad beside the phone and copied down the address as Pitman gave it to him.

"Sure you're up for it, Frank?" Pitman asked.

"Yeah, I'm fine," Frank said, trying to bring some lightness into his voice. "Just a little tussle."

He hung up and glanced at Alvin, who was poised, waiting, at the door.

"What is it?" Alvin asked.

"A body."

Alvin smiled wearily. "Oh," he said, "one of those."

———————

Caleb Stone was already at the scene when Frank arrived. He was the old man of the division, full of what appeared almost ancient wisdom about the ways of men and murder. He'd been born into a tenant farmer family in south Georgia, and his early years had been spent picking a rich man's cotton from dawn to dusk. He'd moved to Atlanta at the age of twenty, brought there by his mother, who worked in the huge brick textile mill which still stood at the border of Cabbagetown, and which, in a sense, served as its monument, towering over the unpainted wooden tenements in which its workers lived.

Caleb lumbered over to meet Frank and squinted hard. "Heard you had a little trouble," he said, "but I didn't figure you for this kind of whupping."

"Three of them," Frank explained.

They were standing at the edge of a large deserted lot. The surrounding buildings were squat, brick constructions, an evangelical storefront church stood at one corner of the lot, a small auto parts store at the other.

"Nice neighborhood," Caleb said with a slight grin. "Ask God what the trouble with the Ford is, then march right over and buy the part."

"What have we got here, Caleb?" Frank asked.

"What we got, Frank," Caleb says, "is something that gives new meaning to the phrase 'shallow grave.' "

"Meaning what?"

"Meaning we got a body dumped in a hole and sort of covered over with dirt and grass and garbage, whatever was around that could be thrown on her."

"Her?"

"A woman. From the look of it, more like a girl."

"I see," Frank said.

"Young girl. Pretty," Caleb said. "That sort of puts the cherry on top."

"How'd she die?" Frank asked.

"Don't know yet," Caleb said. "Photo car didn't get here yet, and we can't move a thing till after the pictures." He turned and pointed toward the center of the lot. A few patrolmen could be seen erecting crime-scene barriers and roping off the entire area. Knots of people, all of them black, stood staring at them from across the adjoining streets.

Caleb lit his pipe and eyed the crowd. "People do love to stare, don't they?" He smiled. "I remember back in the forties, Frank, why, hell, a few cops would take off through a neighborhood like this at full steam, siren louder'n hell, just shooting their pistols into the air." He laughed. "Hiyo Silver, away." He chuckled. "No more of that."

"You didn't ever do that, did you, Caleb?" Frank asked.

Caleb turned from the crowd to look at Frank. "Once or twice," he said softly, "but I stopped before I lost my soul. There's not a black in this division don't come to me for help now." He turned back toward the vacant lot. "Funny thing is, the girl, she's white." He looked back at Frank. "It's little things like that, Frank, that make life interesting."

Frank did not answer. He looked away from Caleb and over to the vacant lot. It was high with summer weeds, dandelions and goldenrods. Kudzu twined about the rusty hulk of an old car at the far rear of the lot, and two patrolmen were already slogging through the thick growth of ragweed and briar to search it.

Caleb pulled a red handkerchief from his back pocket and wiped his balding head. "Going to be a hot one, looks like."

"They all are, this time of year," Frank said indifferently. "Well, I'll go take a look."

It was only about twenty yards from the sidewalk to the body, but it was heavy going all the way. The ground was pitted as if it had been under mortar fire, and the surrounding weeds grew more and more thickly as Frank neared the small patch of barren ground where the body lay.

"Morning, Lieutenant," one of the uniformed officers said as Frank trudged forward.

Frank instantly recognized him as one of the men who'd pulled him up from the gutter only a few hours before. "You've had a busy morning, I guess," he said.

The officer smiled sheepishly. "Yes, sir, I guess I have."

Caleb came slogging through the brush, still mopping his face and neck. "Goddamn," he blurted, "nothing but briar bushes and huckleberries in this whole damn lot." He stopped, and nodded toward a group of patrolmen who stood at some distance talking quietly and glancing toward the ground.

"Right yonder, Frank," Caleb said, pointing to a break in the undergrowth. "We found her fast, so it's not too bad."

Together, they walked slowly over to a dusty area of ground and looked down.

Caleb pocketed his handkerchief, his eyes fixed, almost lovingly, on the body which lay sprawled before him. "I don't care what they say, you don't ever get used to it," he said. He glanced at Frank. "That's what makes us good, Frank, we don't ever get used to it."

The body lay face up in a shallow gully, and by the time the police photographers arrived, Frank felt as if he had been staring at it most of his life. Caleb stood beside him, pointing out various details, the lack of bloodstains in the parched ground which surrounded her, the lack of cuts or bruises, except on her feet and ankles (which were probably made by the body's being dragged through the briar of the lot), the fact that the wrists were not lacerated, nor the throat. Caleb ticked off the meaning of these things methodically.

"So, from the look of it," he concluded, "I'd say the lab boys will have to put a label on this one. Wasn't shot, stabbed or strangled. Surely wasn't beaten up." He took a draw on his pipe. "What do you think, Frank? Poison?" He tapped his shoe against the ground. "Too hard for footprints."

Frank allowed his eyes to peruse the body head to foot. Summer winds had blown away most of the dust and debris with which someone had hastily covered it. He could make out the facial features quite easily. Her hair was blonde, her eyes blue, her skin pale, almost chalky. She had a full mouth with rather thick lips, and Frank could even make out that her teeth, at least the lower set, were perfectly even. She wore a light blue, shortsleeve blouse and a dark blue skirt with a white belt and gold buckle. There was a leather sandal strapped loosely to one foot, but the other was bare. She was of medium build and medium height. Frank guessed her at about five-four and one hundred ten pounds.

"What do you think, around sixteen?" Caleb asked.

"About that," Frank said.

The photo crew were all around him now, taking shots from all directions. Frank and Caleb stepped back slightly to give them the angles they demanded.

Caleb tapped the pipe against the heel of his shoe, spilling the rest of the tobacco onto the ground.

"They'll find that damn tobacco and bag it as evidence, Caleb," Frank said.

"Naw, they won't," Caleb said, with an old-pro smile, "because I'll tell them it's Prince Albert from my own bowl." He glanced about, taking in the few structures which stood in the vicinity. "No bedroom window for some sleepless bastard to be standing at last night when the body was dropped." He placed the pipe in his jacket pocket. "They'll canvass their asses off, but it won't do any good. Just for looks, that's why they'll do it." He smiled. " 'Cause we fucked up that child-murders thing." He looked at Frank. "Everything by the book from now on. But it won't make a goddamn bit of difference, and it'll waste a hell of a lot of time." He lifted his head slightly and called to one of the patrolmen. "Hey, tell the boys from the lab crew that this tobacco down here belongs to Caleb Stone."

The patrolman nodded, then gave him the thumbs-up sign.

Caleb turned back to Frank. "That ought to cover my ass." He slapped his behind. "And this old ass needs a lot of covering."

He ambled away then, tramping through the waist-high brush until he had made it back to his car.

Frank watched him as he drove away. Caleb was one of the few men in the department whom he either liked or respected. He wasn't very bright, but he was full of a kind of noble doggedness. He did his job well, and kept his troubles to himself. He had never asked about Sarah or the divorce, never pried into Frank's private life or opened up about his own. Even after years in the city, he had held to that backwoods silence in which Frank himself had been reared, and which he still admired, almost as a lovely artifact; it was a rare individual in modern, bustling Atlanta who still possessed it.

"We'll be through in a moment, Lieutenant," Charlie Morton, the police photographer, said.

"Take your time," Frank said casually. "Do it right."

Charlie stepped to his side and took a shot. "Looks like she just laid down and died," he said. He stepped around to the other side of the body, bent forward and snapped another picture. "Just walked out here and found herself a little spot of ground and laid right down," Charlie repeated.

"With just one sandal?" Frank asked.

Charlie looked up quickly and smiled. "I guess that's why I just take the pictures, right?" He snapped another picture. "Pretty much caught her from every angle now, Frank." He looked at the body. "Well, maybe one more." He took a final photograph, waved that he was finished and hurried away to the photo car.

Frank motioned to a stretcher team which stood by. "All right, you can take her out."

The two men moved in and slowly lifted the body onto the stretcher. Frank walked over and gently checked the girl's clothes for identification. There wasn't any. Only a class ring on her finger, which he removed and placed in a plastic bag. He lifted the bag, twisting it right and left. The ring was from Northfield Academy, Class of 1987. He handed the bag to one of the patrolmen who stood near him.

"Take it to the lab," he told him, "then radio headquarters to send a car over and pick up a copy of their latest yearbook. We'll need to ID her right away."

"Yes, Lieutenant," the patrolman said as he hurried away.

Frank looked down at the body once again. The bearers had lifted the stretcher from the ground and were standing motionless in the growing heat, waiting for the signal to take it to the morgue. They

26

had waited in the same rigid way after they'd picked up Sarah's body, and he could not help but remember the silence that had gathered around him at that moment. It was as if the world had gone suddenly mute. The bearers had said nothing. Alvin had said nothing. And two hours later when he broke the news to his wife, she had simply sunk down on the sofa, stared vacantly at the empty fireplace and said absolutely nothing. Now, as he nodded quickly and the bearers moved forward through the bramble, it struck him that that first, terrible silence had not yet been broken, that he was still locked in it, as his wife was and Alvin was and as Sarah must have been for many years before she died. He could remember her alone in her room, in the front yard, by the living room window, always distant, unreachable, born to that deep, brooding silence which he'd feared in his father and then in himself and which had been passed down to Sarah like a poison in the blood.

He watched as the bearers pushed the stretcher into the back of the ambulance. One of the girl's arms had dropped over the side and now dangled loosely toward the ground, palm out, fingers open, as if silently begging him for help.

3

It was only an hour later when Caleb lumbered into headquarters and dropped a single slender volume on Frank's desk. It was ice blue with gold lettering: Northfield Academy.

"Page eighty-seven," Caleb said.

Frank opened the book and flipped through it until he reached the right page.

"Third column down, fourth one over."

Frank's eyes followed the line of photographs until he reached the picture of a young girl whose smile beamed back at him from an open, innocent face.

"Right pretty," Caleb said, "before the devil took her."

She was considerably more than pretty, and as Frank continued to gaze at the photograph, he was struck by how much death had slackened her flesh and dulled her eyes until all her former beauty had been drained away.

Caleb's eyes held sadly to the photograph, then shifted to the one of the girl as she lay on her back in the dust. He seemed to sink into the picture, or soak it up. Then he shook his head wearily.

"Dead folks always look like they been left out in the rain," he said.

Frank glanced at the column of names which bordered the left side of the page.

"Laura Angelica Devereaux," he said softly.

"Most folks called her Angelica," Caleb told him.

Frank glanced up from the book. "Who says?"

"Principal over at Northfield," Caleb said. "Fancy school. They call them headmasters over there." He shrugged. "Guess they don't have principals at rich-kid schools."

"What's his name?"

"Albert Morrison."

"What else did he tell you?"

"Well, a few things," Caleb said. He pulled a chair over from another desk and sat down. The early morning light that beamed in from the large windows swept over him, casting one side of his face in deep shadow. "Her parents are dead," he added casually, "but she's got some family. A sister, named Karen. Age approximately twenty-seven; the sister, I mean. Lives at Two-fifty-five West Paces Ferry Road." He smiled. "Ever been out that way?"

Frank glanced down at Caleb's large, beefy hands.

"Don't you carry a notebook?" he asked.

Caleb shook his head, then tapped one side of it with his index finger. "Keep everything up here, Frank. Know why? 'Cause if you do, it means nobody else can get at it." His eyes rolled up toward the ceiling. "Where was I? Oh, yeah. Two-fifty-five West Paces Ferry Road. Ever been out that way?"

"For a Sunday drive," Frank said indifferently. He glanced back down at the photographs on his desk, and suddenly Laura Angelica Devereaux came back into his mind, walked into it like a beautiful woman into an empty room, and he saw the flash of her eyes, felt, very softly, the touch of her young breath.

"Heard anything from the lab?" Caleb asked.

"No."

"Doing a quadrant search?"

Frank nodded. "They're stringing the wire now."

Caleb looked away and called to a passing patrolman. "Hey, Teddy, put a star in your crown and bring me a Coke, will you?"

He turned back to Frank. "What are you planning to do about those guys that bummed you up?"

Frank continued to stare at the photograph. For an instant he thought he saw her lips curl down in a thin, frightened line, and he glanced up quickly at her dead eyes, as if he might find some image of her killer still lingering like a phantom on the tightly closed lids.

"You going to get even with them, Frank?"

"I'm just going to file a report, Caleb," Frank told him.

Caleb laughed.

"No, I mean it," Frank said. "I'm just going to file a report and let it go. Hell, they're probably in Mexico by now."

Caleb shrugged. "Could be, Frank, could be. But it's been my experience that you make them pay real early for something like this. 'Cause if you don't, it just gets worse. They start off with something small like whipping the shit out of a cop; then, before long, they're running out on their rent, or not paying the power bill." He laughed again. "You just can't trust people. That's a true fact, unrecorded, Frank." He shook his head. "If I was God, I'd keep one free hand on everybody's balls."

The patrolman appeared with Caleb's drink.

"Thank you, son," Caleb said. He took a long, slow pull on the bottle, then wiped his mouth with his fist. "I can drink whiskey like this, too."

Frank drew his eyes from the photographs, then squinted slightly in the hard summer light. "Did Morrison say anything else?"

"I didn't press him much," Caleb said. "He was a nervous little shit. The type that likes to keep his job, you know?" He took another swig of Coke. "Anyway, I told him you'd be dropping by one day soon." He smiled. "I'll let you handle this one, Frank. Your record could use a good collar."

"If I can get it."

"Well, if he's a drifter, forget it," Caleb said. "But if he's got a little house somewhere, and a car payment, a whole lot of little shitty things he's got to keep track of . . ."

"Then we've got him," Frank said.

"If he's like us, only just a little different," Caleb added, "then the hook's already in his mouth." He drained the last of the Coke, then set the bottle down on Frank's desk. "It's your case, Frank, but if you get something solid, let me know. I'll help you work it."

"Okay."

"Unless you'd rather share the pie with Alvin?"

"Fuck Alvin."

Caleb smiled. "Lord, I'd hate to be the one that does." He grabbed the edge of Frank's desk and hauled himself to his feet. He groaned loudly, then stood quietly for a moment, as if trying to secure his balance. "Little top-heavy," he said, patting his stomach. Then his eyes drifted slowly over to the photograph of Angelica's body as it lay sprawled in the lot. He shook his head despairingly. "Brotherly love," he said. "Ever see any of that, Frank?"

Frank looked up at him. "Yes, I have."

Caleb smiled knowingly. "Good for you. It's only the bullshitters that say no." He turned slowly and walked away, his great frame crashing through the shaft of light as if it were a pane of glass.

Frank looked down at the pictures once again, but only for an instant. There was nothing to see, a girl alive, a girl dead, one in color, the other in black and white. The faces hardly seemed to belong to the same person, and their bodies to the same world: one was held rigidly before the camera, the chin lifted proudly, the eyes staring straight ahead; the other was laid out in the grimy lot, the fingers, toes and arms already beginning to assume death's grotesque contortions.

He took a pair of scissors and cut out the picture of Angelica from the Northfield yearbook. The photo lab could print thirty or forty of them for distribution, but he would keep the original, as if there were something in it which could not be duplicated, which might speak to him suddenly or rise from it like an accusing finger, pointing directly at her killer's eyes.

Once he'd cut the picture out, he shoved it into his coat pocket, leaned back in his chair and allowed his eyes to roam the surrounding room. He'd felt alone after Caleb left, but he suddenly realized that the room was dotted with plainclothes and uniformed policemen. They milled about in the far corner, and stood idly by the water fountain. He could hear the low hum of their conversation and the clatter of their typewriters as they moved through the motions of their separate investigations. The air was thick with the heavy smell of cigars and cigarettes. There was something raw and terribly male in the atmosphere, a grim potential for sudden, annihilating violence against which the pastel, parti-colored wall seemed as hopelessly out of place as a circus tent in a slaughterhouse.

To escape, he retrieved the photograph of Angelica and laid it flat down on his desk. For a moment he concentrated on her face. She had the beauty of a young girl on the brink of womanhood, waiting for experience, perhaps hungry for it, but still in some odd, indiscernible way, innocent and unknowing. It was a quality he'd seen in girls far less well-off than Angelica must have been. He'd seen it in the faces of fifteen-year-old hustlers. It didn't matter what they'd seen or done, or what had been done to them. The innocence remained. It was in their youth, and it stubbornly maintained itself in every young girl's face. It was a look in their eyes, a sense of something still salvageable no matter how much it had already been ruined, abused, wasted. It stayed as long as youth remained, and left when it was gone. There were times when he'd looked up from his newspaper and caught that same look in Sarah's eyes. He'd seen it unobserved as she'd sat, staring vacantly at the television, her legs drawn up into the big orange chair, and he thought now that the birds must have seen it too as they leaped about the limbs above her, and watched that innocence fade day by day to black.

He stood up quickly and walked out onto the street. The heat closed around him like a fist, and for a moment he wanted only to plunge through it into another, cooler world. He imagined the wide boulevard of West Paces Ferry Road to be exactly that kind of world: spacious green lawns, bright blue swimming pools that glinted in the summer sun, a place where the grit of the city fell away as surely as the heat, and there was only the deep, consoling quiet and the cool, engulfing shade.

Angelica Devereaux had been born into such a place, Frank thought, as he made his way down to the garage and pulled himself in behind the wheel of his car, but she'd ended up in a different world altogether, a seedy, vacant lot on Glenwood Avenue.

As he pulled into the steady downtown traffic of Peachtree Street,

Frank realized that the most logical explanation for Angelica's journey from West Paces Ferry to Glenwood Avenue was also the most obvious: she was a rich girl who had a taste for slumming. He'd seen that before, too, an attraction for the low-rent world of seedy hotels and backstreet clubs. Something flourished in such places that lay dormant in the stately mansions of the Northside, a rough, teeming life that cocktail parties and debutante balls could not match for action and adventure. From time to time, young boys or girls would dip their toes into that seamy current, then a foot, then a leg, until they were way over their heads in the swirling peril of a life whose lethal undertows they could not possibly imagine. They washed up on strange shores, gambling dens, crack parlors, redneck bars and whorehouses. He'd seen perhaps a hundred such people in his time, girls named Porsche or Mercedes, as if for the family cars, and boys named Carlton and Royal, "hotel names," as Caleb always called them. "Hotel face down," he'd say, when one of them would not go home again.

He pulled out his small green notebook and flipped open the first page. He jotted down the name and address Caleb had given him: Karen Devereaux, 255 West Paces Ferry Road. Beside Laura Angelica, Karen sounded as blunt and snub-nosed as Frank's own name, and he almost immediately imagined her as the ugly duckling with the beautiful sister, the one for whom the family had never had much hope.

He pressed down on the accelerator as the traffic cleared slightly near Buckhead. Karen Devereaux. He repeated the name but could find nothing to go with it. He knew only that whoever she was, her life was about to take a dreadful turn. She would soon be told of her younger sister's death, then be driven back downtown to identify the body. He had seen men and women snap like small twigs at such moments. Years before, he had brought a middle-aged woman downtown. She had been small, slight, so weak that she'd appeared almost breathless at the top of the stairs. Her son had been killed by a drunken driver and his body lay in one of the refrigerated vaults the police used as makeshift morgues. She'd stared at her son's face for a long time, utterly silent as she gazed rigidly at the half-crushed skull. Then suddenly, she'd whirled around with terrific speed and slapped Frank's face with all her womanly might. He had actually staggered backward, the heat of her hand still on his skin, his eyes watching, startled, as she'd pressed her back against the wall, slid slowly down and crumpled to the floor.

He was still vaguely thinking of her as he arrived at the Devereaux house. The driveway was circular, and it curved gently in a wide arc around a broad field of neatly pruned shrubs. A line of azaleas bordered it, their bright red flowers shining brightly.

The house looked as if it had been built with something religious in mind, and as he stepped out of the car and stared up toward its tall white columns, Frank thought of the tiny wooden church in which his father had struggled to save the souls of those tormented, guilt-ridden farmers who came to him. The Devereaux house gave off the sense of people who had already been saved from most of the ordinary trials of life. Here no one had ever worried about an early frost or too dry a summer. It rose over the surrounding green as if it held dominion over everything around it. The tall columns stretched up to a wide portico, and the white facade which rested in its shade seemed almost smug in its serenity. It looked like the kind of grand, spacious place which invading armies chose to house their commanding officers, and Frank could easily imagine the conquering Yankee generals who might once have tethered their horses to its tall pillars.

An enormous oak door opened at the second ring of the bell. Frank had expected to see a butler in a black coat, but instead he found a young woman in a paint-dappled artist's smock and tattered blue jeans. She wore unpolished brown loafers, and her long black hair was gathered casually in the back, where it hung in a wild confusion of unruly curls.

She looked at him questioningly, as if he'd ended up at the wrong entrance.

"Yes?" she said.

"Is this the Devereaux house?"

"Yes, it is."

"I'm looking for Karen Devereaux."

"And you are?"

Frank took out his badge. "Frank Clemons."

The woman nodded slowly. Her dark eyes narrowed somewhat as if she were putting it all together, the dusty, battered car, the dusty, battered man in his rumpled brown suit, his swollen, bluish eyes, the bent and tarnished badge.

"I'm Karen Devereaux," she said finally. "What's wrong?"

"Would you mind if I came in?" Frank asked hesitantly.

"All right," Karen said. She stepped back and allowed Frank to walk into the foyer. It was painted white and decked with the portraits of what he guessed to be the more distinguished figures of the Devereaux family, senators, judges, planters, members in good standing of what Caleb always called "the moonlight and magnolia crowd."

Frank reflexively took off his hat and twirled it awkwardly in his hands.

"I'm afraid I have some very bad news for you," he said.

She drew in a slow, calming breath. "I've been through this before," she said.

"Through what?"

"Bad news," Karen said. "My parents were killed in an air crash in Europe. I was just a young girl at the time. A man like you came to the house. He took off his hat like you did, and he kept it in his hands. He kept glancing down at it while he told us." She lifted her face slightly, as if trying to brace herself. "What is it this time?"

"Your sister."

"Dead," Karen said. It was not a question. It was a statement of fact.

"Yes."

Her reaction was a silence so absolute that it seemed to draw everything else into it. Her eyes stared placidly into Frank's, and her lips tightened, as if in a determined effort to hold back the scream that might have broken through them.

"We found her body early this morning," Frank said.

Karen stepped back and grasped the edge of a small table. Her eyes darted from one portrait to another, as if she were communicating this latest family tragedy to the lost, ancestral dead.

"We're not sure what happened to her," Frank added after a moment.

36

She looked at him. "Not sure?"

"No."

"It was some sort of accident?"

He decided to go easy. "We don't know," Frank told her. "We just found her body early this morning." He waited for her to speak. She didn't. "Off Glenwood Avenue," he added.

"I see."

"Did you notice that she didn't come home last night?"

"No."

"Does she live here, Miss Devereaux?"

"Yes, she does," Karen said. "A room upstairs." She drew her hand from the table, and Frank could see the marks her nails had left on its polished surface.

"You'll have to come downtown and identify the body," he said.

"Officially, you mean?"

"Yes."

"So there's no doubt that it's my sister?"

"No doubt. We have a tentative identification from the yearbook at Northfield. She did go to Northfield, didn't she?"

"Yes."

"I could take you downtown now, Miss Devereaux," Frank said. "Or, if you'd rather wait . . ."

"No," Karen said immediately, "I'd rather go now. I don't want to wait."

"All right."

"Just let me change," Karen said.

"Of course."

"I'll be right down."

"There's no rush," Frank told her. He smiled sadly. "I'm very sorry to have to tell you all this."

Karen turned quickly and darted up the stairs.

Alone in the foyer, Frank allowed his eyes to settle on the room. He noticed the immaculately polished table, and the large porcelain vase that rested on top of it. There was a large enameled box beside the vase, black, but with a scene of what looked like European peasants painted on it. Absently, before he could stop himself, Frank opened it. It had a dark red velvet lining, and he ran his finger over it quickly, then closed the lid. He turned his head slowly to the right, and looked at a large portrait of a tall, gray-haired man in a dark blue wing-backed chair. The man sat in a large, book-lined room, and there was a look of enormous pride in his eyes. Perhaps the pride came from his money, or his power, or even from the books which surrounded him, all the vast learning they represented. It was a hard face to read, but in that, it was simply like every other human face. They came in all sizes and configurations, and they divulged nothing. The proud gray man in the book-lined room might be anything, anything at all.

Frank drew his eyes from the portrait and down toward the oriental rug at his feet. He saw Angelica Devereaux's pale, dangling arm as if it were lying among the swirls of red and blue, distinct, yet indistinct, part of an indecipherable intricacy. "Farther along we'll know more about it," he heard his father sing madly at the altar of his mind. "Farther along, we'll understand why."

4

Karen Devereaux looked quite different when she reappeared a few minutes later. The soiled artist's smock had been replaced by a long black skirt and dark red blouse. She had unpinned her hair, and it now hung loosely at her shoulders. She looked somewhat younger because of that, but the emotions Frank had seen rising into her face now seemed even more forcefully contained.

"I'm ready to go now," she said, almost stiffly, and with an air of quiet command.

Frank stepped to the door immediately. "We'll take my car," he told her.

"Yes, all right," Karen replied, "I'd really prefer not to drive right now."

For a time, Frank kept quiet as he drove back toward the city. The wide, shaded lanes no longer seemed as imposing as they had earlier. It was as if something of their invulnerability had been taken from them. The armor of wealth had not been able to protect one of their youngest and most beautiful, and the failure reduced their grandeur, brought them down to human scale once again.

"It is beautiful out here," he said quietly.

Karen said nothing.

"Never seems as hot as it is in the city."

"We have our days," Karen said crisply.

Sitting beside him, her large dark eyes fixed on the road ahead, she seemed extraordinarily composed, considering the news he'd just brought her. She kept her shoulders lifted slightly and her hands folded gracefully in her lap, and as he looked at her, Frank thought that perhaps in a continually shifting and uncertain world, she had learned that only her dignity could be kept in place, that it was the only thing in her life over which she truly had full and personal control.

"There'll be questions, of course," he said.

Karen continued to stare straight ahead. "Yes, I suppose so."

"And it's important to move quickly in something like this," Frank added.

"Yes."

"I'm sure you have a few questions, too," Frank said, still hoping to draw her out, but without coming on too fast.

"You said you didn't notice that she didn't come home last night," he said, finally.

"No, I didn't."

"Is that unusual?"

"That she didn't come home, or that I didn't notice it?" Karen asked.

"Both."

"She had her own room," Karen said stiffly.

"And her own life?"

"Yes, that too."

"What did you know about it?"

"That she kept it to herself."

"What about friends?"

"I don't know if she had any."

Frank looked at her doubtfully.

"I mean, if she had friends, I don't know who they were," Karen explained.

"Other kids, maybe. Didn't anyone ever come by to see her?"

"Not that I know of," Karen said. "I have a studio in the back of the house. I spend a lot of time there. People could come and go; I wouldn't see them." She shrugged. "But as far as I know, Angelica was very isolated."

"It sounds like you are too," Frank said, before he could stop himself.

Karen looked at him sharply. "Maybe I am. So what?"

"Look, I know how people can lose touch," Frank said quickly. "In families, I mean. They can lose touch. My own daughter. It's just that it was only the two of you in the house. That's right, isn't it? Only the two of you?"

"Yes."

"So you had to have some contact," Frank said. "No matter how little, there had to be some."

Karen said nothing. She turned back toward the street and stared straight ahead.

"When a doorbell rings," Frank went on, "someone has to answer it. Was there ever someone there who was looking for Angelica?"

"No," Karen said crisply.

"Never?"

"Not when I was there, no," Karen repeated firmly. "Maybe somewhere else, she had friends."

"On the Southside?" Frank asked pointedly.

Karen did not reply.

"Do you know what Glenwood Avenue looks like?" Frank asked.

"Vaguely," Karen said, almost in a whisper.

"Then you know it's not exactly West Paces Ferry."

"I'm aware of that, yes."

"We don't know exactly what happened to your sister," Frank said, "but she ended up a long way from home."

Karen said nothing. She kept her eyes on the road ahead.

As he glanced at her from time to time, Frank tried to come up with some idea of what she had felt for her sister. He'd had enough experience to know that it was hard to tell where love began or ended in a family. His own mother had appeared to love his father, and yet on one raw afternoon she had simply disappeared, left him with two boys on the brink of manhood and not so much as a note to tell them why.

"I know how it is sometimes," Frank said tentatively. "Sometimes, people just don't get along. Blood's not everything. I know that, believe me. But you did live in the same house as your sister."

She turned toward him. Her eyes widened somewhat, as if she were seeing him for the first time.

"What happened to you?" she asked.

For an instant he thought she meant his life, what had happened to his life, but then he realized that she was asking about his face, the scars and bruises. He touched his left eye and winced slightly.

"I had some trouble," he said.

"In the line of duty?"

"No."

She turned away from him very quickly, almost fearfully, as if she'd found something terribly disturbing in his answer.

They reached the morgue a few minutes later. It was very clean. The tile floors shone brightly and the walls were sleek and white. There was no clutter, no mess, much less any signs of blood or tissue. It was as if the staff was determined to stand up against the terrible disorder which swept up and down its corridors, in and out of its dissecting rooms; murdered wives and husbands, children suffocated in their tiny closets. The broken bodies were little more than the physical remains of something already broken long before, and which the gleaming hallways could not hide.

"How you doing, Frank?" Jesse said as he moved down the long corridor to where Frank and Karen stood beside a small wooden desk.

"Hello, Jesse."

Jesse sauntered up to the desk and took a seat. "Got a problem?"

"We're here to see Angelica Devereaux," Frank told him.

"Got a number?"

"Not yet. The lab work wasn't in when I left headquarters."

"How about a description?"

"Young."

Jesse looked at Frank questioningly.

"Pretty," Frank added.

"Oh, yeah," Jesse said. "She's just come down to us." He looked at a large open accountant's book. "Laura Angelica Devereaux," he repeated, "Number Fifteen." He looked quickly toward Karen. "You with him?"

"Yes."

"Oh," Jesse said softly and with a hint of surprise.

"Miss Devereaux's sister," Frank explained.

Jesse smiled quietly. "Sorry, ma'am. She looked like a nice young girl."

Angelica was the sort who didn't fit the morgue's usual cast of characters, and Frank could see Jesse's curiosity as clearly as if questions were written on his forehead. How had she been caught up in the general web? How did her body end up drenched in a light which usually swept down upon the poor, the deranged, the ones for whom the last wound was very much like the first?

Jesse shifted slightly in his chair. "Anyway, she's in Number Fifteen. I guess you'll be going with her, Frank?"

"Yes."

"Fine, then," Jesse said quietly. "You know where it is. Last door on your right."

"Thanks, Jesse," Frank said. He stepped around the desk and glanced back toward Karen. "This way."

She followed him immediately, keeping to his pace.

Frank opened the door and walked to the wall of refrigerated units which stood at the rear of the room. They were made of stainless steel, and he could see Karen's face reflected in the door of Number Fifteen as he placed his hand on the latch.

"Sometimes, they look a little different," he warned.

"Open it," Karen said.

The latch clicked sharply as Frank drew open the door, and he noticed that Karen's body stiffened at the sound, then held that stiffness as he pulled out the long, metal carriage which held Angelica's body.

"I am sorry," Frank whispered as he drew down the zipper and exposed Angelica's upturned face. It was bloodlessly white, except for the purplish lips.

Karen drew her eyes slowly down to her sister's face. She held them there for a long time, as if trying to explain some facet of it, the long, graceful arch of her eyebrows, the smooth line of her nose, the large, slightly oval eyes.

"She was so beautiful," Karen said softly. She continued to gaze at Angelica's face. "So beautiful."

"Yes."

"At every moment beautiful. A beautiful baby. A beautiful child."
Frank nodded.

"A beautiful woman," Karen said. She looked at Frank. "There's
nothing more powerful than that."

Frank closed the black plastic bag over Angelica's face. "I have
to ask you. It's a technical thing. Is this your sister?"

"Yes."

"We can go now," Frank said. He pushed the carriage back into
the wall and closed the door.

Karen did not move. She continued to look at the closed door,
as if studying her own marred reflection.

"Miss Devereaux," Frank repeated. "We can go now."

She shook her head. "Not yet," she whispered. Her eyes remained
on the stainless steel door, but it was as if they were passing through
it, were still in the dark cold vault gazing at Angelica's face. "Sparks
flew from her," she said. "My father used to pick her up in his arms
and laugh. 'Sparks fly from you,' he'd say." Her eyes remained on
the closed door, but Frank could tell that her mind was somewhere
else, and that everything in her life was passing through the dark
funnel of this moment. Her body grew even more rigid, and slowly
her hand lifted toward the latch.

Frank took it quickly. "No," he said, then released it. It fell
limply to her side.

"Why not?" she asked.

"Because it won't help anything."

"How do you know?"

"I've been here before."

"All right," Karen said. She turned slowly and walked straight
down the corridor.

"Just go on out to the car," Frank told her, once they were back
at the entrance. "I want to talk to Jesse for a minute."

She was standing beside the car smoking a cigarette when he
joined her a few minutes later.

"I'm sorry to keep you waiting," he told her.

"What did you talk to him about?" she asked.

"A few things. Technical."

"What? I want to know, exactly."

Frank took out his notebook and flipped to his last entries. "Well, the body came down about a half-hour ago. The lab report should be on my desk by now." He turned the page. "No outside inquiries about her."

"Do you keep everything in that book?" Karen asked.

"It helps my memory," Frank said. He closed the book. "You took it well, Miss Devereaux."

A slender black eyebrow crawled upward. "Did I?"

"Better than most."

"With less feeling, you mean?"

"With less show of feeling."

"Is there a difference?"

"I think so," Frank said. He opened the car door. "Come, I'll take you home."

It was late afternoon, and the traffic had begun to build steadily toward its rush-hour snarl. Frank knew that it would be a long tangled line from downtown to West Paces Ferry, and given what Karen had just been through, it seemed unnecessarily brutal to add at least an hour of stop-and-go traffic to the day's ordeal.

"We could stop somewhere if you like," he said.

She looked at him curiously. "Stop somewhere?"

"And let the traffic die down a little," Frank explained.

"All right."

A few minutes later, Frank pulled into a small tavern on Peachtree Street. He felt the need for a drink, but he felt even more that he needed a dark, quiet room, a place away from the heat and traffic.

"We can talk about anything you want," he said, after they'd ordered their drinks. "I mean, you don't have to . . ."

"Was she murdered?" Karen asked immediately.

"Probably. We don't know."

"But wouldn't it be easy to tell?"

"If she were shot or strangled, yes, it would be easier to tell. As it is, any number of things could have happened to her—some sort of accident maybe, hell, even a heart attack, I don't know. If someone was with her at the time, and that someone panicked, didn't know what to do, finally just brought her to that lot and left her there—well, it wouldn't be murder. It's not likely, but it's possible."

"Her body then, it wasn't . . . ?"

"There were no signs of a struggle," Frank said, putting it as mildly as he knew how. "And she was fully clothed when we found her." He shrugged. "Except for a shoe."

"A shoe?"

"We found it a few feet away," Frank said.

The drinks came and Frank looked at his, but did not taste it. "Look," he said, "we don't know exactly how Angelica died. We only know that certain common things didn't happen to her."

Karen watched him from over the rim of her glass. "Common things?"

"For me, common."

The waitress bounced over and took the orders of two men in business suits who sat at a table a few feet away. Frank's eyes involuntarily followed her. She was young, and she had a light, exuberant step, the sort he noticed in people who still thought their luck might change.

Karen glanced around the room. "I've never been here," she said.

"Neither have I."

"You just picked it at random?"

"The first one on the right," Frank said. "It looked nice. Better than the traffic." He looked at his watch. "Things'll clear up in about an hour. We'll leave then."

Karen pulled a pack of cigarettes from her purse and offered one to Frank.

"No, thanks."

Karen lit her own. "You look like a smoker."

"I do? How do smokers look?"

"Like certain things don't really matter to them."

"Health, you mean?"

"Too long a life," Karen said.

"Then give me one."

Karen held the pack up to him. "Angelica and I didn't get along very well," she said.

"I gathered that," Frank said. He lit the cigarette. "Of course, that's nothing new."

"But I have no idea what happened to her," Karen said, "and if she was murdered, I don't know who killed her."

"It's her life I'm looking for right now," Frank said.

"Why?"

"So I can trace it."

"To its end?"

"That's the way it works when you do it by the book," Frank told her. He took a sip of Scotch, and the warmth hit him suddenly like a sweet promise of relief. He realized he'd want another after this, and then another. He placed the glass firmly down on the table. *to true!*

Karen looked at him oddly. "What's the matter?"

"Nothing," Frank said quickly. He leaned back in his seat, drawing himself away from the beckoning glass. "Did you really not know anything about how Angelica lived?" he asked.

"I tried to watch out for her. I was her sister, after all. But she resented the intrusion."

"Well, the only things I know right now are that she was rich and beautiful."

Karen leaned forward. "Does that make it more likely that she was murdered, money and beauty?"

"Less likely, I'd say," Frank told her. He took a draw on the cigarette. "There's a saying in a homicide investigation: Follow blood or money."

"Which means?"

"Well, in most cases people kill each other over money or some family matter."

Karen shook her head gently. "I didn't kill my sister, Mr. Clemons."

"I was thinking more of money," Frank said. "Did Angelica have much of her own?"

"Yes. She had a trust fund."

Frank took out his notebook. "She had access to it?"

"Not until recently," Karen said. "Arthur Cummings administered it. He was my father's lawyer. And he was, you might say, Angelica's guardian. At least, he was the guardian of her money."

"Did he keep tabs on her?"

"I don't think so," Karen said. "I don't think she would have let anyone do that."

Frank wrote Cummings' name in his notebook. "Where can I find Arthur Cummings?"

"Cummings, Wainwright and Houstan," Karen said. "Have you heard of it?"

"No. Should I have?"

"Well, not really. It's a major law firm, that's all."

The sort of high-powered legal muscle that people in Karen's circle knew about, Frank realized immediately, and people in his circle didn't.

"I know mostly bailbondsmen and ambulance chasers," he said.

"You think Cummings is any different?" Karen asked.

"Better suits," Frank said. He allowed himself to smile with her for the first time. "With the guys I deal with, it's mostly K Mart."

Karen snuffed out her cigarette, but said nothing.

"Was Cummings your guardian, too?" Frank asked.

"For a few years," Karen said. "I was almost of age when my parents died. He was my guardian until then."

"How well do you know him?"

"Not very well," Karen said. "I recognize his signature. It was always on my checks."

"And nothing else?"

"He was my father's best friend. That's all I know."

"And as far as you know, Angelica was no closer to him than you?"

"As far as I know," Karen said. She took a sip of wine. "Besides, if Angelica was murdered, it could have been anybody."

"Why?"

"Because she was beautiful," Karen said firmly, "and anyone could have desired her: Arthur, the taxi driver, the kid with the groceries, the stranger in an elevator." She paused. "Even you, Mr. Clemons." She picked up the now-empty glass of wine and twirled it in her hands. "Anyone could have desired her, and because of that, anyone could have killed her." She placed the glass back down on the table and leaned slowly toward him. "Was my sister raped?"

"I don't know," Frank said.

For what seemed a very long time, she simply continued to look at him. Then, slowly, a line of moisture gathered in her eyes.

5

When Frank got back to headquarters, he found Caleb already waiting for him, his huge frame slumped in a padded metal chair beside his desk.

"Two things for you," Caleb said.

"What?"

"Message from your wife."

"Ex-wife."

"In my opinion there's no such thing," Caleb said. He shrugged. "Anyway, from Sheila."

"What's the message?"

"She just wants you to drop by after work."

"Okay, what else?"

"This," Caleb said. He took a thin manila folder from his lap and dropped it on Frank's desk. "Lab work on Angelica Devereaux."

"Have you read it?"

"Just finished."

"Any surprises?"

"Well, she wasn't raped, if that's what you mean."

"Does that surprise you?"

Caleb shook his head. "Not much. In my experience, you don't have to be a looker to get raped. Fat or thin, old or young, it don't matter." He smiled sadly. "Like the saying goes, Frank, beauty is in the eye of the beholder." He slid the folder across the desk. "Take a look."

Frank picked it up. "I met her sister," he said. He looked at Caleb. "The two of them had lived together since the plane crash." He shook his head. "Now she has nobody, as far as I can tell."

Caleb stared at him, unmoved. "When you get down to the wire on it, not many people do. That's a true fact, unrecorded." He nodded toward the still-unopened manila folder. "Anyway, we've got a cause of death now." His eyes seemed to withdraw into their large round sockets. "Drano."

"What?"

"Drano, or something like it," Caleb repeated. "A lye-based poison. That's what the lab boys call it." He took the report from Frank's hand and opened it. "Here it is," he said. Then he read directly from the report. "A lye-based poison administered by multiple injection within the pubic region." He closed the folder. "What do you think?"

Frank eased the report from Caleb's hands and began to read it. Very little was out of the ordinary. There was no rape, just as Caleb had said, and neither were there any drugs present in her bloodstream.

"Didn't have so much as a drink for the road," Caleb said.

Frank continued to read while Caleb stood over him, staring down.

"I can save you some time, Frank," he said at last.

"What do you mean?"

"She was pregnant," Caleb said bluntly.

Frank lowered the folder to his desk.

"Meaning it could be something simple," Caleb added.

"Like what?"

"The law calls it 'wrongful death.' "

"Meaning what?"

"Maybe she was trying to give herself an abortion."

50

"With lye?" Frank asked unbelievingly.

"Anything," Caleb added. "Some friend at school could have said something, just a line about how lye'll get rid of a baby."

Frank continued to watch him doubtfully.

"Remember that Johnson kid, remember him?"

"The kid who hanged himself."

"That's right. Everybody but his parents thought it was a suicide."

"Well, that's what you think, Caleb, when you've got a kid swinging from the rafters with a knocked-over stool right under him."

"But it wasn't suicide, Frank," Caleb said. "His mother kept telling me that, and I believed her."

"I thought it was the fact that he was naked that bothered you."

"That, too," Caleb said. "So, anyway, I checked around and found out that a few kids on the basketball team had told him how great it was to jerk off while you're just at the edge of consciousness. That's what he was trying to do."

"And so now you figure the Devereaux girl for a botched abortion?"

"Maybe," Caleb said. "She could have done it herself, given herself those injections."

Frank looked at him pointedly. Caleb smiled. "Yeah, I know. She couldn't have dragged her own dead body across that field, could she?"

"No."

"I bet I know who did."

Frank waited.

"The daddy," Caleb said. He nodded sagely. "Mark my words, you find the daddy of that baby, and you'll find the poor lost soul who killed that girl. Or helped her kill herself. Whatever. You get the daddy, you get the story."

"Maybe," Frank said. But even as he said it, he found that he did not feel certain of it. He had seen too many cases where the general rules did not apply, where nothing ever reduced to its most common elements. For an instant, as he glanced back down at the folder, he thought he heard a voice rise from it. He knew it was only a trick of the mind, but he could not refuse to hear it. It was wordless, almost inaudible, and yet he could hear it, a low, with-drawing moan.

Caleb placed his hand on Frank's shoulder. "Find the father, you'll find everything."

Frank nodded and opened the folder once again.

"You doubt it?" Caleb asked.

"I don't know."

Caleb looked at him scoldingly. "You make things too complex, Frank." He laughed slightly. "You don't ever see the simple things."

"Maybe I just don't like them," Frank said, as his eyes once again scanned the first page of the report.

Caleb released his shoulder. "Well, I got to go home. Big Hilda's waiting." He leaned forward and tapped on the report. "Raise a joyful noise, Frank. The fact that the girl was pregnant is the best thing that could have happened on this case." He stood up straight. "And while I'm full of advice, stay away from the Bottom Rail."

"I never liked it that much," Frank said casually.

"And places a whole lot like it, stay away from them, too."

Frank looked up at him. "You're beginning to sound like my brother."

"Oh, shit," Caleb said with a shiver. "Blessed Jesus, save me from that." He laughed loudly and walked out of the room.

Frank turned his eyes back toward the report, but his mind remained for a time on Alvin, and for a brief moment he allowed his thought to settle almost tenderly on his brother. He thought of all the things that were clean and clear in Alvin's life, the unwavering line he walked from work to home, then back to work again. He could see Alvin mowing the grass in the summer, trimming the hedge, tossing a bowling ball on the one night a week he took for himself, and as he considered these things, he realized with sadness that only the crude coincidence of blood connected him to his brother. They had grown as distant from one another as two bits of debris floating in separate galaxies, and now Sheila floated in one more separate still, and his father in yet another, and Sarah had gone even beyond those, beyond recall, forever.

After a while, he found himself staring at the lab report again. He opened it slowly and read it once more, this time more closely, his notebook open beside it, his pencil poised over the small blank page. It was always possible that something lay hidden in the clean, scientific language. He read the first page, then the second, and behind the crisp, matter-of-fact sentences, he could hear the blade of the scalpel as it sliced into Angelica's stomach and then the slosh of its contents as they spilled out into the stainless steel pan. She had eaten a ham sandwich not long before her death and had drunk some milk. There were no drugs, no alcohol. She had died cold sober. Cold sober she had felt the needle as it pierced her skin, felt the lye flow into her blood. The report surmised that she could have administered the poison herself. It would have been painful, but not impossible. There were no signs of her having been in any way restrained, no rope burns or marks of violence. But the vision which rose from these facts was odd, a beautiful young girl sitting in a chair, filling a hypodermic needle with poison again and again, injecting it into her pubic region again and again. "Seven hypodermic injections," the report concluded, and then added in a final statement as flat as the sound of a hammer nailing shut Angelica's coffin: "Death by misadventure."

The last word continued to sound in Frank's mind: misadventure. But if she had accidentally killed herself, then someone had helped her do it, then dragged her body into that vacant lot and dumped it.

And there was something else. Dirt had been found in her mouth. As Frank recalled the position of her body, the way it lay face-up on its back, he could not see how any dirt had gotten there. Had Angelica been dragged by the feet and on her stomach, then it was possible that her mouth might have picked up some of the loose earth of the lot. But her face would have been scarred, and it had not been. The front of her blouse was not soiled.

The more Frank thought about these things, the more he felt himself drawn back to the vacant lot. For a few minutes, he fought the impulse to return to it. It had already been thoroughly searched. His eyes were no better than anyone else's. And yet, the field seemed to urge him toward it, call to him as if its very silence was a strange, imploring voice.

It was dark by the time he pulled the car up to the curb, and he could almost feel the moment when, the night before, someone else had done the same thing, had pulled up to the curb, quickly snapped off the headlights, and then stepped out into the shadowless darkness.

Frank stepped out of the car and looked around. The yellowish light of the few surrounding houses died away before it reached the edge of the lot, and it was as if this vacant field rested in a darkness which it had itself conceived and which no mere human light could penetrate. He could feel that darkness like a heavy robe across his shoulders. It hung all around him, more dense than air, a thick black shroud.

He walked slowly to the very edge of the lot. Brown weedy grasses inched their way over the edge of the cement walkway. Frank reached down, pulled a single drought-stricken blade from the ground and put it into his mouth.

As he looked out over the lot, he could sense the route the man had taken as he straggled through the bramble with Angelica's body in his arms or over his shoulder. The same briar that had scraped her ankles now grabbed at his trousers as he moved out toward the center of the field. In his mind, he could hear the heavy breath of the man who carried her, hear the whisper of his body as it plunged through the bramble, the thud of Angelica's shoe as it dropped from her foot to the ground.

He stopped and looked down at the ground. Her shoe had been found exactly where he stood, and for a moment he stared at the ground beneath him, as if trying to absorb some vibration from its depths. But the hard, littered earth gave nothing back, and after a moment he moved on through the thickening brush until he stood once again over the shallow ditch where Angelica's body had been found. He stood very still and looked all around him. The lot was so bleak and abandoned that it gave everything around it a deeper, more intractable bleakness. To the left a squat, rust-colored warehouse stood in the faded light of a single streetlamp. It was built of plain, yellowish brick and half its black-painted windows had been broken. It seemed to lean to the left, as if it were sinking slowly into the ground. At the rear of the lot, a group of unpainted wooden tenements, half of them boarded up and abandoned, groaned in the summer breeze. One of them drooped forward, as if ready to collapse, and the single light that shone from its second-story window

seemed to stare at Frank with a half-closed eye. The other surrounding blocks were almost entirely leveled. On one, nothing but
a cinderblock church remained, and on the other was nothing but
a dilapidated auto parts store.

He glanced back down to the place where Angelica's body had
been found. He could still see it lying before him, the legs bent
slightly at the knees, one arm slung outward from her body, the
other tucked neatly at her side. It was as if the imprint of her body
still remained like a stain on the ground, and as he looked at it, he
could imagine that whoever had brought her here had not picked
this spot by accident. It seemed to have been chosen for its ugliness,
for the ways its ugliness further humiliated and offended Angelica.

For a while, Frank remained in place, hoping that something
would come to him, some idea that the physical evidence alone
could not provide, an intimation, however faint, which could nonetheless serve as a kind of guide. But in the end, he felt nothing but
the cold reality of Angelica's death, and he turned around and
walked slowly back to the car.

All the lights were blazing in the house when Frank got there,
but that did not surprise him. Sheila had kept them on more or
less continually since Sarah's death, as if tragedy were some sort of
marauding jungle beast which a campfire could keep away.

"I expected you a little earlier," she said crisply as she opened
the door.

"I have a new case," Frank told her.

"So Alvin said. A young girl."

"Yes."

"Do you know how it happened yet?"

"A little. Not much."

She nodded quickly, then stepped out of the door. "Well, come
in," she said.

Frank walked directly into the living room, but he did not sit
down. It did not feel like his house anymore.

Sheila walked to the fireplace and pressed her back up against it.

She wore a plain blue dress, slightly wrinkled, and her hair hung in a disheveled tangle at her shoulders. She looked drawn, as if she'd been sleeping badly.

"I've decided to leave Atlanta," she said.

"All right."

"I'm going to sell the house."

Frank said nothing.

"I thought I'd give you the first chance to buy it."

"I don't want it."

Sheila's eyes darted away, as if in rejecting the house they shared together, he was once again rejecting her. "All right, then," she said stiffly, "I'll sell the house and give you half the money."

"I don't want the money," Frank said.

Sheila looked at him disapprovingly. "You look like you could use a new suit."

"I don't want the money, Sheila," Frank repeated.

"You could buy yourself a new place," Sheila said.

"I like where I am."

"Renting that place on Waldo? You like that? Frank, it's a slum."

"You've never been there."

"Alvin's described it."

"Alvin has his own way of looking at things," Frank said. "It may not always be the best one."

"Well, he told me about it," Sheila said. "And when I think that we could still be living . . ."

"No," Frank said flatly, and watched as she turned away to face the hearth.

"I didn't mean to get into that again," she said softly. "I always promise myself that I won't get into that, and then I do."

Frank struggled to smile. "So, where are you moving to, Sheila?"

She eased herself around to face him. "Back home."

"Fort Payne?"

"You seem surprised."

"I am . . . a little."

"I don't see why," Sheila said. "I never liked Atlanta, Frank. I never wanted to come here." There was a fatal accusation in her voice. He had taken her where she didn't want to go, and after that, one disaster had led to another, until there was nothing left between them but the memory of disaster.

"You going to buy a place of your own?" Frank asked.

"Not right away," Sheila said. "At first, I'm going to stay with Papa. He needs looking after, you know."

He tried to smile again. "I wish you luck, Sheila. I really do."

She glared at him with a sudden fierceness. "You son of a bitch," she hissed.

Frank walked to the door. "I'll spread the word about the house. Somebody in the department might want it."

Sheila marched to the sofa and slumped down on it. "Save yourself the trouble," she said bitterly.

Frank opened the door and glanced back at her. For a moment he wanted to find some way to ease the bitterness between them, to draw her softly back—not as a wife, for that was gone forever— but as someone he had loved more deeply and for a longer time than he would ever love again. But it was useless, and he knew it. In the end, there was nothing left but to close the door.

It was after midnight before he got back to the house. Hours of driving through the streets had not helped much. He slumped down on the sofa and turned on the light beside it. He could see his unmade bed in the adjoining room, and its disarray echoed the accusation he'd heard all his life, that he couldn't finish things, that he drifted along with the flood, with no direction of his own.

The accusation didn't always seem fair. After all, he'd moved to Atlanta at Alvin's urging, and for years they'd walked a beat together, two brothers in blue on the gritty, noisy streets. He remembered the pride he'd once had in his uniform, the shining buttons and brilliant silver badge. It had taken him many years to exchange it for the gold shield of a detective, and although Alvin was older, and had been with the department longer, they'd done it the same year. The two brothers in uniform became the two brothers in Homicide, and for several years after that, they'd even worked a few cases together. Then Sarah had died at sixteen, and two years later, Sheila had dropped away. More and more since then, Alvin had worked his own beat, both at work and in his life, and now, as he thought of it, Frank found that he couldn't blame him in the least.

He stood up and walked out onto the small porch. It was barely large enough to hold a single wrought-iron chair, but it sometimes felt like the only place in the city he still enjoyed. From its high perch, he felt that he could look down and take it all in with just enough distance and perspective to see it with more clarity. He'd spent hours in the little chair, thinking of his father, his daughter, his wife. The old man was always there, preaching to high Heaven about goodness and salvation. But where had the old man's wife gone to? Why had she left him with two boys and a clapboard church with a congregation so poor they often put bags of peas or berries in the collection box? At times, as Frank thought about it, he felt that he could grasp it. He could remember his mother's drawn, dark, infinitely unhappy face, stripped by his father's rigid saintliness, withered away so completely by it, that she'd sometimes seemed little more than a naked carcass, something the birds had picked to death. "Well away, Mother," he thought now. "Well away from him."

But he and Alvin had had to stay, and he remembered how, after his mother's departure, the old man had grown more and more intemperate in his sermons, more and more frantic, desperate, frenzied. Sunday after Sunday, he'd whipped the dusty congregation into a rage for glory. Even Alvin had taken up the trumpet by then. And so it was only himself, shifting on the bench, silent among the howling host of believers who swayed and wept and cried out for redemption.

Sheila had been his redemption, and he could remember the touch of her long brown legs as if they were still wrapped around him. Her warm breath had redeemed him, and the feel of her fingers as they pulled at his hair. During those long, twining nights, he had not been able to imagine that he would ever lie down next to her without desire. And yet, as the years had passed, so had their passion, until, in the end, it was only the house they shared, little square rooms with pictures of seascapes hanging from the walls. Only their house, and their daughter.

She'd been born only a few years after their marriage, and he had named her Sarah as a last concession to his father: Sarah, after Abraham's faithful and long-suffering wife. Her birth had transformed him, or had at least made him feel transformed. He'd discovered something hidden in himself, an immense and primitive capacity for love. It was as if she possessed a density which nothing else possessed, not his wife or his work, or anything else imaginable. He came to realize how small women lifted huge trucks off the shattered legs of their children. There was something primordial in the bond between a father and his daughter, and he had felt it more powerfully than he had ever felt anything before, and when, year by year, it began to slip away, he felt as if he were slowly being drained of some essential force.

And yet, it had, in fact, slipped away. Slowly, her moodiness had overwhelmed her, and he could not change it. By the time she was nine, she played almost entirely alone. By eleven her eyes had taken on a strange, unfathomable vacancy. By thirteen he had lost her. And three years later she was dead.

He did not know why. The school psychologist had called it "congenital loneliness," as if, by giving it a name, he had solved the mystery. But it remained a mystery to Frank, one that sank into him like water into the open veins of broken wood. For two years he'd thought of almost nothing else, thought about it as his cases lay unsolved on his desk, as his esteem in the department shrank to nothingness.

Now, it seemed to him, he had only the city and its unending streets. From his position on the small porch, he could see the skyline as it rose like a wall of stars against the night. There was still a kind of magic in its life which appealed to him. There was something wondrous in the concentration of so much humanity in such constricted space, and it was this amazing compression which created the wild, insatiable energy of the streets, an energy which spilled into them each summer night and held there, hour after hour, as if certain that the life which generated it could go on this way forever. At times, as he stood alone on the porch, gazing out at the glittering city, Frank thought that he could actually comprehend its people, as if the diverse and hidden forces which drove them forward were the product of a single, central longing that, by some tragic and mysterious code, urged one man to save his brother, and another to destroy him.

6

Frank awoke early the next morning, just as the first gray light had begun to inch its way into his room. He showered, dressed quickly, then headed for his car. The early morning traffic was lighter than he'd expected, and because of that he found himself alone in the detective bullpen. He pulled out the lab report and read it once again. He was still reading it when Asa Brickman, the head of Homicide Division, walked up to his desk.

"Morning, Frank," he said.

"Morning, Asa."

Brickman nodded toward the lab report. "That about the girl over on Glenwood?"

"Angelica Devereaux," Frank said.

"Yeah, that one. Gimme."

Frank looked at him, puzzled. "You want to read it?"

Brickman laughed. "Naw, I don't want to read it," he said. "I want to give it to somebody else." He reached down and took the edge of the folder in his huge black hand.

Frank did not release it. "Why?"

Brickman shook his head. "Oh, come on, Frank, you know when a rich white girl like this gets wasted, we got to jump on it fast."

"I am on it."

"We're talking old-time white money here, Frank. This Devereaux piece is not just some whore in a back alley."

Frank said nothing. He still did not release the folder.

Brickman let it go and straightened himself. "You going to give me shit on this?" He looked at Frank menacingly. "We're talking old white money, goddamnit."

"That what you are, Asa?" Frank asked. "Old white money?"

Brickman sighed heavily. "Yeah, right. And don't I look it?" He shrugged. "Look, the fact is, the bluebloods'll be watching us on this one. I want my best men on it." He smiled knowingly. "And your record's spotty to say the least, my man. Know what I mean?"

"I have a feeling about this one, Asa," Frank told him.

"A feeling?"

"Yeah."

"What do you mean? You got something on this case already?"

Frank shook his head.

"Then forget it," Brickman said. He reached for the report again, but Frank did not let it go.

Brickman's voice hardened as he once again released the folder. "What the fuck you think you're doing, Frank?"

"I want this case."

"Since when does it matter to you what case you're on?"

"Since right now."

"You got some connection to it?"

"No."

"Some special expertise, something like that?"

"No."

"Any reason I could give for keeping you on it? I mean one that would hold up on the top floor?"

"Nothing. Just a feeling."

Brickman stared at him quietly. "You know Harry Gibbons?"

"Yeah."

"Would you say he's the best detective in Homicide?"

"Yeah, I guess he is."

"Takes these special goddamn courses all the time, right? Goes to night school? A real top-gun?"

"That's what they say."

"Just like the Mounties, always gets his man."

Frank nodded.

"Well, Gibbons wants this case, too, Frank," Brickman said. "Now what would you do in my situation? Think about it. You've slouched around here, pissing away month after month." He stopped. "And by the way, what the fuck happened to your face?"

Frank said nothing.

"Ran into a swinging door?" Brickman asked dryly.

"Personal business," Frank said. "It has nothing to do with my work."

"Uh huh," Brickman said unbelievingly. "Anyway, if you had a case you needed to break, wouldn't you hand it to Gibbons?"

"Probably," Frank admitted.

"So why shouldn't I?"

"Because in his heart," Frank said, "Gibbons doesn't give a damn about anything."

"That don't mean a goddamn thing to me, Frank," Brickman said.

Frank looked steadily into Brickman's eyes. "Years back, Asa, if some peckerwood mayor had told Gibbons to go waste some big-mouthed, agitating nigger, what do you think he'd have done?"

Brickman's face softened slightly, and a slow smile stretched across his lips. "All right, Frank," he said, after a moment, "I'll let you hold on to it for a while. But I don't want you on it alone."

"I won't work with Gibbons," Frank said flatly.

"How about Alvin?"

Frank shook his head. "Caleb Stone."

"That old fart?"

"Yeah."

Brick laughed lightly. "That old bastard have a feeling for this case, too?"

Frank shrugged. "I can work with him, that's all."

"Okay. I'll put Caleb on it. You want to tell him, or you want me to?"

"I will."

"You working anything else?"

"That guy who killed his wife over on Highland."

"That's pretty open and shut, right?"

"Yes."

"Mind if I throw it to Gibbons?"

"No."

"Okay, done," Brickman said. "You just work this one, nothing else. But don't fuck it up, Frank. You won't get another chance." He turned quickly and walked back out of the room.

Frank returned to the lab report and began to scan its findings once again. Slowly, his mind shifted from Angelica to her sister, and he remembered the forceful way in which she had managed to control herself. He wondered if Angelica had shared that characteristic, if she had been able to sit in a chair and calmly inject her own body with poison seven times. It seemed beyond anyone's capacity, no matter what the lab report said. The method was too protracted, the results, as he imagined them, too unendurably painful. He had seen his share of deaths: crudely slashed wrists deep in bloody water, faces blown away by shotgun blasts, bodies slumped limply to the side, the smell of gas still rising from their clothes. The reasons were almost always the same, a loneliness and isolation so complete that it closed them off from the rest of the world, locked them in a dark drawer from which they could not even imagine an escape.

He tried to picture Angelica with the hypodermic needle in her hand, but found he could not. He saw her picture in the yearbook and her body sprawled on the ground, but could imagine nothing between the ordinariness of the one and the perversity of the other.

He was still struggling to find some line that might connect the two when Caleb walked up to his desk.

"Saw Brickman downstairs," he said, his lips fluttering around the stem of his pipe. "He said you wanted to see me."

"We're going to be working together on the Devereaux case."

"Well, that's real nice, Frank, but I'm pretty damn busy already."

"Your cases will be reassigned."

Caleb frowned. "Who's going to get them?"

"Gibbons is getting mine," Frank told him. "I don't know about yours."

Caleb shook his head resentfully. "You know what's the matter with this department? They don't ever let you get rooted in anything. They're always shifting things around. Half the time, there's no sense to it at all."

"That's the way it is," Frank said dryly.

"Five people get axed to death in a holdup, they're liable to hand it over to robbery detail."

Frank handed him the lab report. "Read this."

"I already have," Caleb said. "You know that."

"Read it again."

"Why?"

"Because things jump out at you," Frank said. "Things you didn't notice before."

"Not in this one," Caleb insisted. "I know the answer to this case." He dropped the file on Frank's desk. "Here's the way it happened. A pretty rich girl got pregnant by a pretty rich boy. Nobody wants this kid. Lots of bullshit involved, maybe even some very pissed-off parents, the kind that take away your new car, along with all those big plans for college."

"So the father of the child killed Angelica?"

"If she was murdered," Caleb said. "It could have been just what the lab boys said, a bungled abortion." He blew a column of smoke past Frank's head. "What have you got on it?"

"I brought her sister down to identify the body."

"She tell you anything?"

"Not much. They lived together. A big house on West Paces Ferry."

"Anything else?"

"I didn't try to press her," Frank said. He took out his notebook. "She did tell me that Angelica had just come into a lot of money. Before that, it was all handled by her guardian." He flipped another page. "Arthur Cummings. He's with some big law firm."

"A real big firm," Caleb said. "Didn't he think about running for mayor a few years back?"

Frank nodded. "Yes, I remember that."

"But he never tossed his hat in the ring," Caleb said. "Hell, it wouldn't of mattered if he had. Old money. White money. They got the power, but they don't get the office anymore, not in this town."

"I was thinking of going to see Cummings this morning," Frank said.

"Want company?"

"No. I want you to get copies of Angelica's picture to give out on the canvass."

"You won't get a thing from that," Caleb said confidently.

"Try it anyway," Frank said. "Headquarters would want that covered."

Caleb tugged wearily at his drooping trousers. "This shit'll take all day, you know."

"Let me know what you find out."

"Yeah," Caleb said, as he turned heavily and trudged out the door.

Frank pulled the telephone book from his desk and looked up the Cummings law firm. It was in one of Atlanta's glittering midtown towers, and he quickly wrote the address and phone number in his notebook. Then he glanced at his watch: nine-thirty. If Cummings were like most ambitious, hard-driving Southern lawyers, he'd have already been in his office for two hours.

He was on his way toward the door when Gibbons suddenly came through it.

"Hey, Frank," Gibbons said, slowing as he came nearer. "Got a late start this morning." He smiled cheerfully. "Anything on the night beat?"

"Nothing."

Gibbons straightened his bright yellow tie. "No untimely deaths, huh?"

"No."

"What about that girl they found over on Glenwood?" Gibbons asked. He shifted his own personal volume of the FBI Uniform Crime Report. "That a kill?"

"We don't know yet," Frank said.

"If it's a kill, it's a prime collar. You still on it?"

"Yes."

A glimmer of surprise passed over Gibbons' face, and Frank suspected that someone at headquarters had already tipped him off that the case was going to be shifted to him. Gibbons always had a jump on everybody else when it came to knowing what was coming down from the top floor. He played tennis with the chief of detectives and handball with the head of Vice, and on Sunday, he ended up at the Mount Pyron Church of God wailing for salvation from the same pew as two members of the city council. There wasn't a wheel of government he hadn't greased, and because of it, information flowed down to him like manna.

"Well, let me know if you need an assist on this one," Gibbons said cheerfully. "I mean, we're all in this together." He smiled thinly, and just behind his lips, Frank thought he could see the pale, starving features of his soul.

7

It was almost ten when Frank got to the offices of Arthur Cummings. They spread out across the top floor of one of the city's most elegant towers, and as he stepped into its spacious reception area, Frank could almost hear the rustle of the hundreds of briefs and motions and appeals which had paid for it. The carpet was scarlet, and very thick, and the paneled walls were decked with a lavish display of paintings. A brass chandelier hung from the ceiling, and its bright light fell over an array of flowers and potted plants.

The receptionist sat behind a large wooden desk, her fingers moving nimbly over a bank of phones. She was dressed in a skirt and blouse that were almost as red as the carpeting, and she had the pliant, yet calculating look of a woman who knows that she is surrounded by rich and powerful men.

"May I help you, sir?" she asked as Frank stepped up to her desk.

Her tone was a bit stiff, and Frank noticed that her eyes gave him a quick, dismissive glance, the sort that falls on all the wrong things, the slight stain on his tie, the unpolished shoes, the suit from so many seasons past that she seemed to be surprised that such relics still survived in her more modern world. It was the kind of look that reduced one kind of man while it exalted another, and under it, Frank felt himself utterly reduced, a ragamuffin cop with a swollen eye and a pocketful of loose change.

"You wish to see someone?" the woman asked.

"Arthur Cummings," Frank said crisply.

"Mr. Cummings?" the woman asked doubtfully.

"Yes."

"Do you have an appointment?"

"No."

"Well, I'm afraid you'll have to make one."

Frank shook his head. "I don't have time for that."

The woman stared at him lethally. "What was that?"

"Is Cummings here?"

The woman did not reply. Instead, she looked at him as if she knew quite well that any further discussion would be held in the lobby between Frank and the building's largest security officer.

"As I mentioned," she said in a cool, measured tone, "Mr. Cummings does not see anyone without an appointment."

Frank took out his badge and waved it in front of her face.

The woman leaned forward and looked at it closely, checking to see if it were authentic, or just some tin star he'd bought at a novelty store.

"You're with the Atlanta police?" she asked finally.

Frank nodded. "Badge number one one four seven, if you want to take it down."

The woman sat back stiffly. "That won't be necessary." She paused a moment, her eyes checking him out once again. "May I know what this is about?"

"No," Frank said, "I think that Mr. Cummings would want that to remain confidential."

"Very well," the woman said. "Please be seated. I'll see what I can do for you." She stood up quickly, then walked back into one of the suites of offices at the rear.

Frank turned slowly and strolled around the room. The paintings drew his attention and he walked from one to another, carefully looking at each in turn. They were all of places in what Frank took

70

to be Paris, street scenes of cafés and expansive boulevards, huge arches and sweeping parks. The colors were bright, even garish, and he didn't like them very much. There was too much peace and gaiety pushing out the facts of life as he saw them, and for a moment he tried to imagine why anyone would hang only such pictures. He wondered if Cummings himself had selected them, and if so, why? To relieve the gray monotony of corporate law, perhaps, or to present a view of life which seemed possible for him once he'd won enough cases, garnered enough fees and could then sit back and sip a glass of wine in a street café exactly as thousands of far less wealthy and distinguished people did quite absently and without a thought every single day.

He was still brooding over the general tone of the paintings when the receptionist returned.

"Mr. Clemons," she said, "Mr. Cummings will see you now."

"Thank you."

"Just follow me, please," the woman said. Then she turned briskly and led Frank down a long, very wide corridor which finally spread out into yet another large reception area. There was another woman behind another wooden desk. She was young and very elegantly dressed, and she flashed Frank a pleasant smile which he instantly distrusted.

"I'm Mr. Cummings' executive secretary," she said. She glanced coolly at the other woman. "That'll be all, Amy."

Her eyes shifted back to Frank. "I understand you're with the police."

"That's right."

"And this is some sort of official visit?"

"Yes."

"Are you interested in engaging the firm in some way?"

"What do you mean?"

"Are you seeking legal counsel? For yourself, I mean?"

"No," Frank said.

The woman jotted down a note, and Frank wondered just how many layers of the servant class he was going to have to penetrate before he reached Arthur Cummings.

"I don't have all day," he said finally.

The woman looked up. She looked as if he had spit in her face. "What's that?"

"I want to see Arthur Cummings," Frank said bluntly. "And I don't have all day."

"Well, Mr. Cummings usually sees people only by appointment."

"This is a murder investigation," Frank said.

The woman's eyes widened.

"Now why don't you press that little button on your phone there, or whatever it is you press, and tell Mr. Cummings that I'm coming in."

The buzzer was still sounding in Cummings' office as Frank came through the double mahogany doors.

Arthur Cummings looked as if his fortress had been breached by a barbarian army. He stood up slowly, glaring into Frank's eyes. He was dressed in a dark blue suit that looked as if it had never been worn for more than forty minutes. He was tall, slender, with a head of blindingly white hair.

Frank displayed his badge. "I don't mean to be difficult, Mr. Cummings," he said quietly, "but I have a lot to do, and seeing you is first on my list."

A slight smile swept over Cummings' face. "I see," he said. "Well, why don't you sit down?"

Frank sat down in one of the chairs opposite Cummings' desk.

Cummings continued to stand behind his desk, his back to an enormous window. The light that came through it turned his hair to silver.

"I must tell you, Mr. Clemons, that I'm a bit at sea as to what all this is about."

"It's about Angelica Devereaux."

Cummings' eyes darkened, and he lowered himself into his chair. For a moment he simply stared at Frank, then he leaned forward and snapped up his phone. "No calls," he said. He placed the phone back in its cradle. "Now, what do you mean?"

"She's dead," Frank said. "We found her body in a vacant lot off Glenwood."

"Off Glenwood?" Mr. Cummings asked, as if the location of her body was a good deal more incomprehensible than her death.

"We don't know exactly how she died," Frank said, "but we know that she couldn't have gotten to that lot by herself."

Cummings looked puzzled. "You mean you don't know if she was murdered?"

"We don't know what happened," Frank repeated, "but we do know that at least one other person had to have been involved." He stopped, trying to gauge how much information he should hold back. "Her death involved injection, and there were no hypodermic needles near her body."

"So others must have been involved."

"At least one."

Mr. Cummings nodded. "How terrible," he said. He seemed genuinely saddened. He folded his hands quietly over his desk and gazed at them. "She'd just begun to live." He looked up at Frank. "So young."

"Yes," Frank said.

Mr. Cummings shook his head mournfully. "So very, very young."

Frank took out his pen and notebook. "You were her guardian, I believe."

"Who have you been speaking to?"

"Karen Devereaux."

"Yes, well, guardian is a legal description in this case," Cummings said. "It is a technical term."

"What do you mean?"

"I administered her trust fund," Cummings said, "but that's about all."

"Do you still administer it?"

"No. Angelica turned eighteen a few months ago. She's her own guardian now."

"How much money was involved?" Frank asked.

"Almost three million dollars in assets," Cummings told him. He smiled sadly. "More than a young girl should have control of."

"Was that cash?"

Cummings looked at Frank as if he were a small child. "Of course not. There were stocks, bonds, that sort of thing." He shrugged. "Of course, these things are easily convertible into cash. And, along with them, there was a sizable amount of what you might call 'ready cash.' That is to say, purely liquid assets."

"How much?"

"Two hundred thousand dollars."

Frank wrote it down. "What did she do with that money?"

"I have no idea."

Frank looked at him doubtfully.

"It's quite true," Cummings said. "I have absolutely no idea. That's what I meant by calling my guardianship purely technical."

"Purely technical?"

"It means that I was her financial caretaker," Cummings explained. "But as far as a personal relationship with Angelica went, I had none whatsoever. So, when she became eighteen and took charge of her own finances, we ceased to have any relationship at all."

"She took full charge?"

"Full charge, yes," Cummings said. "And I must admit that I didn't think that was very wise. But as you know, Mr. Clemons, the law is the law. And in matters of this kind it is explicit. At eighteen, Angelica assumed full control of her entire inheritance. That's that."

Frank nodded. "When did you see her last?"

"On her birthday, as you might expect," Cummings told him.

"When was that?"

"June seventeenth."

"Here in your office?"

"That's right. My legal connection to Angelica ended at that time. And, of course, there was no personal connection."

"How did you happen to become her guardian?"

"I was named executor of the estate left at the death of Angelica's parents."

"Why?"

"I was a friend of her father."

"And that was your only personal connection?"

"Yes. Angelica was, as you will probably discover, a somewhat headstrong person. I think she always rather resented my guardianship. She certainly severed it at her first opportunity."

"Which was her eighteenth birthday."

"Yes," Cummings said. "I must say that I'm sorry Angelica and I never developed any kind of rapport." He smiled quietly. "But that's rather the way of things. I mean, I was the wall that kept her from her money."

"How old was she when her parents died?"

"Five years old," Cummings said. "Karen was almost eighteen. They never lived with anyone else. They simply lived together in that enormous house." He shook his head. "I don't know why. But I did try to be more than simply a financial advisor. They were young girls. They needed a father. I suppose I made certain efforts to play that role."

"But they never accepted you?"

"No, they didn't," Cummings said. "Of course, that wasn't entirely their fault. After all, I couldn't be much of a father. I don't know how to be one."

"You don't have any children?" Frank asked.

"I have three," Cummings said, "but I rarely see them. They live at home with my wife." He lifted his arms slowly. "And I live here." He allowed his arms to drift back slowly toward the desk. "I learned a long time ago that you cannot make people love you. You cannot even make them seek your counsel." He pushed a polished wooden box across the desk. "Would you like a cigar?"

"No."

Cummings took out one for himself and lit it. "I deal with the law. It's something I can understand. People? They are a mystery to me."

"Was Angelica a mystery?"

"One of the deeper ones," Cummings said. "Have you learned much about her?"

"I'm only beginning."

"There may be nothing to learn," Cummings said.

"Why do you say that?"

"Well, I'm no great judge of character, but I do know when there's nothing there, when someone is rather empty."

"Was Angelica like that?"

"She seemed unformed," Cummings said. "That was my only impression."

"Did you know that she was pregnant?"

For a moment Cummings did not answer. His eyes grew almost childlike, wondering. "Yes," he said. "I could hardly have been more surprised."

"Why?"

"Because of exactly what I mentioned," Cummings said. "The fact that she seemed so unformed. I could not imagine her making love. So beautiful, yes. Very desirable, no doubt. But actually making that flesh-and-blood decision, and then going through with it? I couldn't imagine Angelica doing that." He smiled gently. "I can't imagine that it was pleasurable for her."

It seemed so odd a comment that Frank wrote it down in his notebook.

"I wouldn't put too much stock in what I say, however," Cummings added dismissively. "I'm not a very good student of mankind."

"How did you know she was pregnant?"

"She told me."

"When."

"On June seventeenth, when she came to take control of her inheritance. It was one of the reasons she gave me for wanting full control of her assets. She planned to keep the baby, or so she said. She wanted to support it herself."

"She planned to keep it?"

"Yes," Cummings said.

"You didn't get the impression that she was going to get an abortion?"

"No, why?"

"Well, one idea is that she died while trying to give herself one."

Cummings laughed. "That's ridiculous."

"Why?"

"My God, if Angelica had wanted an abortion, she could have gotten one from the finest doctors in the world," Cummings said. He leaned forward slightly. "We're talking about a very wealthy young woman."

Frank wrote it down.

"Did she mention an abortion at all?"

"No," Cummings said. "She said that she planned to have the

76

baby, raise it herself, and at the same time—we're talking about a young girl here—she was going off to New York to be an actress."

"New York City?"

"That's right, that paradise for exiles," Cummings said. "She was going there."

"Did that surprise you?"

"Not really. She was drifting, I could tell."

"In what way?"

Cummings tapped his head. "In here. She was drifting inside her mind." He shook his head. "I don't think she had much to stand on, but I think, in whatever naive way she could, she loved that unborn child." He was silent for a moment, his eyes gazing at his hands. "Who knows about Angelica's death?" he asked, after a moment.

"Her sister. You."

"Her killer," Cummings added quietly.

"Yes," Frank said, sure for the first time that there was one.

Cummings shook his head. "They've been through so much, those two. First the plane crash, now this." His eyes drifted for a moment, then returned to Frank. "She's all alone now, Karen."

"Yes."

"Angelica's money will go to her, of course."

"How do you know?"

"Well, I doubt that Angelica had a will," Cummings said. "She'd had to have made a will right away, and I don't think that was a top priority for her. And, of course, if there is no will, then it's all Karen's now."

"But she doesn't really need it, does she?"

"Need?" Cummings said. "No, she doesn't need it. But need has very little to do with whether someone wants more money. That's one of the few things I've actually learned about life." He took a long drag on the cigar. "I don't need a Cuban cigar, but I want one." He watched the blue smoke curl upward toward the ceiling. "Lovely house they have out on West Paces Ferry Road. Have you seen it?"

"Yes."

"Quite elegant. Did you notice the paintings?"

"No."

"The Devereauxs were quite avid collectors," Cummings said. "Always going to Paris, Rome. The art in the foyer, it was all given to me by Charles, Karen's father."

Frank nodded.

"Karen is quite a painter, actually," Cummings added.

Frank closed his notebook. "Well, that's all I have for now," he said. He stood up. "Thanks for your time."

Cummings seemed hardly to hear him. "You should see some of Karen's work the next time you're over there. I even have one of hers in the foyer."

"I will," Frank said. "Thanks."

"Miss Carson will see you out," Cummings said from across the room as Frank closed the door.

Once in the foyer, it took him but an instant to recognize the painting that had been done by Karen Devereaux. It was an oil of a little girl standing by a vase of flowers. He stared closely at the swirling colors, his eyes drawn toward the face, the pale, flawless skin and deep blue eyes. It was Angelica's face, he realized immediately, and it watched him vacantly, its lips faintly blue. Without doubt, it was Angelica, and he felt his eyes move from her face down along her body to her small white legs. He half-expected to find one bare foot and a sad, scraped ankle.

Karen had signed her name in the lower right corner, and as Frank continued to look at the painting, he was surprised that it had not caught his attention earlier. Its colors were darker, its mood more somber; the portrait was vastly different from the ones that surrounded it. Instead of cheerful crowds and gay scenes, there was only the body of a little girl, and a face that seemed larger than the body. It was the face which drew him toward it now, very beautiful as Angelica certainly had been, but with a beauty that now seemed misplaced, misshapened, and which brooded over its own features rather than radiated from them. It was as if Angelica had already known that she would never be allowed to live out her life. Somehow, Karen had painted this knowledge into her sister's face, a knowledge, Frank realized with a sudden, dreadful chill, that had, in fact, been Karen's, and not her little sister's at all.

8

Caleb Stone was sitting at his desk when Frank returned to the detective bullpen. Propped back in his chair, his large belly drooping over the thick black belt of his trousers, he looked like a god of misspent youth.

"Well, I beat on some doors for you," he said dryly.

"Turn anything up?" Frank asked as he ambled up to Caleb's desk.

"By the grace of God, I did," Caleb said. "You ever work Vice, Frank?"

"No."

"It's an eye-opener, let me tell you. You walk around the streets, checking out this guy in a high-priced double-breasted suit. He's got a sweet little wife in Ansley Park, and a son who's doing just fine at Emory." He smiled sadly. "Thing is, this is the same guy who likes to tie a woman to the bedstead once a month and beat the shit out of her."

Frank turned away slightly. "What'd you turn up, Caleb?"

Caleb leaned back in his chair. "Well, when I was in Vice, I used to keep my eye on this little house on Glenwood. A guy people called Sancho used to run a string of whores out of it. One of them was named Beatrice, and dear God, Frank, she was the cutest little thing in the world." He smiled, almost wistfully, as if his memory were turning faintly sweet. "Black as the ace of spades, and with a wild look in her eye. But goddamn was she cute." Suddenly the sweetness fell away, and Caleb's voice took on a dangerous edge. "Anyway, the guy in the suit, he used to pay the price once in a while and Beatrice would meet him at this cabin he had on Black Mountain. For the whole weekend, you know. A real fly-me-to-the-moon sort of thing." He shook his head gently, and his voice grew darker and more somber. "Well, he used to give Bea a slap once in a while, just for the fun of it, you might say. She let it go. It was just part of the deal, nothing serious. She didn't like it, she told me, but whoever asked a whore what she liked? One weekend, though, things turned real sour up on Black Mountain, and this fuck did a real nasty job on Bea." Caleb's eyes shifted away, as if he were trying to hide what the story made him feel. "Well, I sort of liked Beatrice. She didn't exactly have a heart of gold, and she'd probably rolled more than one conventioneer in her time, but there wasn't a really mean bone in her body." He looked back toward Frank. "Hell, even old Sancho was a stand-up guy. About as good as a pimp can ever be." He laughed slightly. "Fat bastard with two buck teeth. Like the saying goes, he could eat a ear of corn through a keyhole."

Frank smiled.

"When things got hot for him, Frank," Caleb went on, "he did one thing I never knew a pimp to do. He spent his last goddamn dime bailing out his stable, and when he had to leave Atlanta, he run all the way to Kansas City, took every single whore with him, gave them some money, and then you know what?"

Frank shook his head.

"He cut them loose, Frank," Caleb said. "Just said, 'Good luck. Hope you'll have a nice life.' And then he just disappeared."

"What are you getting at, Caleb?" Frank asked finally.

"Well, after the double-breasted suit beat up on Bea, Sancho came to me," Caleb said. "He told me the story, and he said he was going to make sure this guy stayed clear of his girls." Caleb shook his head. "And he tried to do that. But the suit was hot for Beatrice. Something about her skin, the way it bruised, maybe. Anyway, he wouldn't leave her alone, and after Sancho said to stay away from Beatrice, just about everybody he knew got busted by the cops."

"So he looked like a snitch," Frank said.

"That's right," Caleb said. "That's a dangerous thing to be."

Frank nodded.

"So Sancho came to me," Caleb said. "He figured the suit was in on it, that the suit had plugs into the cops, and that they were helping him set Sancho up." Caleb smiled. "But he was wrong. The suit had a connection to a newspaper, to a reporter on the cophouse beat. That's the guy that was feeding him." He leaned even further back in his chair. "Well, it wasn't long till somebody worked over Beatrice. It wasn't the suit. It was somebody who thought Sancho had snitched on him. So the way I looked at it, it might as well have been the suit. Know what I mean?"

"Yes."

Caleb smiled broadly. "Ever heard the expression 'to take the law into your own hands'?"

"Yes."

Caleb lifted his arms into the air. "These old hands right here, son," he said. "One night they grabbed that fucker in the double-breasted suit, and they just didn't stop working on his face until he was really sorry he'd ever been nasty to a nice little black girl."

Frank smiled indulgently. "And this all has something to do with Angelica Devereaux?"

"It has to do with me knocking on a few doors around that lot," Caleb answered. "When one of them opened, it was little Bea behind it."

"She lives around there?"

"No, she lives in Kansas City," Caleb said. "Right where Sancho cut her loose. Claims she's a computer operator. Says she's long gone from the whorehouse business."

"You believe her?"

"Yeah," Caleb said confidently.

"What's she doing back in Atlanta?"

"Her sister's just got married for the fourth or fifth time," Caleb said. "She wanted Bea to come down and mind the kids while she went on her latest honeymoon."

"And you don't doubt any of this?"

"Nope," Caleb said. "Know why? Because she didn't give me that look whores always give men, even the ones they like. Lord God, Frank, you don't know what disgust is until you listen to whores talk about men. I know. I listened to a lot of them when I was working Vice."

Frank took out his notebook. "Beatrice, you said?"

"Beatrice Withers's what she goes by."

"And what did she tell you?"

"Well, Beatrice don't much like kids," Caleb said. "Fact is, she don't know a thing about them. So they've been running her ragged for the last few days. She's been walking the floor a lot. She was walking it at around three in the morning the day we found Angelica Devereaux."

"Tuesday morning," Frank said.

"That's right."

Frank could feel the skin of his fingers tighten slightly, as if they were already stretched out and reaching for the killer's throat. "What'd she see?"

"I thought you might want to hear it from her own mouth."

"Where is she?"

"At her sister's house, like I said," Caleb told him. He glanced at his watch. "She said she'd be there until around noon, then she was planning on taking the kids to the park so they could have a go at the squirrels. She's probably there now." He stood up immediately. "Ready to go?"

On the drive to the park, Caleb sat leisurely in the front seat, his large thighs spread out across the seats like thick rolls of dough. An enormous cloud of blue smoke ringed his head as he puffed at his pipe and, despite the open window, it seemed to coil around in the car, increasing the already stifling heat. It was as if it had become a part of him, this tumbling blue smoke, a swirling, indefinable cloud that marked and identified him like his own personal badge.

"She said she'd be near the playground," Caleb said as Frank turned the car onto Grant Street, then made a right and headed into the park. "She's wearing a bright yellow dress," he added with an appreciative smile. "That's something that hasn't changed much about Beatrice."

The bright yellow dress was visible from a great distance, and Frank saw it almost immediately. He guided the car slowly over to the curb and glanced toward the playground.

"That her?" he asked.

Caleb's eyes were already on her, and they seemed to soften as he looked at her. "Oh, yeah, that's her," he said, almost in a whisper, "sitting by the swings." He looked at Frank. "You might say she always did love things to be in motion."

It was well past noon, and as he got out of the car and headed down the small, bare hill toward the playground, Frank could feel that the steadily building summer heat had already turned everything dull and slow and sluggish. Even the children who dotted the playground moved ponderously through the thick, pulsing air. They hung like overripened fruit from the climbing dome, or swung slowly back and forth, as if moving through layers of gelatin.

"Hey, Bea," Caleb called as he walked up to her.

The woman looked up immediately, saw Caleb, and smiled sweetly as she looked at him. "Didn't think you was coming back."

"I said I would," Caleb told her.

She shrugged. "Well, you know what I'm used to." She leaned gently against the tree, as if it were a source of cool air. A wave of dark perspiration swam out from beneath the arms of her dress. Another hung in an almost perfect crescent over her upper chest.

"Kids still getting to you?" Caleb asked.

Beatrice smiled languidly. "They more than I can take, Cal." She waved her hand over her face. "And this heat. I almost forgot what it was like down here."

"You'd get used to it, if you didn't rush back up North," Caleb said, as if he were trying to persuade her to linger in the city.

Beatrice shook her head. "Naw, I got to get back." She glanced at Frank, but said nothing.

"This is Frank Clemons," Caleb told her. "He's in charge of the case."

Beatrice grinned at him. "Top man, huh?" She winked at Caleb.

"That's good. I like working with the man on top." She laughed. "Hey, Cal, you tell this white boy about me?"

"I got nothing to hide, Bea," Caleb said somberly. "You know me when it comes to things like that."

"So he told you I was once a working girl?" Beatrice asked Frank.

"Yeah."

"Way back when, though. Long gone from now."

"You work with computers these days," Frank said.

"Right, computers," Beatrice said. "Them other times is passed me by." She nodded toward Caleb. "He was skinny as a rail back then. Wasn't you, Caleb?"

"I was, yes."

"Handsome, too," Beatrice said. She shook her head despairingly. "But so thin. Lord, you could just about see through him." She leaned forward and patted his belly. "Look like somebody done knocked you up, Cal." She glanced back at Frank, and he saw the wildness in her eyes. "But he could go all night back in them days." She turned back toward Caleb and smiled affectionately. "Could 'bout wear a girl out, couldn't you?"

"With the right help, I could," Caleb said, and the two of them laughed softly.

"I understand you've been staying at a house near Glenwood?" Frank said.

"That's right," Beatrice told him. "I been takin' care of my sister's kids. She on her honeymoon. I never figured she'd get married again, but she done it, so I come down to see after the kids."

"Caleb says they keep you up at night?"

"That's right, too," Beatrice said. "They don't got much sense, them two. They run all over me. Like wild animals." She pointed toward a small dirt hill. Two children were tumbling down it, spewing waves of dry dust into the air. "See 'em. Like monkeys." She shook her head. "Shit, if I'd acted like them two, my mama would have nailed my bare feet to the kitchen floor."

Frank took out his notebook. "So you were up early on Tuesday morning?"

Beatrice nodded, her eyes looking closely at his face. "You had a talk with the wrong guy, looks like."

"More than one," Caleb said.

Beatrice smiled. " 'Member when them two got after you that time? You was all busted up."

"Tuesday morning you were up, is that right?" Frank repeated.

"Till the break of dawn."

"What did you see?"

"Well, they ain't much traffic on them sidestreets that time of the morning. So, I heard a car, and I looked out the window, sort of hoping it was my sister. It was a crazy thought, like maybe she done got tired of that fat bastard and left him on the beach. It was a crazy thought, but you know, when you want something bad, it does things to your mind."

"What kind of car was it?"

"Fancy car," Beatrice said, "like you don't see much around here."

"Do you know what kind it was?"

"It was a red little thing. What they call a 'coupe,' I think. It looked like a foreign car."

"Did you happen to notice what model it was?"

"I don't know models much. Used to, I did. Back when they was just a Buick and a Ford. They got too many of them foreign cars now."

"Was it new?"

"Oh yeah, it was new. Real shiny. Red as a rose. Only brighter. Bright red."

Frank wrote it down. "Which way was the car coming?"

"Up from Glenwood," Beatrice said, "going sort of slow."

"So you were facing the headlights?"

"Yes," Beatrice said, "shined right in my eyes. But then he flashed them off, and it was black night again." She looked at Caleb. "Black as my old ass, right, Caleb?"

Caleb took out his pipe. "Double or single headlights, Bea?"

"Two of them," Beatrice said. She looked scoldingly at the pipe. "So you still smoking that thing?"

"Just like always."

"How's your poor wife stand it?"

"Just like always," Caleb said, and again they laughed together.

"Where did the car stop?" Frank asked.

" 'Bout halfway up the street," Beatrice said. "It circled a time or two. Then it pulled up to the curb right by that empty lot. Then the lights went off."

"Could you see the car clearly?"

"It was pitch black, except for that one streetlight down on Glenwood."

"But you're sure about the color?"

"Yeah, I could see it good enough for that."

"Could you see any people in the car?"

"One guy. He was behind the wheel."

"Could you describe him?"

"You mean his face?"

"Yes."

"Naw, he was too far away for something like that," Beatrice said. "He waited a while before he got out, just set there behind the wheel. Then he got out and sort of looked up and down the street." She smiled. "White guy, though. I could tell that much."

"Could you tell what he was wearing?"

"Work suit, something like that," Beatrice said. "You know, one of those one-piece things that sort of go on like my daddy's overalls used to."

"Did he just stand by the car?"

"Uh huh."

"For how long?"

"Oh, maybe a minute, maybe two. I wasn't timing him."

"Then what happened?"

"He went around to the dark side of the car and opened the door."

"The door on the passenger's side?" Frank asked. "Not the trunk?"

Beatrice nodded. "Then he pulled something out. It looked like an old carpet. I figured he was dumpin' it in the lot. Nobody supposed to do that, but that old rusty car, God didn't put that there, you know? I figured that's why he's looking all around, 'cause he ain't suppose to be dumpin' no trash in that lot."

"Did you see anything in the carpet?"

"Nah, I didn't," Beatrice said. "But it was rolled up real loose like, and from the way he was walkin' it seemed a lot heavier to him than it ought to have been." She looked at Caleb. "It must have been real heavy. 'Cause one time, he dropped it."

"Where did he drop it?" Frank asked immediately.

"Oh, maybe a few yards into the lot, just about in front of that old car."

That was about where Angelica's shoe had been found, and Frank made a note of it in his book.

"He didn't put the carpet up on his shoulder no more after that," Beatrice added. "He just sort of drug it along, pulling it as he walked backwards." She glanced toward the children. They were now beyond the hill.

"Stay close now, Raymond," she called loudly. "And you watch out for Leila."

"Where did he take the carpet?" Frank asked.

"Into that lot, like I said."

"Where in the lot?"

" 'Bout the middle of it."

Which was about where the body had been found, Frank realized, and which meant that she probably had seen the things she described.

"What did he do in the lot?" Frank asked.

"I seen him lay the carpet down in the weeds," Beatrice said. "That's the last I seen. One of them kids started some shit, and I had to go tend to them."

"So you stopped watching him?"

"That's right."

"You didn't see him leave?"

Beatrice shook her head. "Next time I seen that street, it was maybe an hour later. Car was gone by then."

Frank wrote this last statement down in his notebook and ended it with a large black period.

"Thank you," he said.

Beatrice smiled faintly. "Don't guess it adds up to much, does it?"

"It's very helpful," Frank told her truthfully. He pocketed his notebook. "How long do you expect to be in Atlanta?"

"Maybe another week."

"Let us know before you leave."

"I'll tell old Caleb here." She smiled. "We're old buddies, ain't we?"

"Yeah, we are," Caleb said.

Moments later, when the two of them were back in the car, Caleb glanced wistfully toward the playground, his eyes lingering for a moment on the woman in the bright yellow dress. She seemed like a spot of light in the surrounding green. "You know, Frank," he said softly, "there's nothing like the past to make the future look like hell."

9

"It was murder, Caleb," Frank said determinedly, as he and Caleb made their way through the lunchtime crowds on Peachtree Street. The great towers loomed over them, a thousand small suns winking in a thousand separate mirrors. The heat rose from the street in steamy waves and rippled upward.

Caleb swabbed his face with a red handkerchief. "With malice aforethought," he said. He pocketed the handkerchief and elbowed his way around a strolling couple. "You know what tipped me off? The way he dumped her. You don't do that to someone you care about." He shook his head. "My daddy was full of shit, but I remember that when he was laid out in his coffin, my mother reached over and straightened that poor bastard's tie."

They reached the small, treeless park at the center of the city. It was made of cement blocks, with little triangles of closely cropped grass. A large lunchtime crowd of clerks and office workers was munching sandwiches. A few scattered derelicts elbowed their way through the crowds, and to the far end of the park, a small area had been taken over by poor, unemployed men who slouched about in fishnet shirts and drank beer from cans wrapped in paper bags.

"The heat don't make them nicer," Caleb said with a small, thin smile. He sat down on one of the few wooden benches and patted it softly. "Take a load off, Frank."

Frank sat down. "Headquarters would love it to be an accidental death," he said.

"Fuck them," Caleb said. He swabbed his neck again. "They got a low attitude about life, and they always have. Top floor's black now, but nothing else has changed. There's only one rule: cover your ass."

Frank watched the long line of barely moving traffic that circled the park: taxis, delivery vans, private cars, and here and there a bicycle that whizzed by everything else. For an instant, he felt a strange envy for the men and women on their bikes, for everything that seemed less stranded and bogged down.

"They don't see the bigger thing," Caleb said, "the top brass. It makes them crazy 'cause they don't." He crammed the handkerchief in his coat pocket. "So you get this murder and then that one and then the one after that." He shook his head. "Things blur."

"Not much of a way around that, though, Caleb," Frank said.

"I know one," Caleb said. "You got to do a trick in your mind. You got to think that every murder is the first one that ever was." His eyes shifted over to Frank. "In every one, there's some little thing that strikes you," he added. "I saw a little boy who'd been murdered once. His big brother had shot him. He was laying on the floor, and there was a little toy pistol still in his hand. That did it for me, that little pistol. I kept thinking about it, and in the end, it was all I needed to track that son-of-a-bitch brother down."

Frank nodded slowly.

"Now with Angelica, it's her hair," Caleb said, "the way it was all laid out around her head. Just like a gold fan."

Frank looked at him unbelievingly. "You think about that? About her hair?"

"Yeah," Caleb said. "It's what keeps the fire going in me."

Frank turned away and looked at the stream of traffic again. He could not think of small things to sustain him, as Caleb did. For him, it was just the opposite. Instead of a toy pistol, a fan of hair, such small, incidental things, he sensed something infinitely large which lived in the darkest quarters of the city or swept out like a prairie wind across barren, dust-covered fields. It was something which fed on the shadows in which it lurked, and then, suddenly, without warning, stepped out of them and into the adjoining world, swept out like a gnarled hand and pulled someone back into it, leaving only traces behind, a toy pistol for Caleb to remember, or a strand of golden hair.

In his mind, he suddenly saw Angelica's hair. But he did not see it as Caleb did, but as Karen had painted it in the portrait on Cummings' wall. Something in the portrait clung to his mind like a silver hook. Slowly, delicately, he tried to bring each feature into view: the shining black shoes and white socks, the gently tapered ankles, the red velvet dress and the lace that curled about its hem then rose in a swirl of white to her chest, where it gathered gracefully in a small white pool. He could see Angelica's neck rise from the lace collar, and then her face, so beautiful, framed by the blonde hair, each feature so perfectly wrought that it seemed separately made. He noted the ears, the full red mouth, the lines of her chin and cheekbones. Then, at last, he settled upon her eyes. He could see them very clearly, the blue irises, the black pupils, the oval pools of white. It was the irises that drew him back. Something was missing, the tiny white specks that give the eyes their light, They had not been painted in the portrait, and because of that, Angelica's eyes looked dead. Years before, her sister had painted her this way, but even now, as Frank felt a cold wave pass over him, he could not imagine why.

He was still thinking about it when he got home several hours later. For a long time, he stood on the little porch and watched night fall over the city. He stared first at one cluster of lights, then another, but always through the cloudy haze of Angelica's painted face.

He glanced down at his feet, as if hoping to find a clue clinging like a piece of street debris to his shoes. But there was nothing there, nothing anywhere but in his mind, feelings the facts could not warrant, vague, half-formed intimations. There were times when he was sure his father had been plagued by such odd sensations, times when his deep-lined face would look so wounded that everything around him seemed to grow quiet, and the world would appear as some small, crouching animal, huddled, frightened, sleeplessly listening for the footfall of a larger, predatory beast.

For relief, Frank lit a cigarette. He allowed it to burn for a while, then tapped the ashes and watched them fall slowly toward the ground. They twirled gracefully in the heavy summer darkness, lightly, playfully, as if there were no earth beneath to catch their fall. But the earth came up quickly, and even from several feet above, Frank could see the ashes as they collided with it and shattered into feathery specks of white.

Suddenly, in his mind, he saw Angelica's face shatter in exactly the same way. It was as if something had exploded beneath it, blowing its separate parts in all directions and leaving only the already lifeless eyes to spin like two dull marbles in the empty air.

He started to go back into the apartment, but as he turned, he felt a tremor move through him. It came from the ground beneath him, and he tried to imagine its source, a slight shift in the foundation, some tiny burrow caving in. He glanced at the window, to see if he could detect any trembling in the glass. But it was still. Everything was still. It was only in him, and so he simply waited for it to pass.

When it was over, he looked back into his apartment. It was an unappetizing clutter of fast-food boxes and newspapers. He could not bring himself to go inside.

The car was his escape, and within a few seconds he was moving down the city streets. Driving at night renewed and invigorated him. The flow of light, the feel of the air as it rushed through the open windows, worked on him like a tonic. For it was as if the streets belonged to him in some special way. He sometimes felt like the sole survivor of a bombed-out and abandoned kingdom, a ghostly presence, silent, restless, with nothing for thought but his own inchoate feeling, nothing for guidance but his hands on the wheel.

It was almost an hour later when he found himself far past the midtown towers. On his left, he could see West Paces Ferry Road as it came to an end at Peachtree Street. As he turned onto it and headed north, he could see Karen's portrait of Angelica as if it hung like smoke in the passing web of trees.

He slowed down as he approached the Devereaux house, then edged the car over to the curb. The wrought-iron gate had been closed, sealing off the driveway, but to its left Frank could see a small hinged entrance gate. When he pushed against it, it opened immediately, and he walked into the grounds.

As he walked slowly up the graveled driveway, he could see the house very clearly. All the lights were out, but its outer walls glowed softly white in the full moon. For a while he stood beneath a large oak and watched the house. He could see no movement at all behind the darkened windows, and after a while he turned quietly to leave.

But suddenly the front door opened, and Karen walked out onto the grounds. She was dressed in a white blouse and long white skirt, as if she had decided to embrace the opposite of mourning. There was a single white ribbon in her hair, and the wind lifted it gently as he stepped out of the shadows and walked toward her.

She saw him instantly, and there was enough light for him to tell that her face did not change when she saw him. She stood very still, her arms at her sides, and waited as he neared her.

"The gate was open," he said.

"Yes," Karen said. She moved a few paces to the right, toward an enormous spray of summer roses. Their red petals had curled tightly for the night. She took one of them in her hand. "My father planted these for Angelica," she said. She pointed toward another bush of white roses. "And he planted that one for me." She looked at him closely. "Why are you here?"

"I'm not sure," Frank said. "I went for a drive. I ended up here."

"And the gate was open, as you said."

"Yes."

"I have a telephone, Mr. Clemons."

"I know I should have called."

"Why didn't you?"

"I didn't want to," Frank said.

93

He waited for her to answer back, perhaps insult him. But she didn't. Instead there was just silence, without so much as a whisper of wind.

"I went to see Arthur Cummings today," Frank said finally.

"About the trust fund?"

"About that, and about Angelica."

"You won't learn anything from him," Karen said dryly. She released the flower and it sprang from her hand. "Why did you come here?" she asked again.

For a moment, Frank tried to come up with an answer that would satisfy her, something that would make sense either to her or to Brickman when she complained about him the next day.

"The portrait," he said at last, "the one you painted of your sister."

"The one in Cummings' office?"

"Yes," Frank said. "When did you paint it?"

"When she was eight years old."

"And so you were . . ."

"Twenty-two," Karen said immediately. She took a slow, hesitant step into the darkness, like one testing the water of a pool. "Twenty-two," she repeated. She moved again, this time slightly backward, and fixed her gaze on the lush summer grounds. "We used to play here," she said, "the two of us." She looked at him. "All those childhood games. I can look over there and remember tying her up, Indian-style." She nodded to the right. "And under that tree was where they set up the buffet at her third birthday party." She laughed quietly. "My father loved to do that sort of thing, throw a grand party." She shook her head. "Some people look for money, and some people look for ways to spend it. My father loved to see money flow away from him, rivers of money into the arts, schools, all sorts of things." She drew in a long, slow breath. "I think it was his way of being good. It was probably the only way he knew to be good."

"Was he good to Angelica?" Frank asked.

"Yes, he was. And he was good to me, and to Mother."

Frank resisted the impulse to pull out his notebook. "Angelica's face, the one in the portrait." He stopped, waited, then let it drop. "The eyes."

He could see a little shiver of emotion run through her body, then gather in her face.

"You noticed them?" she asked.

"Yes."

She smiled. "You're the first."

"I don't believe that."

She looked at him as if he had insulted her. "I don't lie, Mr. Clemons." Her eyes settled on him thoughtfully. "And to tell you the truth, I'm surprised you noticed." She shrugged. "Some people have commented that the painting seems a little odd. But no one has ever realized that it's all in the eyes."

"They're dead," Frank said.

"Yes, they are."

"Why?"

"I don't know," Karen replied. Her eyes swept over him. "The most I can say is that somehow I expected something terrible to happen to Angelica. When our parents died, I thought that that was it, the terrible thing. Then, later on, I knew that it wasn't."

"So you weren't surprised by her death."

"No," Karen said.

"But if you—"

"We have a garden in the back," Karen interrupted. "Do you like gardens?"

"I don't know much about them."

"You don't have to," Karen said. She smiled delicately. "I'm glad you came tonight. I guess you can understand that. I never thought it would feel this odd."

"What?"

"To be absolutely alone."

Frank nodded. "I'd like to see the garden," he said.

"Good," Karen said. "Come with me."

He followed her around the side of the house to where the garden swept out before them, wet and gleaming in the evening dew. It was softly illuminated by small, bluish floodlights. There was a circular marble fountain, and here and there assorted pieces of statuary rose from flowerbeds or peeped over slender walls of carefully manicured hedge. It was beautiful, and for a moment Frank found himself oddly moved by it, as if the garden were a beguiling vision of an order and a contentment that were beyond his own grasp.

"We don't cultivate anything that's really exotic," Karen explained. "The demanding ones just require too much." She glanced at Frank. "Only the really hearty ones can make it on their own."

"Do you have a greenhouse?" Frank asked.

"No. Only the garden."

"Did Angelica like the garden?"

Karen's eyes narrowed. "You don't ever forget where you are or what you're doing, do you?"

Frank felt himself bristle slightly. "There aren't too many things worth doing," he said.

She turned away from him. "Well, do you like the garden?"

"It's all right."

"So you don't like it?"

"It's nice," Frank said.

"What do you like, Mr. Clemons?"

"The streets."

"Why?"

"They're not like this," Frank said, nodding toward the garden. "They're not controlled." He shrugged. "I don't know, maybe I think that once in a while everybody ought to have to put everything on the line. Maybe that's why I like the streets."

"Violence, you mean?"

"If it comes to that."

"But violence doesn't solve things, does it?"

"I've seen it solve a few."

She waited a moment, as if considering her next question.

"Was Angelica murdered?" she asked finally.

"I think so," Frank told her.

"Yes," Karen whispered. She shivered slightly, despite the warm, musty air that surrounded them. "I think I'd better go in, now."

Together, they walked back around the house.

"That's Angelica's room," Karen said. She pointed to a single dark rectangle. "She always kept the shade drawn."

"I'll have to go through it sometime," Frank told her. "Is tomorrow all right?"

"Yes."

"What time?"

"It doesn't matter. I'll be here all day."

Karen walked up the steps, then turned back toward him. "Go ahead," she told him. "I'll wait until you're gone."

It seemed an odd request, but Frank did not hesitate to honor it. As he walked toward his car, he knew that she was watching him, but he did not know why. And yet, he believed that he had somehow managed to break through to her. He could feel her eyes upon him as he walked away, and he knew that there was no hostility in them. He could feel some sort of line uniting them, one that stretched beyond the approaching gate, and farther still, to the other side of the city where the streets still clung to their anger, and his room waited for him like a lonely child.

10

It was almost nine the next morning when Frank arrived at North-field Academy. It was located only a few miles from Angelica's house, and its grounds were shaded by similarly elegant trees. A rich summer greenness swept out all around the few buildings that dotted the campus; their exteriors looked as if they'd been designed to remind students of the glory that was Greece. The main building was larger than the rest, and its tall, Doric columns looked down upon a wide, cobblestone driveway.

The summer session had already begun, and Frank made his way toward the building through a steady stream of students. They were very well dressed in the latest teenage fashions, and in their midst, Frank felt like some bit of flotsam that had somehow managed to enter a bright, shimmering stream.

The crowds of young people thickened as he entered the building. They flowed around him in all directions, glancing at him indifferently and continuing their own daily routines. But one of them finally took pity and stopped in front of him.

"You look lost," she said.

"I am."

The girl smiled cheerfully. "Maybe I can help you."

"I'm looking for the headmaster's office."

"Oh, that's easy," the girl said brightly. "Just go straight down this hallway. It's the last door on your right."

"Thanks," Frank said, and did as she had told him.

A single desk confronted him as he went through the door. A well-dressed middle-aged woman sat behind it. A short, slightly overweight man in gold-rimmed glasses stood over her, pointing something out in a letter. "Just change that one line," he said, "and then get it out right away. Mr. Douglas has been expecting it for a while." He laughed lightly. "I think we've sunk the hook in pretty deep on this one, and it's time to reel it in."

The two of them laughed conspiratorially, then the man looked up at Frank.

"May I help you?" he asked.

Frank pulled out his badge. "Frank Clemons," he said.

The man's face whitened. "Oh, yes, so sad," he said. "Please come in." He hustled Frank into an adjoining office and quickly closed the door. "The other detective said you'd be coming by. I can't tell you how sorry we all are about Angelica."

Frank took out his notebook. "Of course," he said.

"There's some talk of a memorial gift, actually," the man said.

"You're Albert Morrison, right?" Frank asked. "The headmaster?"

"That's correct," Morrison told him. "And as I was saying, a memorial gift has been discussed. Arthur Cummings has expressed an interest."

Frank looked up. "You know Cummings?"

"Of course. He's one of the trustees of the Academy."

Frank wrote it down.

"And of course," Morrison went on, "he's very interested that the school be protected."

"Protected? From what?"

"Well, to use an old Victorian word, scandal," Morrison said. "I mean, she had been a student here. As you know, she was a member of the senior class. She only graduated a few weeks ago." He smiled thinly. "One other thing, I want you to know that Northfield will cooperate fully with your investigation. After all, we consider every student, whether past or present, to be a member of our extended family."

"When did Angelica graduate?"

"June first."

Frank wrote it down.

"On the grounds of the Academy," Morrison added. "That's been our tradition."

"How old is the school?"

"Fifteen years old," Morrison said. "Angelica was a good student here. Her death is a tragic loss for the entire community of Northfield. I do think a memorial gift would be appropriate. I was thinking of a flagstaff, or, if the donations warrant it, perhaps even a new addition to the theater."

"How many students were in her graduating class?" Frank asked.

"Twenty-five," Morrison said. "It was a beautiful ceremony. We had a string ensemble. They played Mozart."

Frank nodded dully. To celebrate his own graduation, he and a few of his classmates had bought an old car and pushed it off a cliff. It seemed now to have fallen as quickly and resoundingly as their own ambitions.

"How well did you know Angelica?" he asked.

"I try to know all the students here. And I mean more than just their names."

"How well did you know Angelica?"

Morrison seemed lost in thought. "She was very beautiful."

"How well did you know her, Mr. Morrison?" Frank asked, this time with a slight edge in his voice.

"Well, less than most," Morrison admitted. "Less than any, if you want to know the truth. She was not a terribly approachable human being."

"Did she have many friends at the school?"

"I really don't know."

"Well, did you ever see her with other students?"

"Rarely."

"But sometimes?"

"Yes, I suppose."

"Who were they?"

Morrison hesitated. "You mean, the names?"

"Yes."

"What would you do with them?"

"I'd look them up in your little student directory," Frank told him coolly, "and then I'd go talk to them."

"That could be embarrassing."

"One of their friends is dead," Frank reminded him. He waited for this to sink in. Then he fired again. "She was pregnant, did you know that?"

Morrison winced. "Yes."

"How?"

"Arthur told me," Morrison said. "He felt Northfield should be warned."

"About six weeks pregnant," Frank said, "which would mean that she was pregnant at her graduation."

Morrison's eyes lowered mournfully. "Yes, of course."

Frank leaned forward slightly. "Do you have any idea who the father might have been?"

"None at all," Morrison said. He shook his head worriedly. "One incident like this can have a terrible effect upon a school like Northfield." His lips curled downward. "All you need is one rotten apple."

"Is that how you thought of Angelica?"

Morrison looked like a child who'd been caught using bad language. "Well, no," he sputtered, "of course not. I mean, she was very—"

"Beautiful, yes," Frank interrupted. "What else?"

"Odd, that's all."

"In what way?"

"She didn't participate in school activities very much," Morrison said. "We stress community life at Northfield. We like joiners."

"And Angelica wasn't one?"

"Hardly," Morrison said with barely concealed disapproval. "She was very much to herself most of the time. I don't think she ever attended a school dance, or any other school function for that matter." He thought a moment, and something caught in his mind. "Except one."

"Which was?"

"The senior play," Morrison said. "She was in the senior play."

"When was that?"

"You'd have to ask Mr. Jameson; he directed it."

"Where could I find him?"

"He's probably in the theater right now," Morrison said. "We do have a summer theater program."

Frank wrote it all down.

"She was quite good, actually," Morrison added. "Everyone was impressed." He shook his head. "I do wish we could have helped her more."

"In what?"

"In life," Morrison said. "When you teach children, you realize how unprepared they are for life." He smiled gently. "We send them into a wilderness, Mister . . ."

"Clemons."

"Mr. Clemons, yes. We do the best we can, but it's not always enough."

"Would you say that Angelica was withdrawn, moody, anything like that?" Frank asked.

"From the life of this campus," Morrison said. "She was very withdrawn from that. Perhaps she had something else. Other people who were pulling her away from us."

"Toward the Southside?" Frank asked.

"Well, that's where she was found, after all."

"How did you know that?"

"It was in the paper," Morrison said. He took a folded newspaper from the table behind his desk and handed it to Frank. "See?"

Frank opened the paper. Angelica's Northfield photograph stared up at him from the front page.

"She should have been in the paper," Morrison said, "but not like this. As an actress, perhaps, or something else equally meaningful." He shook his head. "But not this."

Frank handed the newspaper back to him.

Morrison glanced at it again, then allowed his eyes to drift toward one of the Civil War portraits that hung on the opposite wall. It seemed to calm him, as if he had discovered something sweet and beautiful within it which the hectic world of upper-class education could not give him.

"I believe in tradition, Mr. Clemons," he said, finally. "I don't believe I should have to apologize for that." He looked back toward Frank. "When I think of Angelica, I think of someone who was drifting, who had no traditions to stand on."

"Maybe she didn't like them," Frank said.

"Of course, that's possible."

"Why did she go to this school?"

"It was not her choice."

"Whose was it?"

"Arthur Cummings chose the school."

"He made her go here?"

"He administered her trust fund," Morrison said. "Part of it was allocated for Angelica's education. Arthur elected to spend that money at Northfield."

Frank wrote it down.

"And may I add that I think Arthur made a wise choice?" Morrison said. "He was trying to help Angelica. But some people simply cannot be helped."

From the tone of his voice, Frank would have thought that he was talking about the kind of girl who ended up on her back, waiting for the next trick.

"What did Cummings want her to be?" he asked.

"Responsible," Morrison replied. "A credit to her family. A woman of some standing in the community." He looked at Frank sadly. "Isn't that what everyone wants for his children?"

Frank said nothing, but in his mind he suddenly asked himself what he had wanted for his own daughter. It struck him that he'd wanted only for her to live through all the stages of life, and, at the end, to have had some sense that it had been worthwhile.

"If she'd just allowed herself to join in with the other people at Northfield, she'd have been all right," Morrison said confidently.

For a moment, Frank actually tried to see the world as Morrison did, but he found that he could not comprehend his vision of a clearly divided world where a human being remained safe in one place and was imperiled by another. Instead he saw it as a constantly melding landscape, one in which there were no isolated lands, no insurmountable walls, no places so high that the tide could not rush in and sweep everything away.

"I'll need copies of the student and faculty directory," he said.

"I hope you'll use them discreetly," Mr. Morrison told him.

"And could you tell me where the theater is? I need to talk to this Mr. Jameson."

"The building just behind this one," Morrison said. He walked Frank out of the office and stood with him a moment in the corridor. "I am sorry about Angelica," he said. "I hope you understand that."

Frank nodded. There seemed nothing left to say.

11

As he entered the theater, Frank could see a tall, lean man who stood quietly on stage. He adjusted a microphone, then glanced up toward the back of the theater.

"All right, hit the spot," he called loudly.

Instantly a shaft of bright light cut through the dark interior of the theater. It enveloped the man on the stage, and threw a dark shadow almost to the rear wall of the stage. The man looked at the shadow, studying it closely, as if it were a dark pool of water which had just risen from beneath the boards.

"I like that," the man said. "Orchestra won't notice, but it'll be a nice effect for the people in the balcony."

Once again he looked up toward the back of the theater.

"Okay, drop it," he called, and the light flashed off immediately.

It was only then that he caught Frank in his eye. He leaned forward and squinted. "Can I help you with something?"

Frank walked down the center aisle and flashed his badge.

"I'm here about Angelica Devereaux," he said. "Are you Mr. Jameson?"

"Yes, I am."

"Well, I guess you've—"

"Just a minute, please," Jameson said hastily. He looked up toward the balcony again. "Okay, Douglas, you can finish up later. Just leave the spot in position and go on to your class."

Jameson waited until the boy had left, then he made the small leap from the stage to the floor. "The whole faculty had a private meeting about it this morning," he said. He smiled slightly. "All that matters is that Angelica not be associated with Northfield."

"Does everyone feel that way?"

"The board feels that way," Jameson said. "That's all that matters. As for the teachers, they're a bunch of cowards, afraid for their jobs." He shrugged. "Of course, Morrison has a point. Angelica had already graduated; she really wasn't a part of the school anymore."

"She was in a play, I understand," Frank said.

"That's right."

"Which you directed?"

Jameson laughed. "Does that make me a suspect?"

"We're not sure how she died."

"Well, what does that make me then?"

"Just someone who had contact with her," Frank said. He let his eyes drift down slightly. Jameson was dressed in a plain sweatshirt, spattered jeans and worn, unwashed sneakers. It was the sort of outfit that singled him out as a good deal less straitlaced than Northfield appeared to be.

"You did know her, didn't you?" he asked.

"Yes, a little. Like you said, I was her director."

"Did you know she was pregnant?"

"I heard she was."

"From whom?"

"Morrison," Jameson said. "That's got them more uptight than her being dead."

"Do you know who the father might be?"

Jameson shifted lightly on his feet. "Not me, if that's what you're thinking."

It wasn't beyond imagining, and Frank had already considered it. Jameson was young, perhaps thirty-five. He was handsome in a rough-and-tumble, scraggly-clothed sort of way, and he seemed to have a definite energy in his body and his eyes, the sort that might draw a young girl to it.

Jameson smiled slowly, and as he did so, Frank caught the unevenness of his teeth. It gave him an odd, predatory look.

"Do you really think I might be the father?" Jameson asked.

"I don't know," Frank told him. "Are you?"

"Isn't there some sort of test you can do if you really want to find out?"

Frank said nothing.

"Well, Mister . . ."

"Clemons."

"Clemons. You can test me until the cows come home, but I didn't fuck Angelica." He waited for Frank to answer, peering intently at his face. "By the way," he said, after a moment, "what happened to you?" He smiled. "You look like a mine blew up in your face."

"When was this play?" Frank asked.

"Two months ago."

"And rehearsals before that?" Frank asked.

"Yes."

Frank took out his notebook. "For how long?"

"Six weeks."

"Were they during the day or at night?"

"Both," Jameson said. "When it got close to opening night, we had more evening rehearsals."

"Did she come to most of them?"

"Yes, she did," Jameson said, "and that surprised me. Kids sometimes burn out. I thought she would be one of the first. You know how it is, kids have different priorities than adults."

Theories of child development were not what Frank was after, especially from a man who seemed to have an odd leer in his eye.

"Did she miss any particular night?" Frank asked.

"What do you mean?"

"Well, like every Thursday night, or every Friday night?"

"No. What would it mean if she did?"

109

"I don't know Angelica," Frank said. "It would help if I could pin down some pattern in her movements."

Jameson thought about it for a moment. "Well, I can't remember exactly when she did or didn't show up." His eyes continued to stare intently into Frank's face. "You really got pounded, didn't you?" He laughed. "Happened to me once, too. Only it was the cops who gave it to me." He smiled proudly. "Little place called Chicago, nineteen sixty-eight."

Frank did not bother to write it down. "What role did Angelica play?" he asked.

Jameson's face stiffened, as if he'd been rebuffed. "The lead."

"Which was?"

"Medusa. Ever heard of her?"

Frank nodded.

"Her hair was all snakes," Jameson said with a thin smile. He placed his fingers on his head and wriggled them wildly. "Much abused by men, that was Medusa's story. The snakes were to ward off rapists." He drew his hands down from his head and dropped them to his sides. "I wrote the play myself. I figured it would shock the hell out of the old blue-haired grandmothers who usually show up at Northfield Academy productions." He grinned childishly. "And it did, too. Poor Morrison must have gotten twenty calls about it."

"How was she in the part?" Frank asked.

"Pretty good."

"She wanted to be an actress."

"Doesn't everybody?"

"Did she have any talent?"

"Not really," Jameson said dismissively. "She fit the part, that's all."

"Did you know she was planning to go to New York?"

Jameson laughed. "Isn't everybody?"

"To be an actress."

"I repeat: Isn't everybody?"

"Did she speak to you about it?"

"She might have thrown the idea out a couple of times," Jameson said.

"Did you get the impression that she meant it?"

110

"I didn't get any impression one way or the other," Jameson said, "but I'll tell you one thing, that little girl would have ended up with her back on the casting couch more than once." He patted the pockets of his trousers. "You have any cigarettes? I'm fresh out."

Frank handed him his pack.

"Been trying to quit, but I can't," Jameson said. He lit a cigarette. "You know, I've always been interested in cops." He lifted his hand up near Frank's face then slowly made a fist. "It's sort of a hands-on profession, don't you think?"

Frank jotted down a few of the things Jameson had already told him.

"Not exactly Sherlock Holmes, are you?" Jameson asked haughtily.

Frank ignored him.

"I thought of writing a mystery once," Jameson said. "A sort of parody, you might say, I was going to call it 'The Deductive Detective.' "

Frank looked up. "Do you have a copy of the play?"

Jameson smiled happily. "Yes, since I wrote it. It's an adaptation from mythological sources. I have copies of it at home. I could send you one."

Frank handed him one of his cards. "Send it to me at that address," he said.

"Happy to," Jameson said. "I hope you find it interesting."

Frank glanced back down at his notebook. "How many other people were in the cast?"

"Five," Jameson said. "A few of them are right outside. They're in the summer production, too."

"Was Angelica close to any of them?"

Jameson smiled thinly, and Frank caught the leer again.

"Well, what do you mean by close?" Jameson asked.

"Whatever you want it to mean."

"Well, as a matter of fact, Angelica didn't really associate with the other kids very much."

"No one at all?"

"Not that I ever saw," Jameson said. "She was quite aloof, that one. Most of the kids thought she was sort of snobby."

"So she had no friends at all here at Northfield?"

"I don't think so."

"How about acquaintances, people she hung out with in the hall?"

Jameson shook his head.

"Are you telling me that she was entirely isolated at the school?"

"She seemed that way."

"From both the girls and the boys?"

"Come on," Jameson said, "you're not really looking for a girl friend. You're looking for the guy who knocked her up."

"I'm looking for anyone who might have known her in a personal way."

"Personal?" Jameson laughed. "Right, personal." He shrugged. "Well, as far as I could ever tell, she was alone."

"Even from the cast of the play?"

"Even from them."

Frank wrote it down. "Why do you think she was isolated?"

"Because she wanted to be," Jameson said, with a slight, resentful edge in his voice. "She thought she was better than everybody else."

"Why?"

"Why?" Jameson asked, as if the answer could hardly be more obvious. "Have you ever seen a picture of Angelica?"

"The one in the yearbook."

Jameson shook his head. "That stupid picture doesn't even begin to suggest how beautiful that girl was." He looked at Frank as if he were an innocent. "She had a quality, a way of walking, something like that, and it made people take notice, let me tell you."

"What kind of notice?"

"Come on, you know what I'm talking about."

Frank said nothing.

"Sex, man," Jameson said. "She gave off this incredible sexual thing. It was a wave of heat coming right off her body." He stopped, as if sensing that same heat in the air around. "Everybody wanted her."

"Did you?" Frank asked bluntly.

Jameson's eyes squeezed together. "That's none of your business."

Frank looked at him intently. He could see something crumbling behind his eyes. "Everything about Angelica Devereaux is my business," he said.

112

"Look, if you're after horny stories, why don't you go over to the boy's locker room?"

Frank said nothing. He could see Jameson's agitation building steadily, and he waited for it to crest in a wave of sudden truth.

"Don't you think they talked about her, those boys?" Jameson said. "Don't you think they dreamed about her?"

Frank continued to watch him closely, his pencil held motionless above the page.

"Oh, you can bet they talked about Angelica," Jameson sputtered. "And you can bet Angelica knew the things they said."

Frank still said nothing. He kept his eyes steadily on Jameson's face.

"It was like a spotlight was always on her," Jameson went on. "And she wanted that light. She knew what it was. She knew everyone turned around when she came into a room. She knew what they whispered when she walked by them." He nodded frantically. "Oh, she knew, all right, and she loved it." He stopped suddenly, and his lips squeezed together tightly, as if in a desperate effort to hold something back. He took a deep breath, trying to calm himself, then wiped a line of sweat from his upper lip. "That kind of beauty," he said quietly, at last, "it can fuck you up."

"You, or her?" Frank asked pointedly.

Jameson's eyes flashed toward him. "Look, I didn't fuck that girl. What happened between us, it was nothing."

"What was it, exactly?"

"This is in confidence, right?" Jameson asked cautiously.

"If it doesn't pertain to her murder," Frank said.

Jameson's eyes narrowed. "Murder? I thought the cops weren't sure about how she died."

"I'm sure."

Jameson's eyes darted about nervously. "Well, I can tell you that I didn't have anything to do with a murder."

"Just tell me about you and Angelica," Frank said.

"It's got to be between you and me," Jameson insisted.

Frank glared at him icily. "If you withhold one thing from me," he said, "it's obstruction of justice, and I'll nail you for it."

Jameson sucked in a quiet, desperate breath. He seemed to think about it all for a moment, calculate what was to be gained or lost.

113

"All right," he said finally. "It's not what you think. I mean, I really didn't fuck her. I didn't knock her up, you understand."

Frank lowered the pencil to the page.

"We were working late one night," Jameson began. "We were up here on the stage. Everyone else was gone. I don't know why Angelica decided to hang around that night. She was usually the first one out of here." He drew in a long breath, then let it out slowly. "Anyway, she hung around for a while, so we started to run lines together. She was standing right next to me. She was so beautiful. Unbearable." He glanced toward Frank, as if for sympathy. "You know what I mean?"

"She was seventeen," Frank said.

"But worldly," Jameson said quickly. "I mean, she knew what she had. She knew what people wanted. I mean, she gave it to somebody, right?" He shrugged. "Well, the fact is, I had a weak moment."

Frank said nothing. He suspected that Jameson's life had been made up of a long string of weak moments. "What happened, exactly?" he asked.

"Well, like I said, we were on the stage together," Jameson said. "We were running lines. She was about three feet from me, I guess. Then something happened. I don't know what. I heard the back door of the theater open, or something else distracted me, and when I looked back, she seemed so close. To tell you the truth, I don't know if I moved, or if she moved, but she seemed to have gotten closer to me." He stopped and shook his head wearily. "Well, when I looked back at her, she sort of smiled. We started running lines again, but it was different. She kept smiling and her voice changed. It was like she was talking to *me*, not to the character I was playing." He pointed to himself. "To *me*, those lines I had written for her." Then he quoted them: " 'For you, this beauty, arrayed in wanton fire.' " He fell silent again, as if to recall the folly of the moment. "And then I leaned toward her and kissed her." He shook his head despairingly. "I could hardly believe I'd done it."

"What did Angelica do?" Frank asked.

"She just drew back and looked at me. There was this expression on her face—I hardly know how to describe it. It was a look of triumph, you know?—and at the same time of utter distaste. It said, I made you do what I wanted . . . and you disgust me." He made a small noise, half-grunt, half-sigh. "Talk about a Medusa stare."

"Then what happened?"

"She just walked away. Neither of us ever mentioned it again."

Frank started to write it down.

Jameson grabbed his arm. "Please," he said, "you've got to keep this in confidence."

Frank pulled his arm from Jameson's grasp. "I'm not your priest," he said.

Jameson's body grew tense, but he said nothing.

"You said that some of the kids who were in the play with Angelica were still around, is that right?"

"Yes," Jameson said stiffly.

"Where are they?"

"Just outside the auditorium. They usually laze around under the trees out there until I call them in."

"What are their names?"

Jameson stepped over to one of the empty chairs and pulled a piece of paper from a rumpled stack. "Here's the program for the performance. All the names are in it."

Frank took the program and put it in his pocket.

———————

They were exactly where Jameson had said they would be, slouched around a large oak tree just outside the auditorium, two boys in white tennis outfits, and a girl in a white blouse and bright red shorts.

Frank pulled out his badge as he stepped up to them.

"You've all heard about Angelica Devereaux," he said.

The three students nodded and glanced apprehensively at each other.

"Were all of you in the play with her?" Frank asked quietly.

"Yes," the girl said.

Frank took out his notebook. "What is your name?"

"Danielle Baxter."

Frank looked at the two boys. "And how about you?"

"Philip Jeffers," the taller boy said.

"Aaron Shapiro," said the other.

"There were six people in the cast," Frank said. "Where are the other two?"

"Joanna's in Europe for the summer," Danielle said. "She's spending it with her father."

"And Stan Doyle couldn't do the summer show," Aaron added.

"Yeah," Danielle said, "he had to take a summer job." Her voice was almost mournful, as if no worse fate could be imagined.

"I'm trying to find out as much as I can about Angelica," Frank said. "And to tell you the truth, so far I haven't been able to come up with very much."

Danielle nodded. "Yeah, well, she was sort of strange."

"In what way?"

"She wasn't friendly," Philip said. "She wasn't a joiner."

"She joined this cast," Frank noted.

"Well, that's the only thing," Danielle said, almost scornfully.

"She wasn't very well liked then?" Frank said.

Aaron shrugged. "We'd probably have liked her if she'd given us half a chance," he said defensively. "But it's like Philip and Danielle said, she was sort of strange, and she didn't really socialize very much." He thought about it for a moment. "I don't think she liked *us* very much. The kids at Northfield, I mean."

Philip laughed. "I mean, the way she looked, you can bet she would have been popular. Especially with the guys, right, Aaron?"

"Yes," Aaron said. He looked at Frank. "All the guys were hitting on her."

"Yeah, like crazy," Danielle said. She smiled cunningly. "Even you, Philip."

Philip bristled slightly. "That was before Tina."

"How did she react to being hit on all the time?" Frank asked, trying to get them back on track.

Aaron faked a shiver. "Brrrrrrr. She was a cold fish."

Philip sighed painfully. "Yeah. It was tragic, the chill she could put on you."

Danielle laughed self-consciously.

Frank turned to her. "How did the girls feel about her?"

"Maybe a little jealous at first," Danielle admitted with some reluctance. "I mean, the way she looked, she was a sort of threat to everybody. Philip and Aaron are right, all the boys were hitting on her. But then, when she froze them out, she just sort of disappeared in our minds."

"Because she wasn't a threat anymore," Aaron said confidently. "Right, Danielle?"

"I guess so," Danielle said. "I guess that's the way it was."

"Did she have any friends at the school?" Frank asked.

"Not really," Danielle said.

"How about during the play?" Frank said. "Did she get close to anyone in the cast?"

Almost simultaneously, the three students shook their heads.

"When rehearsals were over," Frank said, "didn't the cast go out together?"

"Sometimes," Aaron said, "but not Angelica."

"Where did she go?"

"She always left by herself," Aaron said.

"What about teachers?" Frank asked. "Was she friendly with any of them?"

"No," Danielle said. "She didn't really talk in class." She looked at the two boys. "Were her grades any good?"

Aaron shrugged. "I don't know."

"I never saw her name on the honor roll," Philip added, "so I guess they couldn't have been that great."

Frank could tell that the well was drying up, and that if he were going to find out anything about Angelica Devereaux, he would have to look outside the campus of Northfield Academy. Still, he decided to try one more question.

"We have reason to believe that Angelica had a boyfriend of some kind," he said curiously. "Any idea who that might have been?"

The three faces stared back at him blankly.

"Maybe a boy from college," Frank added. "Somebody like that."

The blank stares remained in place.

"Okay," Frank said wearily. "If you think of anything that might help me, give me a call." He gave each of the students one of his cards. Then he stepped back and looked at each of them pointedly. "I know that none of you was close to Angelica," he said, "but remember that she was young, like you, and that she had her whole life ahead of her, like you do. Now she won't get a chance to live that life, maybe even to turn into someone you would have liked better." He stopped, and allowed his eyes to settle on them. "I need to find out why that chance was taken from her."

The three young faces softened somewhat, and for the first time, Frank thought he saw something other than the self-centeredness of youth in them: a little bit of sympathy, a little bit of fear.

12

It was almost noon by the time Frank reached the downtown headquarters, and the streets were already baking in the same unrelenting heat that had plagued the city for the last few days. The cool of the air-conditioned interior of the building swept over him soothingly as he entered it, and for a moment he wondered why he'd not been able to live the life of an office worker or junior executive, a calm, climate-controlled life in rooms where blood never dripped from the walls.

The elevator door opened and Caleb walked out into the lobby. "I left a note on your desk, Frank," he said.

"What'd it say?"

"Just to let you know where I was headed."

"Where are you going?"

"Toward Marietta. A little past the Chattahoochee."

"What for?"

Caleb grabbed Frank's upper arm and tugged him forward. "Come on along with me," he said, "I'll fill you in." Frank had intended to go out to Karen's to check Angelica's room, but he let Caleb carry him along instead.

Traffic was moving briskly on the northbound side of the expressway, and before long, even the faintest outline of the city had disappeared behind them.

Caleb flung his arm out the window as he drove, and the rushing air flapped loudly in his sleeve.

"Anybody ever mention to you whether or not Angelica had a car?" he asked.

"No."

"Turns out she did," Caleb said. "But that's getting a little ahead of things."

"What do you mean?"

"Well, about an hour ago, I got a call from an old hometown buddy of mine," Caleb said. "Name's Luther Simpson. A regular good old boy. He moved to Atlanta about the same time I did. We was both just kids. I got hooked up with the police, and Luther, well, he took a different way altogether."

"What way was that?"

"A life of crime, you might say," Caleb told him. "Oh, nothing big-time or really that bad. Petty stuff. A whole yellow sheet of it wouldn't add to much. We're talking about a little bootleggin', maybe some gambling on the side." He looked at Frank. "Nowadays, he's mostly a car cutter."

"Where does he do it?" Frank asked.

"He don't steal them, you understand," Caleb said, "he just cuts them."

Frank nodded. "Out this way?"

"About ten miles out," Caleb said. He pressed down on the accelerator and the car surged ahead. "He works for Dave Goggins. Goggins runs four or five cut operations. He's been doing it for years. Everybody knows it, but nobody's been able to nail him yet." He stared about the steadily thickening countryside. "Sometimes I do think about getting back to the woods, Frank," he said. "Just think how nice it would be to have a place out here."

Frank stared straight ahead. He could see a line of gently rolling hills in the distance and, beside their quiet beauty, the city did sometimes appear as little more than a steel and cement canker on the surface of the earth. Perhaps that was why Sarah had chosen to leave it behind, to take the very same road out of town and head toward the very same rolling hills that stretched before him now. They were calm, green, utterly silent. But as they grew larger as he approached them, they also seemed to take on an odd, stalking life. He could feel a puzzled rage building in him, squeezing his throat. He had felt it before, and it seemed little worse now than at those other times, when he'd relieved it with a long night in some grim, honky-tonk bar.

"Well, Luther gave me a call about an hour ago," Caleb said.

"What for?"

"Because he got a car in this morning that gave him a little scare."

The man who'd stumbled upon Sarah's car had been scared too, Frank remembered. But by then the car hardly mattered. Sarah had been gone for days, and he'd already convinced himself of the worst, that she was dead, dead, dead, and that nothing could reclaim her. It was Alvin who'd finally come to tell him, his hat in his hand, standing glumly in the doorway: *We found her, Frank.* He had not needed to say another word, and Frank had only answered: *Where?*

In those hills, he thought now, as they began to loom sullenly above him. He'd gotten into the car with Alvin, and sat silently for the short ride. Then he'd gotten out and staggered off into the woods, slowly at first, following Alvin, then more quickly, passing him and moving still more swiftly until he was running at full speed toward a place he had never seen and could not have known about, running so fast, plunging through the thick undergrowth so loudly that he could barely hear his brother struggling far behind him, and then could not hear him at all, but only the sound of his own body as it crashed through low-slung limbs, until, at last, he broke through the last of them and saw her in the little clearing, her body framed by the river, and rushed to her there, dropping to his knees, lost in a silence that seemed to last forever and that was broken only by the breathless, exhausted sound of Alvin's voice: *Sweet Jesus, Frank, how did you know she was here?*

"Just over the river, here," Caleb said as the car nosed down a small hill and headed toward a narrow, concrete bridge. "That's where Luther does the cutting."

Frank struggled to bring his attention back to the case. "What about the car, the one that's bothering him?"

"Well, Luther'd read about Angelica in the paper," Caleb said.

"And early this morning a red BMW comes in, and it's got the initials LAD right on the dashboard, and inside the glove compartment, there's a program of some play or something that was given at Northfield."

"So he thinks the car's Angelica's?" Frank asked.

Caleb turned toward him. "Yeah," he said. "And it turns out he's right."

"Angelica had a car?"

"Yes, she did," Caleb said. "I called her sister. What's her name?"

"Karen."

"Yeah, Karen. She knew about it. She figures Angelica bought it with her new money."

"Why didn't she report it missing?"

"I guess she didn't think about it," Caleb said. "But I asked her to check the garage, and when she got back to me, she said the car was gone. That's when I went back to Luther and got the serial numbers on the BMW. I ran them through the computer and it comes up owned by Angelica." He gave the wheel a sharp turn to the left and the car headed off onto a dusty, unpaved road. "Cutters don't exactly stay right on the beaten track," he said.

The car lurched forward down the winding road. Low-slung limbs slapped loudly against the windshield, and glancing in his mirror, Frank could see a long trail of dust as it wound behind like a furry orange tail.

"Guess you haven't been on roads like this since you left the piney woods, have you, Frank?" Caleb asked. He pressed the accelerator a little harder, and the car slammed loudly into an enormous pothole, then plowed out of it effortlessly.

"I did a little dirt racing," Frank said, "but we stuck to better roads for that."

"There was a few nights in those days, Frank, when I'm not sure we even bothered with a road."

Frank smiled, but his youth now seemed so far away that he felt as if it had been lived by someone else. "How far to this place?" he asked.

"Maybe another mile or two," Caleb said brightly. He slammed down into another hole, and a huge smile spread across his face. "God, I love this," he said with a laugh.

Frank closed his eyes for a moment, and felt himself go back involuntarily to the farm country of his youth. He remembered the clear, cold streams and granite cliffs, the long summer nights with Sheila beneath him, her back on the cool ground, her breath in his face, the moon above them like a kind, unsleeping eye. His mind shot forward and he saw Karen in the darkness before her house, her arms at her sides.

"Yonder it is," Caleb said.

Frank opened his eyes. Through a wall of thick leaves he could see a large building. It was made of corrugated tin, and much of it had rusted over the years. Several cannibalized cars rested here and there in the surrounding brush and gave the woods the eerie appearance of a long-abandoned town.

A man in gray work pants and a green khaki shirt walked out of the building as Caleb brought the car to a halt.

"Howdy, Caleb," he said as the two of them got out of the car.

"Hey there, Luther," Caleb said. The two of them shook hands. "This is my partner, Frank Clemons."

Luther offered his hand. "How you?"

"Fine," Frank said as he took it.

"Me and old Luther here, we've seen some times," Caleb said. He glanced at his friend. "You look like you've shed some weight since I saw you last."

"Must of gone right to you, then," Luther said with a smile.

Caleb rubbed his belly. "Well, what the hell. Like the song says, I ain't built for speed."

"How's Hilda?" Luther asked.

"She'll do," Caleb said dryly. "Listen, Luther, I told Frank here about the car and everything. He'd like to take a look at it."

Luther nodded. "Like I said, the minute I thought this might have something to do with that girl, I called you right up."

"And we appreciate it, Luther," Caleb said. "Ain't that right, Frank?"

"Yeah, that's right."

"I don't keep nothing from my partner, Luther," Caleb said. "He knows you've not exactly walked the straight and narrow."

"But I ain't never hurt a soul," Luther said.

"I told him that, too."

"Just so that's all clear. Sometimes, the cops, you know, they just decide they want somebody, and they go get him. I've seen it happen, Caleb."

"Well, Frank's not like that," Caleb assured him. "Now, where's that car?"

"Well, if you say so," Luther said. He slowly turned toward the building. "Come on, I got it in here."

The red BMW could be seen clearly at the back of the shed. It glowed like a bright fire among the other cars, somber late-model luxury automobiles in their conservative blacks and grays.

"Minute I saw it, I got a little click in my mind," Luther said as he stepped up to the car. "It came in early this morning, and I'd already read about that girl." He walked over to the driver's side and opened the door. "I started to look her over, and that's when I saw them initials." He pointed toward the dashboard. "See, right there."

Frank leaned in. The LAD initials were gold-plated and they were attached to the leather dash.

"Now me, I got girls of my own," Luther said. "I wouldn't have nothing to do with hurting somebody like this girl you found dead." He looked at Caleb. "You know me better than that, don't you, Caleb?"

Caleb nodded. "When'd you say this car came in?"

" 'Round nine."

Frank pulled himself out of the car and took out his notebook. "You haven't done anything to it, have you?"

Luther laughed. "Shit, no. If I'd done something to this car, you'd know. This ain't no car wash. We break them down to parts."

"We'll send a tow truck for it, Luther," Caleb told him.

Luther nodded. "That's what I figured. I already explained to the bossman. He don't want nothing to do with it. He said, 'sooner you take it, the better.' "

Frank felt a strong urge to examine the car on the spot, turn it inside out, but he knew they could do a better job on it back at the garage. Instead, he took out his notebook. "Who brought it in, Luther?"

Luther hesitated for a moment. "He ain't a nice guy. Least that's what I hear."

"Who is he?"

"Big nigger. Into quite a few things. I hear he spread some queer around a little bit too much, and drew some time for that."

"We need a name, Luther," Frank said. "We can find out about all the rest."

"He goes by the name of Davon Little," Luther said. "Some folks call him Butt. He's got a big ass on him." He glanced at Caleb and laughed. "Like he's toting a bale of hay."

"Been doing business with him long?" Caleb asked.

"Over the years, he's brought in nine or ten," Luther said, "usually fancy, like this one. He usually joyrides them awhile, then just turns them over to a cutter."

"He didn't joyride this one for very long," Frank said.

"Yeah, well, you know how it is, you kill a girl, you don't want to keep her car."

"You got the keys?" Frank asked. "Or did he hot-wire it?"

"He had the keys," Luther said. "That's another thing that bothered me."

"Where are they?"

"Right here," Luther said. He pulled them from his trousers and dangled them in the air.

"Open the trunk," Frank said.

Luther stepped to the back of the car and opened the trunk. It was empty except for the usual spare tire and jack.

"Clean as a pin," Caleb said mournfully. "Too bad."

Luther laughed nervously. "What'd you boys expect to find, another dead gal stuffed back there?"

"Never know," Caleb said. He looked at Frank. "They'll vacuum the shit out of it. If Angelica lost so much as a hair back here, they'll find it."

Frank closed the trunk. "Do you have any idea where this Davon Little lives?"

Luther shook his head. "People we deal with, they don't make a point of mentioning things like that."

"Have any idea where he did time?"

"He talks funny," Luther said. "Sort of like Johnson used to, Texas-like. Maybe that's where they busted him." He picked up a soiled magazine and fanned himself languidly. "Lord, it's hot in here." He glanced at Caleb. "You remember S. D. Pullens? He used to explode them little fireballs in his mouth?"

"Yeah, I do," Caleb said.

"He got the chair up in Illinois."

"Pullens?" Caleb asked unbelievingly. "What for?"

"He was working one of them factories up there, and he just got roaring drunk. Cops come to cool things down, and he shot two of them." He squinted hard. "I wouldn't have figured him for that, would you?"

"The drinking, but not the killing," Caleb said.

Luther shook his head wearily. "When things turn sour, anything can happen. I guess that's all you can say." He dropped the magazine into a rusty fifty-gallon drum. "Fanning don't do no good." He looked longingly at the square of light which came through the single open door of the shed. "What say we go on back outside."

The heat remained stifling even outside the shed, and Caleb pulled off his jacket and slung it over his shoulder.

"This Davon character, did he say anything to you, Luther?"

Luther thought about it for a moment. "I just noticed one thing."

"What was that?"

"He didn't try to get me down," Luther said. "Minute I give him a price, he took it." He looked at Frank. "This ain't Woolworth's. People usually bitch and moan about the price, and I come up a little, and the next guy comes down. Not Little, though. Not this time. I quoted him about half what I'd have paid him on the up and up, and he looked glad to have it."

Frank wrote it down.

"He must have figured they was a APB on it by now," Luther said, "so he just wanted to dump it. Cutter is the best place. A fence don't want no fucked-up car." He shook his head. "Shit, I wouldn't have bought it either if I'd read the paper yesterday." He laughed. "But I don't ever get to the paper till the next day. When it comes to the news, I'm always a day late."

"Did he say anything at all about the car?" Frank asked.

"They's nothing to say," Luther told him. "I know my business, so nobody bullshits me. Besides, I ain't buying it to take a long vacation in." He nodded back toward the shed. "Them cars in there,

126

they'll be down to parts before morning. I mean right down to parts, nothing but bumpers and carburetors and shit like that." He looked affectionately at Caleb. "Could have been the same with that little BMW, too."

"I know it could, Luther," Caleb said quietly.

Luther turned back to Frank. "I'm a car cutter, and I'm a good one, but I don't have nothing to do with no real meanness, and that's a fact. Anybody hurts a little girl, they deserve what they get." He glanced back toward Caleb. "They deserve·it a hell of a lot more than S. D. Pullens did, I bet."

Frank pulled out his card and offered it to Luther.

Luther didn't move to take it. "I just deal with Caleb," he said flatly.

Frank put the card back in his pocket. "I appreciate it," he said.

Caleb laughed. "Well, Luther, I'd tell you stay out of trouble, but shit, I know better than that." He pulled on his jacket. "You know where to find me."

"Tell your boys to come get this fucking car out of here," Luther said. "Some people I deal with would get pretty bent out of joint if they come driving up and saw a goddamn police tow truck."

"It'll be here fast, Luther," Caleb said. "I guarantee it."

Luther rubbed his sleeve across his face. "And do something about this fucking heat while you're at it," he said.

13

The drive back to headquarters struck Frank as unbearably long, and as the first grayish outline of the city became visible, he felt an urge to turn away from it and drive in the opposite direction, it didn't matter where. Just someplace where he didn't know the pimps or the whores, or even that fresh-faced young traffic cop who waved him through the late-afternoon congestion. He wanted to be a stranger, a silent, invisible presence, nothing more.

A full sheet had already been run on Davon Little by the time they got back to the bullpen. Gibbons was waving it playfully in his hand when Frank and Caleb came through the door.

"This looks hot," he said with a boyish smile.

Frank snatched it from his hand. "We don't know yet."

Gibbons looked at him doubtfully. "You'd let me know if you needed something, I hope."

"Sure thing," Caleb said as he passed by and followed Frank quickly to his desk.

"Davon Clinton Little," Frank said to himself as he began to read the report.

Caleb stood over him, his eyes fixed on the paper.

"Uh huh," he said, after a moment. "Lots of petty shit. Burglary in his youth, then graduating to a little personal assault."

"He drew some time on that," Frank said.

"Yeah, and it looks like it settled him down a little," Caleb added. "So he switched over to flim-flams and car theft." He smiled. "Before long we'll be dealing with white-collar crime."

"Slid back in eighty-two," Frank said.

"And things got raw, didn't they?" Caleb said.

Frank ticked off the descent. "Armed robbery, assault, attempted murder."

"He's not mellowing with age, Frank," Caleb warned darkly.

Frank nodded. "Last known address was on the Southside." He took a map of the city and spread it out across his desk. "Simpson Street." He found the street name in the index then pinpointed it on the map. "Look at this."

Caleb leaned forward, eyeing the map. He watched as Frank's finger moved left about a quarter of an inch and struck the corner of Amsterdam and Glenwood, the vacant lot where Angelica's body had been found.

"Bingo," he whispered.

Frank stood up. "Well, let's go see if he's home."

"When you get older, it's all memory," Caleb said as he pulled himself into the car.

Frank hit the ignition and eased the car from the curb. "What is?"

"Life," Caleb answered. "Like since we found that girl, I've been thinking of all the other bodies. I can remember the first one the best." He pulled out his pipe and began to fill the bowl. "It was on the Southside, too, and it was a young girl. But there was a difference. She'd been buried quite a while, and, you know, Frank, the thing I remember most is how she kept coming apart when they tried to dig her out. Pieces of her would just crumble in your hand." He shook his head. "And I thought, well, the preacher back home, he got one thing right: dust to dust, Frank, that's a fact." He put the pipe in his mouth and lit it.

Frank glanced over at him, and for some reason his eyes lingered on Caleb's face. It was large and jowled. Skin hung flaccidly from the line of his jaw and gathered in rounded puffs beneath his eyes. He was nearly sixty, Frank guessed, and it was as if he could see the thread of his life as it unraveled, hear each fiber as it snapped.

"Now my wife has a different idea," Caleb said after a moment. "Sort of a Holy Roller type. She thinks she's on her way to God."

Frank continued to listen. He was surprised that after so many years, Caleb had suddenly begun to talk about his private life. It was as if there was something in him trying to break out, a small, trapped animal gnawing through his skin.

"She was always off to church," Caleb went on. "Praying we could have a kid, that's what I always figured." He glanced over to Frank. "I don't know why we couldn't. We tried plenty during the first few years." He smiled ruefully. "Then we didn't try that much anymore."

Frank felt himself overtaken by a deep sadness, like a fist out of the darkness, and he had to turn away quickly and fix his eyes on the street ahead in order to keep himself contained. Caleb seemed to sense it, and said nothing else. He simply sat, puffing on his pipe, and watched the line of shops and restaurants until they faded almost imperceptibly into the dilapidated service stations and fast-food joints of the Southside.

"Okay, let's keep our eyes open for Simpson Street," Frank said after they'd gone past the vacant lot.

"Should be on our right," Caleb said matter-of-factly.

It was a narrow, pitted street, and the car rumbled noisily as Frank turned onto it.

"Go slow, now," Caleb said. "We're looking for Two Forty-one." He peered out the window, his eyes darting from one house to the next. "There it is," he said, finally.

Frank guided the car over to the curb and stopped. The house was small and rested on a cement foundation. The red brick facade was chipped, and even from that distance, Frank could see a large tear in the front screen door. A scattering of children's toys lay here and there on the parched lawn.

Caleb's eyes moved from the overturned tricycle to the rusting swings. "I don't like kids around when we're checking a guy out."

He looked at Frank. "Guys like Little, what the fuck do they want kids for?"

Frank got out of the car and joined Caleb on the sidewalk, then the two of them walked to the front door and knocked.

It opened immediately, and a tall thin woman with stringy blonde hair stood facing them. She was dressed in faded jeans and what Frank took to be the upper half of a flowered bikini. She was very pale, and her arms dangled at her sides like strips of white paint.

"Davon ain't here," she said. She raked back her hair with a single, boney hand. "I don't know when he'll be back." A small child in a soiled diaper toddled up from behind and wrapped its arms around her leg. "Get away now," the woman said. She reached down, jerked the child around and shoved it back toward the rear of the house. "This ain't your business."

Frank pulled out his badge. "Where is Mr. Little?" he asked.

The woman stared vacantly at the badge.

"Where is he?" Caleb demanded in a hard voice.

The woman's watery blue eyes shifted over to Caleb. "I don't got to say nothing to you."

"We're investigating a murder," Frank told her.

A thin smile slithered across her lips. "He killed somebody? I figured he would someday."

"We just want to talk to him," Frank said. He pocketed his badge. "Now where is he?"

"The park."

"Grant Park?"

"Yeah," the woman said. "But you don't tell him I told you so, you hear?"

"Where in the park?" Caleb asked.

"Said he was going to the zoo. Said he was meeting somebody over there. He's a liar, though. He could be anywhere. Sometimes he don't come home. He just leaves me with the kids, and he just goes wherever he wants to." She stepped back from the door. "*You* find him. I ain't looking for him no more." She closed the door.

It was only a short drive to the park, and Caleb and Frank rode silently together until they reached the entrance.

Frank took out the mug shot which had been attached to the report. "Want to look at this again?"

Caleb shook his head. "Nah. Once I see a face, I got it forever."

Frank looked at the picture for a moment, then returned it to his pocket.

They spotted him almost at once, a tall black man in a pair of bright yellow pants and a short-sleeve flamingo shirt.

Caleb chuckled to himself. "With a record like his, you'd think he'd try to look a little less conspicuous."

Frank nodded.

"You know, when it comes to guys like Little, we got one advantage, Frank: they're even stupider than we are."

In the distance, Frank could see Davon Little as he slumped against the short storm fence. Beyond the fence there was a moat, and beyond that a small concrete island where two enormous polar bears yawned in the heat.

Little stared off toward a clump of trees in the distance, then straightened himself and moved on down along the storm fence, pausing for a moment at the grizzly bears.

"Swear to God, Frank," Caleb said, "he looks like he's here for the pleasure of it."

A short distance away, Frank could see another man lingering by the fence. He wore purple corduroy pants and an open-collared shirt of bright yellow. He had a hot dog in one hand, and a can of soda in the other.

"I think we may have stumbled on to a drug deal, Caleb," he said.

Caleb peered at the man in the yellow shirt. "That's Jimmy Swift," he said. He smiled. "I bet you a big steak dinner that he's going to mosey over to Davon, chat with him real casual for a moment, and then offer him a sip of that soda. It'll all look just fine, except poor Jimmy won't get that soda back."

"And inside the can . . ." Frank said.

". . . little bag of cocaine wrapped up real tight."

"How does he get the payment to Swift?"

"Probably already dropped it off somewhere," Caleb said. He smiled. "Just watch your line of fire if things get hot. We don't want to waste a polar bear."

Together they moved forward slowly. Almost at the same time, Swift and Little came together at the edge of the bear cages, talked for a moment, then, just as Caleb had predicted, Swift gave Little his can of soda. Little took a swig, smiled, nodded, but did not give the can back to his friend.

"See there," Caleb said quickly. "Little must be losing his grip to use such an old trick."

Swift walked away, leaving Little once again leaning against the fence. He watched the bears for a moment, took another sip from the can, then moved on, sauntering casually along the winding path that led to the reptile house.

"We'll get as close as we can without getting burned," Caleb said.

For the next few minutes they kept pace with Little. Caleb circled to the left, Frank to the right, widening the space between them.

The crowds which were gathered around the bear cages had thinned along the uphill walk to the reptile house, and Frank and Caleb waited for the moment when Little would be most in the clear.

It occurred only a few yards from the entrance to the reptile house, and Frank and Caleb seized the opportunity immediately, rushing quickly up to him, one on his left side, the other on his right.

"Morning, Davon," Caleb said. He dug his fingers into Little's upper arm. "Show Mr. Little your badge, Frank."

Little looked glumly at Frank's badge. "What's this all about, man?"

Caleb smiled. "God, it's hot in the zoo today," he said. "Hey, Davon, how about you give me a taste of that R.C?"

Little's face stiffened. "It's all drunk up."

"Really?" Caleb asked. "Maybe just the last few drops then?" He snatched the can from Little's fingers. "Feels like there's some left."

Little's eyes darted from Frank to Caleb, then back to Caleb. "Small-time, man. I ain't a big horse."

Caleb shrugged. "We don't mind a pony, do we, Frank?"

Frank shook his head. "How long have you been living in this area, Mr. Little?"

"Few years, why?"

Frank pulled out a picture of Angelica. "You ever seen this girl?"

Little glared at the picture. "I don't hunker down with no white pussy." He cocked his head proudly. "Plenty of dark meat without it."

"Like that woman you're living with?" Caleb asked.

Little said nothing.

"Or is she your cousin?"

"She nothing to me, man," Little said. "A friend of mine dropped her off on me. Left her and them screaming kids." He shook his head. "I ain't got the heart to kick them out, that's all."

Frank jerked the picture up toward Little's face. "Have you ever seen this girl?" he asked sternly.

"No, I ain't never seen her."

"What about a red BMW?" Caleb said. "Ever seen one of them?"

Little let out a long, slow breath. "Shit."

"Where'd you get that car, Davon?"

"I found it."

"It's not exactly the same thing as a penny lying in the gutter," Frank told him.

"Well, that's the way it is, though," Little said. "I didn't break into it or nothing." He looked desperately at Caleb. "You can tell I didn't. They ain't a mark on that car." He laughed. "I mean it was just *sitting* there, man, with the keys in the ignition, the windows all rolled down."

"Where was it?" Frank asked.

"Not far from here."

Frank took out his notebook. "Where, exactly?"

"At the edge of the park," Little said. "It was just sitting there one morning."

"Which edge of the park?"

"Sydney Street," Little said. "Right where it meets Boulevard. Right on that corner."

Frank wrote it down. "When was this?"

"Three days ago."

"In the morning, you said?"

"I was out walking," Little added. He looked at Caleb. "That's the truth. I wasn't looking for nothing. It was just there."

"What time in the morning?" Frank asked.

135

"Must have been about four."

"Was it still dark?"

"Just turning light."

"Odd time for a stroll, Davon," Caleb said.

Davon glared at him. "Ain't no law against it."

Caleb waved the can in front of him. "Well, we got something else."

Davon looked at him sourly. "Lucky punch," he said knowingly. "You didn't get a clean bust. You just bumped into it."

"That don't matter to the judge," Caleb reminded him.

Davon smiled contemptuously. "Bust me fine, I do the time."

"A poet," Caleb said with a grin.

"Do me bad, I make you sad."

Suddenly a streak of anger flashed over Caleb's face. He grabbed Little by the shirt and wrenched him forward. "Listen to me, you little shit, you're a thief and a pimp, and in your whole goddamn life you haven't done one good thing." His voice hardened and grew cold. "You fuck with me, and I'll go through you like a spear." He let him go, and Little stumbled backward slightly.

Frank stepped over to him. "You'd better come squeaky clean on this one," he said. "The girl in that picture was the owner of that BMW, and somebody killed her."

Little's eyes shot away from Frank. "I ain't got nothing to say."

"You figured it out, didn't you?" Caleb said. "You knew that car was about as hot as a car could get, and so you dumped it on a cutter."

Little said nothing.

"Didn't you?" Caleb asked loudly.

Little nodded slowly. "But I didn't kill no girl. I didn't even *see* no girl. I just seen that car, all shiny and red, with the windows open and the keys right in it." He shook his head. "It was like ready to be grabbed. I mean it was sitting there just for the taking." His eyes lifted slowly toward Frank. "So I took it," he said. "But I never seen no girl."

"Was anything in the car when you stole it?" Frank asked.

"No. It was clean. Looked like it had been done over real good."

"What do you mean?"

"Cleaned up real nice."

"Did you see anyone around it?"

Little shook his head. "You think I'd took it if I'd seen somebody 'round it?"

"Where did you take it?"

"I rode around a little," Little said. "It's something, a flashy car. I knowed it was dumb not to just let it go to a fence. Car like that, it's easy to spot. But I just couldn't do it for a while. I liked riding in it too much." He shrugged. "So, I took the chance." He smiled. "Don't take a chance, you got nothing in your pants."

"So you rode around awhile?" Frank said.

"That's right," Little said. "I even thought of just heading off up North or something." He looked at Caleb. "I'm righteous 'bout that woman. She ain't nothing to do with me. She a friend's whore."

"When did you decide to drop it?" Frank asked.

Little turned back toward him. "When I seen that girl's picture in the paper. It said she was from that school, what you call it?"

"Northfield Academy."

"That's right," Little said. "And in the glove compartment, well, they was this piece of paper that had the name of the school on it, and her name too."

"The play program," Frank said.

"Is that what it was?" Little asked. "I don't know. I just left it in the glove compartment." He turned to Caleb. "I knew the car was burning when I seen that paper."

"So you took it to the cutters?" Caleb asked.

"Fast as I could drive, that's for sure," Little said. "I didn't want to hang around nothing that girl had. She too hot." He looked back at Frank. "And that's the righteous truth." He shook his head. "I ain't never seen that girl."

"You still living on Simpson Street, Davon?" Caleb asked.

"Yeah."

"Don't pull any deals in that house, you understand? You got little kids living there."

Davon peered toward the soda can. "What you going to do 'bout that?"

Caleb lifted it toward him. "I'm going to toss it into the garbage,

137

Davon, and let the narcs clean up their own house. But if I ever hear of a deal going down around those kids, I'll come get you myself."

Davon nodded vigorously. "Yeah, all right, man."

Caleb shoved the can in his jacket pocket. "Don't fuck with me, Davon."

Frank took out one of his cards. "Call me if you hear anything about this girl," he said.

Little took the card and gave it a peremptory glance. "Yeah, right, okay." He shifted nervously on his feet. "So that's it, then, right?"

"Just don't leave the city without telling me," Frank warned.

"Nah, I won't go nowhere," Davon assured him.

"And stay out of the zoo," Caleb added. "Do your business in a parking lot somewhere."

"I don't like the zoo, noways," Little said. "All them animals, it stinks like shit 'round here." He walked a few feet away, then glanced back tentatively, as if half-expecting to be shot down where he stood.

For a few minutes, Frank and Caleb stood together outside the reptile house. The heat seemed to swirl around them, despite the motionless air.

"What do you think?" Caleb asked.

"I think we got the straight story," Frank told him.

"Me too. He ain't got the guts to kill a girl like Angelica."

Frank drew out her picture and looked at it.

Caleb watched him closely for a moment. "You think about her a lot, don't you?"

"Sometimes," Frank said. He put the picture back in his jacket and glanced around the park. "Sometimes I get tired of talking to people like Little."

"High society's not much better, I bet," Caleb said with a short laugh.

"I wasn't really thinking of that."

"Oh yeah," Caleb said. "What were you thinking about?"

Frank shrugged wearily. "Nothing really," he said, and realized that it was a lie. He had, in fact, been thinking about someone, and not for the first time. As if carried on a current, her image came unbidden, dark hair, dark eyes, with a curled rose still resting in her open hand.

14

There was a black Mercedes parked in the driveway of Karen Devereaux's house when Frank arrived, and he found its presence there disquieting. It was too elegant, and its elegance was something against which he felt utterly powerless. He could not help but compare it to the battered, dusty frame of his old Chevrolet, the unwashed windows and plain blackwall tires. Parked beside it, the Mercedes shimmered brilliantly in the cascading sunlight. It was beautifully polished, and Frank immediately imagined its owner as equally sleek and stylish, a man in a black tuxedo and red cummerbund who knew one wine from another and smoked expensive European cigarettes.

Once at the door of the house, Frank hesitated. He did not want to intrude upon her, but he also felt himself powerfully drawn back to her. It was as if the line connecting them, the one he'd felt the night before, was sturdier than he had imagined, and that it was forever being tugged gently and insistently in some effort to bring him back.

The man who opened the door was exactly what Frank had

expected. He was tall, blonde, and very handsome. He wore dark gray pants and a black velvet jacket, and looked to be in his middle thirties. He seemed at home in his surroundings, utterly natural in clothes that would have looked like a costume on almost anyone else. As Frank faced him silently, he felt his own disarray, the frazzled suit and rumpled hat, but he realized that he did not in the least feel shamed by them, and for an instant he felt a sudden, exhilarating pride in what he wore.

He pulled his badge from his coat and watched as the gold shield glinted in the light.

"I'm here to see Karen Devereaux," he said.

"She's upstairs," the man answered quietly.

"Who are you?"

"My name is James Theodore. I'm Karen's partner."

"Partner?" Frank asked, as if he suspected that this was the sort of word that could easily mean something a great deal more.

"Yes, in the Nouveau Gallery," Theodore explained. "It's an art gallery downtown." He stepped out of the door. "Please, come in."

"I told Miss Devereaux that I would be back some time today," Frank said as he walked into the house. He was annoyed with himself: How had he missed finding out about the art gallery? He took off his hat and twirled it in his fingers. "She should be expecting me."

"I'm sure she is," Theodore said. He closed the door and pressed his back up against it. He looked as if he were guarding a bank vault. "She mentioned you to me," he said.

"Mentioned?"

"That you'd be coming by today," Theodore added quickly. "I'm sure she'll be right down."

"Did you know Angelica very well?" Frank asked.

"Slightly."

Frank pulled out his notebook. He could sense that Theodore was not just some upper-class playboy. He had an air of quiet authority, as if he knew he would be the same person even if the Mercedes suddenly evaporated, along with the velvet coat.

"So you're sort of a friend of the family?" Frank asked tentatively.

"Well, there isn't much of a family," Theodore said mournfully. "I suppose you know what happened to Karen's parents?"

"Yes."

"So it was only the two of them," Theodore added, "just Karen and Angelica." He drew in a deep breath. "Now there's just Karen." He smiled sadly. "But that really doesn't answer your last question, does it?"

"No."

"Sorry."

"How well *did* you know the family?"

"Not at all, as a family," Theodore said. "And as for Angelica, not at all, really. My only relationship is with Karen." He shrugged. "And to be entirely candid, I'm not really sure that I know her very well, either."

"That sounds more like her sister," Frank said.

"What does?"

"That no one seems to have known her very well."

"Is that what you're discovering?"

"Yes."

Theodore looked at Frank curiously. "So you have to live their lives a bit, is that it? The lives of the victims, I mean?"

"In a way," Frank said.

"Fascinating."

"Not really," Frank said. "It's just that most people know the people who kill them. So, you have to find out about the people they knew."

"Do you think Angelica was murdered?"

"Yes, I do."

"And that she knew her murderer?"

"That I don't know."

"You know," Theodore said, "I sometimes think that there is such a thing as a family that simply carries its doom around with it. Like a virus, you might say. It's as if they've been infected, and there's nothing that can be done to them."

Frank nodded.

"The Devereaux family strikes me as very much like that," Theodore went on. "It just doesn't seem possible that mere accident could have generated so much tragedy. It's more like a plague, don't you think?"

"When was the last time you saw Angelica?"

Theodore thought about it for a moment. "That would have been last Friday."

"Two days before she died," Frank said. He pulled out his notebook. "Did she seem different in any way?"

"No, not then."

The "not then" struck Frank as unusual. "But there were other times when she did seem different?"

"Oh, no, not really," Theodore answered quickly. "It's just that I saw so little of her. I hardly knew her."

"Did she seem happy that last Friday?"

"I suppose," Theodore said. "I really saw her for just a few seconds. She sort of passed me in the foyer here. She seemed very busy, but that was nothing odd for Angelica."

"She always seemed busy?"

"Bustling, rushing about, that sort of thing," Theodore explained. "There were times when I suspected that she might be quite a creative person."

"Why?"

"Her energy," Theodore said. "That's the one thing I've noticed about creative people. They may not be brighter than others, and they certainly have no better morals or any more ordered personal lives than the rest of us. But they do have this energy. It's like— forgive the standard image—it's like they're on fire."

Frank wrote it down. "Did Angelica seem that way?"

"Sometimes," Theodore said. He thought a moment, as if trying to recapture some part of her in his mind. "But, at the end of all that energy, there was nothing. I mean, she never really *did* anything."

"She was eighteen," Frank reminded him.

"Of course, you're right," Theodore said. "What can you expect from a young girl?" He walked a few paces away, then turned back toward Frank. His face was very grave, as if some disturbing thought had occurred to him. His lips parted slightly, as if he were about to speak, then closed suddenly, sealing off the words.

"Hello, Mr. Clemons."

Frank glanced toward the stairs that swept down to the foyer and saw Karen as she slowly made her way down them. She was dressed in a long, lavender skirt and white blouse, and as he looked at her, Frank could feel something go soft and pliant within him.

"I told you that I'd be coming by today," he said.

"Yes, I know," Karen said. "James was just leaving."

She stopped on the last step, lingering there, as if to hold herself back from something. Then she moved forward quickly and touched Frank's hand. "I'm glad you came," she said. "The funeral is tomorrow, and I wanted to get as many things done as possible before then. Things having to do with the investigation, I mean."

"Yes," Frank said. His hand tingled where she had touched it.

"I'd better be on my way, Karen," Theodore said quickly. "Nice to have met you, Mr. Clemons."

"Thank you," Frank said. "And if you think of anything that might . . ."

"Yes, yes, I'll let you know," Theodore said as he walked briskly out of the house.

Frank looked at Karen. "Your partner?" he said.

"Yes."

"In a gallery?"

"That's right."

"I didn't know you owned a gallery."

"Of course you didn't," Karen said crisply. "How could you?"

And yet it seemed to Frank that he already knew a lot about her. He had seen her in the garden, with that rose. He glanced down at his notebook, and the facts gathered there suddenly struck him as the least real things in life, little more than an inventory of its debris.

Karen stepped away from him. "Do you want to see Angelica's room now?"

"Yes."

"Follow me," Karen said.

Frank walked directly behind her as she made her way slowly up the stairs. There was an odd weariness in her movement, it seemed to him, a reluctance which all but stopped her at each step.

Angelica's room was at the far end of a long, wide corridor, and when Frank walked into it, he was amazed at what he saw. It looked like the room of a little girl, rather than a young adult's. Frilly curtains hung from the two large windows. The walls were papered with designs that looked as if they'd come from *Fantasia*. There was an enormous canopy bed, all white and lavender, and at the opposite end of the room, a large cabinet filled with exotic dolls. A white wicker vanity sat near the adjoining bath, but it looked as if it had never been used. The tall mirror was polished to a bright sheen, and the ornate embroidered stool showed no signs of wear.

"I came into this room for the first time only a few hours ago," Karen said. "For the first time in many years. I was very surprised by the way it looked. Nothing had changed in all that time. It looked as it had when Angelica was eleven."

"You haven't been in this room since then?" Frank asked.

"Absolutely not," Karen assured him. "It became a real issue for Angelica when she was around eleven. Privacy became an obsession with her. She refused to let anyone in."

"Even you?"

"I think, especially me."

"Why?"

"I thought it was just something she was going through," Karen said, "some sort of prepuberty thing. So I went along with her. But it never changed. Time went by. I didn't make an issue of it."

"But why especially you?"

"Big sister, I suppose."

Frank walked slowly to the center of the room. He remembered the look of Sarah's room, cluttered, strewn with books and records, perpetually disordered. It was as if she had despised the order Angelica had worked so hard to maintain.

"It sure doesn't look like a teenager's room, does it?" Karen asked.

"Not like my daughter's," Frank said, before he could stop himself.

"Oh, you have a daughter?" Karen asked.

Frank turned away slightly. "She died."

"I'm sorry."

Frank glanced at the bed. "Did Angelica ever have people up here?"

"Not that I know of," Karen said. She stepped over to the vanity and opened the top drawer. "I found this," she said, as she handed it to Frank. "It's a diary."

Frank took it from her and opened it. "Where did you find it?"

"It was on her bed," Karen said. "And it was open."

"Have you read it?"

"Yes."

"Is there anything in it?"

"Odd things," Karen said. "But only odd because they're so normal."

Frank began to flip through the pages. "What do you mean?"

"Well, from the diary, you'd get the impression that Angelica was a very average sort of teenager. She writes about going to parties and sleep-overs. She writes about being the treasurer of the senior class. She writes about being on the prom committee, that sort of thing." She shook her head. "But she never did any of those things. It was all a lie." She glanced at the diary. "That's what I mean about it being odd. It's about a normal life that never existed."

Frank continued to flip through the book. The handwriting was extraordinarily neat and precise, the letters carefully formed, the lines utterly straight. It was as if Angelica had drawn the words, rather than written them.

"She lived behind a mask," Karen said. "That's all I can figure out." Her eyes latched on to the diary. "It's as if she lived an entirely mannered life."

"Mannered?"

"Yes," Karen said. "Like when a painting is mannered. There's nothing real about it. It's as if the artist decided to copy a feeling he didn't have himself."

Frank closed the diary. "I'll need to keep this."

"Of course."

He put it in his coat pocket. "How did Angelica take it when your parents were killed?"

"She was too young to understand it."

"Did she play with other children?"

"A little," Karen said, "but I don't think she ever had a real friend." She glanced about the room. "You know, this room isn't strange only because of what's in it, but because of things that are missing."

"What things?"

"Letters. There's not one note to Angelica in this room. There are no books, no records. It's as if nothing has been added to it from the time she was eleven."

Frank turned slowly, eyeing the room carefully. At a murder scene, the area was often divided into quadrants and then searched meticulously. His eyes had gotten used to the same method. They turned the room into a grid, then examined each small square of space.

"It's as if Angelica was some sort of teenage version of Miss Havisham," Karen said, after a moment. "It's like time stopped when she was eleven, and after that it was all a fantasy."

"Unless it was all in secret," Frank said.

"Another life, you mean?"

"Yes."

Karen smiled delicately. "You know, I hope she did. And in a way, it doesn't matter what kind of life it was." Her eyes darted furiously about the room. "As long as it wasn't *this*."

"We can find out what kind of life it was," Frank said.

"How?"

"We can start with this book."

"And do what?"

"Well, for one thing, all those nights she claimed to be at proms and parties, things like that."

"What about them?"

"If she wasn't at those places, where was she?"

Karen thought about it. "Most of the time, she was here, I think."

"Up in her room?"

"Yes."

"But you're not sure?"

"No, I'm not sure," Karen said. "I tried to stay out of her life. I knew that that was what she wanted."

Frank closed the diary. "Maybe."

"What do you mean?"

"Sometimes they want to be watched over," Frank told her. "They want to be told 'no.' "

"I don't think that was the case with Angelica," Karen said firmly.

"All right," Frank said. He lifted the book slightly. "Did you notice any names in here?"

146

"Names?"

"Friends, fellow students, teachers, anything."

"She used initials," Karen told him. "She would write something like 'Had a great time at L's,' or 'Met with Prom staff: B.T.H.' "

"Telephone numbers?"

"I didn't see any."

Frank walked over to the small white telephone that rested on a table next to Angelica's bed. He took out his notebook and wrote down the number.

"Why do you want that?"

"To find out who she's been calling," Frank said.

She looked at him with an odd sympathy. "It must feel odd, to do what you do. I mean, it's something like a Peeping Tom, isn't it?"

"Yes," Frank admitted.

He closed the notebook, put it in his pocket and looked up at her. She was standing in the doorway, her body framed by a soft, purplish light. Her beauty swept over him like a thirsty wind. There was a kind of isolation in her eyes, a separateness from ordinary experience, and he wondered if her sister had felt the same aloneness, had walked down lost, desolate streets and listened to the catcalls of the men she passed until there was nothing to do but return to the innocence of a little girl's room. It was the sort of loneliness he'd known in others, known in himself, and he knew how easily it could turn to rage.

"The play she was in," he said. "Did you see it?"

"Yes," Karen said. "It was the only time she ever invited me to anything." She shook her head slowly. "We're burying her tomorrow. Will you come to the funeral?"

"Yes," Frank said.

"It's part of the routine, I guess," Karen said.

Frank shrugged. "That's part of it," he said, "but it's not the whole thing."

15

I t was almost noon the next day when Angelica Devereaux was buried in one of Atlanta's most exclusive cemeteries. It was the sort of exquisitely kept ground that up until recent years had never received the body of a black or a Jew. It held to a certain rigid dignity, the sort that looked as if money couldn't buy it, even though everyone knew that it was the only thing that could.

"They'll probably bury the mayor here," Caleb said, his lips fluttering around the stem of his pipe. "That'll make integration complete."

To Frank, it had only mattered that Angelica was being buried. He could still remember the feel of her clothing. He'd gone through it the day before, fingering the pockets of her ordered blouses and neatly folded jeans for some note with a name or number on it. The closets had revealed nothing, and so, as Karen stood in the doorway, he had gone through the drawers of the vanity, then the bureau, had peered under the canopy bed and beneath the primly stuffed pillows. The underside of things revealed no more than their appearances, and a little girl's room remained a little girl's room forever.

"Who's the guy with the white hair and black suit?" Caleb asked.

"Arthur Cummings," Frank said.

Caleb leaned against the large elm and sucked his teeth. "Oh yeah, the guardian."

Even from the distance, Frank could hear the low moan of the Episcopalian minister as he began his prayer for Angelica's salvation.

"I recognize that guy on Cummings' right," Caleb said, "the headmaster." He squinted against the bright light. "But who's the blonde guy with the hairdo?"

"James Theodore. Friend of Karen's."

The sound of prayer died away, and Karen stepped forward. For a moment she remained, staring into the open grave. Then she took a spadeful of reddish earth and scattered it over Angelica's coffin.

"From the look of it, Frank," Caleb said, "Angelica didn't have many friends."

"No teachers from the school. No students."

"You think the little papa might be here?"

Frank glanced at one face, then another: Cummings, Morrison, Theodore, and at last, a small, squat man in a gray suit and horn-rimmed glasses.

"The guy in the gray suit," he said. "He looks familiar."

Caleb shook his head. "I think Angelica could have done better than that."

"I've seen him somewhere," Frank said thoughtfully. He was not sure exactly what he remembered, the flabby round face, the short, stocky body, the enormous glasses, but it was something unpleasant. He replayed his past cases, searching for some detail that would sweep the man back into his memory.

Then, suddenly, the man reached in his jacket pocket and fingered the antenna of a small remote receiver.

"He's a doctor," Frank whispered. He looked over to Caleb. "There was a woman, a society woman. They found her dead in her house on the Prado."

Caleb watched him. "This one's new to me, Frank."

"She'd OD'd on something," Frank continued. "Alvin brought the doctor in for questioning."

Caleb's eyes slowly shifted back to the little man in the gray suit.

"It turns out he was one of those Dr. Feelgood types," Frank said. "He was pretty much giving a few rich people anything they wanted. Loading them up on prescription drugs."

"Did they nail him?"

"No, he slipped by," Frank said. "There was some talk about the medical society checking him out, but I don't know if anything ever came of that."

Caleb took out a large handkerchief and wiped the sweat from his neck. "Well, as a group, we got the family lawyer, the family educator . . . maybe we got the family doctor, too."

"Maybe," Frank said. His eyes had shifted over to Karen. She stood beside the grave, her hands folded in front of her, her eyes fixed on the open ground and the coffin which rested in it. She looked sadder than he had ever seen her. It was as if she were mourning everything around her, the bright midday light that swept the grounds, the stifling heat, the enormous magnolia that rose beside the grave, even the small bird that could be heard from somewhere deep in its lush growth.

Within a moment the service was over, and Frank continued to watch as Karen and the rest of them moved toward their waiting limousines.

"Remembered awhile, forgot forever," Caleb said. "That's what my mother used to say."

The doctor was leaving too, and Frank walked over to him immediately.

The doctor's eyes lifted slowly as Frank approached. They were large and brown, and they gave his face a cuddly expression.

Frank flashed his badge.

The man smiled. "I thought you were the police."

"Did you?"

"Like in the movies. They always go to the funeral of the deceased." He thrust out his hand. "I'm Herman Clark, Dr. Herman Clark."

Frank shook his hand quickly. "I'm handling the investigation into Angelica's death." He took out his notebook. "Did you know her?"

"I suppose you could say I was her physician," Clark said. "I suppose you must have discovered that she was pregnant?"

"Yes."

151

"I'm the physician who confirmed that."

"Confirmed?"

"Told Angelica," Dr. Clark explained.

"She came to your office?"

"Yes."

"Did someone recommend you?"

"She said she took my name from the phone book," Dr. Clark told him. "As far as I know, that's how she found me."

"And you saw her in your office?"

"Yes."

"When was that?"

"Well, two days ago, when I read about her death in the newspaper, I went to my files and reviewed the whole case." He smiled. "I mean, you can't be too careful, what with all these malpractice suits." He shifted slightly on his feet. "Well, anyway, I wanted to make sure that I was clear of any negligence in her case. I didn't even want the appearance of negligence. I mean, that's all they need, these people and their goddamn lawyers, just appearance." He breathed a sigh of relief. "But thank God, I'm clear on this case."

"What do you mean?"

"Well, there was nothing to it," Dr. Clark said. "She came for two office visits. She was given a routine examination and pregnancy test. After that she was appropriately notified of her pregnancy. No medicines were prescribed, no course of treatment recommended." He snapped his fingers. "In and out, like that." He looked at Frank pointedly. "So there's no goddamn way any shyster lawyer can nail me on a negligence suit. I'm like Caesar's wife on this one."

Frank continued to hold his pen over a blank page in his notebook. "When did she first visit your office, Dr. Clark?"

"May eleventh," Clark said. "It's all right there in my files. The visit lasted about an hour. I did an examination and a pregnancy test, and she was on the streets in no time."

"Did she know she was pregnant when she came to you?" Frank asked.

"She suspected it."

"She told you that?"

"She indicated that her menstrual cycle was off, that she was late."

Frank wrote it down. "So, May eleventh," he repeated.

Clark smiled happily. "At eleven oh five in the morning, to be exact. I keep very accurate records." Then he noticed that Frank was writing in his notebook, and the smile vanished. "Now look," he said, "I didn't come to this funeral in order to be drawn into the investigation."

Frank looked up. "Why did you come?"

"It's a nice gesture."

"What do you mean?"

"For the deceased person's relatives," Dr. Clark explained. "I always make it a policy to attend the funerals of my patients. It shows my sympathy. The relatives appreciate it." He chuckled lightly. "I think it helps to protect you from lawsuits. The family sees you in your black suit. They see you mourning their dead loved one. It makes them feel grateful to you for being such a caring person. Nobody sues a kind, sympathetic doctor." He laughed again. "I mean, it's an inconvenience, but it's worth it. I figure that over the whole life of a medical practice, it could probably save the average physician close to a million dollars in malpractice claims."

"Where is your practice, Dr. Clark?" Frank asked.

"Midtown, not far from the Hyatt," Dr. Clark said. "I'm in the book. Clark, Herman, M.D."

"Are you an obstetrician?"

"Yes," Clark said. "I usually handle the entire pregnancy. I expected to do that in Miss Devereaux's case." He shook his head. "I mean, if all she'd wanted was to confirm her pregnancy, she could have done that at home and saved herself a lot of money."

"Why didn't she do that?"

"She was very naive," Dr. Clark said. "It was like talking to a little girl. I could hardly believe that she was eighteen." He smiled. "And so beautiful. Her body, I mean, was stunning. Nothing child-like about it." He pressed his hand against Frank's arm. "Between us, she was the most beautiful woman I've ever examined. And let me tell you, my practice being what it is, dealing with the kind of clientele I have, I've examined some beautiful women." His eyes drifted toward the grave. "What a waste." For a moment, he stared at Angelica's coffin, then he looked back up at Frank. His eyes widened somewhat, as if he were seeing him for the first time. "My word, what happened to you?"

"What?"

"Your face, my dear man. What happened to your face?"

"Nothing much."

"Well, I hope you got some medical attention for that," Dr. Clark said. He moved his hand to touch Frank's face.

Frank flinched away.

Clark smiled oddly. "She was like you, jumpy."

"Angelica?"

"Yes," Dr. Clark said. "Of course, that's sometimes the case. An examination of this kind involves a certain amount of intimacy. It isn't unusual for a woman to be a little nervous."

"But Angelica was more than that?" Frank asked.

"A good deal more," Dr. Clark said.

"How long did the examination take?" Frank asked bluntly.

Dr. Clark's face stiffened. "What?"

"How long did it take?" Frank repeated.

Clark hesitated. "About an hour," he said finally.

"You examined her body for an hour?" Frank asked coldly.

Clark's whole body tightened. "It was my medical judgment that a routine examination was not enough."

Frank jotted it down.

"My professional judgment," Dr. Clark added nervously. "There's nothing wrong with a more intimate examination if it is in the professional judgment of the examining physician."

"Why did she need one?"

"I just thought she did."

"Why?"

Clark's lips fluttered rapidly. "What is all this? I'm not on trial here."

"You wanted to see her, didn't you?"

"What!"

"She was beautiful and you wanted to see her . . . touch her."

"How dare you!"

154

Frank stepped toward him. He could feel the rage of every woman who had ever been stared at by a man.

Clark glared at him fearfully. "Now, look, I don't have to submit to this."

Frank realized that he was right, and he drew back and glanced quickly down at his notes.

"I am a professional physician," Dr. Clark said haughtily. "I do not 'look' at women."

"What did you find out in this 'examination'?" Frank asked.

Clark took a deep breath, calming himself. "I'm not sure I wish to continue this discussion."

Frank looked at him lethally. "You said she needed an examination. You gave her one. What did you find out?"

For a moment, Clark did not answer. He seemed to consider his options for a moment. Then he made a decision.

"I discovered that she was a very healthy young woman," he said finally.

"Anything else?"

"Other than that she was pregnant, no."

"Did she say she was married?"

"No."

"What did she tell you, exactly?"

"She said that she'd missed her period, that she had always been very regular, and that she suspected that she was pregnant."

"Anything else?"

"That she wanted everything to be kept in confidence," Clark said. "Of course, that really was not in question. I always keep everything confidential." He hesitated. "You know, it was odd."

"What was odd?"

Clark looked at him. "I really don't want to get into this business of the examination again," he said hesitantly. "I would like to keep our relationship a little less strained."

"What was odd?"

"Well, she seemed rather like a virgin," Clark told him. "Inexperienced. Yet she was pregnant." He smiled. "You know, I actually felt that she'd probably been one of those poor, unfortunate girls who gets pregnant the first time out."

155

Frank wrote it down.

"Did she mention anything about an abortion?" he asked.

"No."

"Did she say anything about what she intended to do about the baby?"

"No."

"Did you think she was going to have it?"

"I assumed that she was, yes," Clark said. "And I assumed that I would be in attendance at the birth." Once again he looked at Frank closely. "You know, you really should get something done about your face."

Frank gave him his card. "I want you to send me everything in your file on Angelica. Tests, consultation notes, everything."

Dr. Clark nodded quickly. "Yes, of course."

"I want them on my desk by tomorrow morning."

"I will have them there," Clark assured him. He shifted about nervously. "May I go now? I have an appointment in half an hour."

Caleb was still leaning against the tree when Frank returned. The heat of midday had already wet the armpits of his light green jacket, and he looked as if he were about to dissolve into the sweltering air.

"It's rougher on the fatties," he said. "Skinny people, they don't ever look hot." He glanced at the figure of Dr. Clark as he scurried down a small hill. "Who was that peckerwood?"

"A doctor," Frank said morosely. "Like I said. She had figured out that she might be pregnant. She went to him to make sure."

Caleb straightened himself. "Well, let's get back downtown," he said.

The two of them headed down the hill toward the car. The bright light swept around the gray tombstones, bleaching them to a pure hard white.

"He saw her for the first time on May eleventh," Frank said. "Then she came back four days later for the results."

Caleb stopped. "May fifteenth? What time?"

Frank looked at his notes. "Three-thirty in the afternoon."

"Well, that's pinpointing it," Caleb said casually.

"If you were a young girl who'd just found out she was pregnant, who would you call, Caleb?"

"Daddy, I guess."

Frank nodded. "Have you done a check on her phone yet?"

"No," Caleb said. "But it would only take a second."

They hurried back to their car, then headed downtown. Once at his desk, Frank ran the check, detailing Angelica's calls on the afternoon and evening of May 15.

"She made three calls that day," he told Caleb, who waited anxiously beside his desk. "They were all to the same number."

Caleb walked away quickly, then returned with the reverse directory.

Frank read him the number, and Caleb looked it up.

"That number belongs to a Stanford K. Doyle," Caleb said. "He lives in Ansley Park."

Frank pulled the program of Angelica's play from his pocket and opened it. "Stanford Doyle was one of the cast," he said.

"Daddy," Caleb whispered vehemently.

A few minutes later, they were in the car, heading down a road that seemed to lead like a single dark thread to the heart of Ansley Park.

16

The Doyle house was located on a small lot in a middle-class section of Atlanta. Ansley Park was a far cry from the shaded boulevards and spacious estates of West Paces Ferry Road. Its modest brick homes seemed to rest exactly between the mansions of the north side of the city and the poverty-ridden hovels to the south.

"Look at that," Caleb said, as he looked at the single-story brick house with its two-car garage. "I bet they got a Buick station wagon with an old travel map of Yosemite National Park in the glove compartment."

Frank got out of the car and waited for Caleb to join him. He could feel a strange tension growing in him, as if he were nearing the dark center of the case, the shadows where the animal lurked.

"Be careful," he said to Caleb.

Caleb looked at him oddly. "Careful? What we got here, Frank—providing we've got anything at all—is an average kid who took something too far." He glanced at the house. "I mean, look at the yard. Somebody mowed it yesterday." He shook his head. "No, middle-class killers will put out their hands and let you snap the cuffs on. It's like something's already missing in them. They don't know how to fight; they don't know how to run." He looked at Frank pointedly. "When you get like that, you're better off dead." He started up the walkway, sauntering casually toward the front door, as if nothing odd ever happened, nothing unpredictable, as if no office worker had ever blown away the typing pool.

Caleb was already rapping loudly at the door when Frank stepped up beside him. It opened immediately, and a tall, thin, redheaded boy stared at them from behind the screen. He had a light, unblemished complexion, and he was wearing a T-shirt embossed with large white letters: NORTHFIELD ACADEMY.

Caleb glanced at the letters, then at Frank. "Daddy," he whispered, as the two of them stepped nearer to the door.

Frank pulled out his badge. "Are you Stanford Doyle?"

"Junior," the boy said weakly, "Stanford Doyle, Junior."

"Is your daddy home?" Caleb asked.

"No, sir."

"You alone?" Frank asked.

"Yes, sir," the boy said. "My father's on vacation for the next two weeks."

"Whereabouts?" Caleb asked.

"Florida. Fort Lauderdale."

"So you're living by yourself?"

"Yes, I am."

For a moment, Frank did not know how to begin. Some things were too tender to be approached, and as far as he could tell, the boy seemed to have no idea what had brought him to his door.

"I see you go to Northfield," he said.

"Yes, sir."

"You like it there, Stanford?"

"Stan," the boy said. "People call me Stan."

"You like it at Northfield?"

"It's all right."

Caleb took out his handkerchief and pointedly swabbed his neck. "It's hot out here. Your place air-conditioned?"

"Yes, it is."

"Suppose we could cool off a little while we talk?"

"Oh, sure," the boy said, as if suddenly attentive to good manners. "Come on in." He swung open the door and Frank and Caleb walked inside.

"Would you like to sit down?"

"I wouldn't mind that," Caleb said.

"In here, then," the boy said. He ushered them into a small living room. The carpet was bright green, the walls pastel green with small white flowers. It looked like the sort of place where the Christmas tree stood for a long time, gathering small red packages beneath it.

Caleb sat down in one of the large, stuffed chairs which faced the sofa. "Nice place," he said. "Lived here long?"

"All my life."

"Lucky you," Caleb added with a big smile. "Lot of people from Northfield live out this way?"

The boy smiled. "Not many. They mostly live farther north."

Frank glanced at a family portrait. It was of a man and his son.

"That's my dad," the boy said.

"Where's Mom?" Caleb asked.

"She's dead," the boy answered. "In childbirth."

"So it's just you and your dad who live here?"

"Yes, sir," the boy said. He looked at Frank. "Don't you want to sit down?"

"No, thanks."

The boy took a seat on the sofa, his eyes darting nervously from Frank to Caleb. "I've never had the police come around here," he said.

As he watched the boy squirming on the sofa, Frank suddenly felt a deep sympathy for everyone who had not yet gone through the later stages of life. They were a mystery, a wilderness that could hardly have been more visible in Stanford Doyle's eyes. He looked as if he'd just emerged from a protective shell.

"You like this area?" Caleb asked amiably.

"I've never lived anywhere else," the boy said. His voice was weak, almost plaintive, and as he spoke he lowered his eyes slightly. It gave him a look of lingering innocence.

"Northfield, that's a pretty expensive place," Caleb said.

"Yes, it is."

"Been going there long?"

"For the last two years."

"What are you now? Junior? Senior?"

"I graduated," Stan said.

"When was that?" Caleb asked.

"Last month," the boy said. "I'm supposed to be going to college in September."

"Which one?"

"Emory."

Caleb smiled broadly. "Well, that's wonderful? Right, Frank?"

"Yeah," Frank said. He paused a moment, then pushed ahead, since there was no other way. "I guess you have some idea about why we're here."

The boy said nothing.

"Angelica Devereaux," Frank added.

The boy nodded slowly.

"She was in your graduating class."

"Yes."

"We're trying to find out a little about her," Frank said. "How well did you know her, Stan?

"A little."

"No more than that?"

"We talked sometimes."

Caleb leaned forward slightly. "Well, that makes you sort of special."

Stan looked at him. "Why?"

"The way we hear it, she didn't talk to anybody over at Northfield."

"That's right," Stan said. "She didn't."

"But she did talk to you?" Caleb asked pointedly.

"Not much."

"Yeah, right. A little, like you said."

"She didn't really have any friends at the school," Stan said. "I don't know why."

"But that's pretty strange, don't you think?" Caleb said. "I mean, a pretty girl like that?"

The boy shrugged. "That's the way she was."

"What way?" Frank asked.

"What do you mean?"

"How would you describe her?"

"Well, she was very pretty."

"Beyond her looks," Frank said. "Her personality."

"I don't know about that," the boy said. "I really don't. I mean, we weren't close." He glanced out the front window to the close-cropped lawn. It was turning brown along its edges, and the heat which blazed down upon it seemed to be sucking at its essential life.

"The thing is," Caleb said. "Here we have a real pretty girl who's been in a school for quite some time, and yet nobody knows anything about her." He looked at the boy piercingly. "Does that make any sense to you, Stan?"

"That's just the way she was," the boy said again.

"Shy, you mean? Aloof?"

"I guess," Stan said. "She acted like she didn't really want anybody to know her."

"Did you know she had a phone in her room?" Frank asked.

"No."

"She only made three calls from that phone during the last three months."

Stan looked at Frank vacantly.

"They were all made on one day, May fifteenth."

Still no reaction. The boy stared at Frank.

"And they were all made to the number at this house."

Stan's lips parted. "To me? She tried to call me?"

"You didn't get these calls?"

"No."

Caleb looked questioningly at Frank, then turned to Stan. "You didn't know she was trying to get hold of you?"

"No, I didn't," the boy said frantically. "I swear I didn't."

"Do you have any idea why she might have been trying to reach you?" Frank asked.

Stan shook his head vigorously. "I hadn't talked to her since the play."

"You were in the play?"

"Yes, sir."

Frank took out his notebook. "She called you three times on May fifteenth," he said. "You have no idea why?"

"I don't," the boy said emphatically. He looked helplessly at Caleb, then back at Frank. "I swear to you, I don't know about these calls. Maybe she just got our answering machine, and didn't leave a message."

That was possible, Frank thought. The call would register even if she didn't say anything.

"Did you know she was pregnant?" he asked.

The boy drew in a quick breath. "What?"

"Angelica was pregnant," Frank told him. "Did you know that?"

"No."

"Takes two, of course," said Caleb pointedly.

Stan's eyes closed slowly. "I didn't know she was pregnant," he said. "I swear I didn't know that."

"She found out on May fifteenth," Frank said, "the same day she called you."

"Now when you think about it," Caleb said, "when you get news like that, there's a couple people you might want to call." He stuck a single finger into the air. "Your best friend, maybe." He looked at Stan. "But you say you didn't know Angelica very well." A second finger shot into the air. "Or maybe the father. You might want to call him."

Stan took a deep breath. "I may be the father," he said.

"*May* be?"

"I slept with her once. I don't know if anyone else did."

"You only slept with her once?" Frank asked.

"Yes."

"So it wasn't exactly a romance," Caleb said.

"No, sir, not at all," Stan said. "When I told you a minute ago that I didn't know Angelica very well, that was the truth. I really didn't. I had practically never said a word to her before that night." He looked at Frank. "The night we did it, I mean." He turned toward Caleb. "We'd just pass in the hallway at school. She might say 'hi,' she might not. It was like that. Until that one time."

164

"When was that 'one time'?" Caleb asked bluntly.

"It was the last night of rehearsals," Stan said.

"When was that?"

"April first."

Frank wrote it down.

"It was a Friday night," Stan added. "The next Saturday was opening night."

"So you had the rehearsal," Frank said. "Then what?"

"We went for a ride."

"In your car?"

"No, Angelica's."

"The red BMW."

"Yeah, that one," Stan said. "What a car. She'd only had it about a month."

Frank looked up from his notebook. "Go on."

"Well, the rehearsal was like always," Stan went on. "Maybe a little more intense, since we were opening the next night." He looked toward Caleb. "It was over around eleven, which was later than usual. Everybody was tired." He leaned back farther into the back of the sofa and let out a long, slow breath. "Anyway, I was headed toward my car . . . my father's car, actually, and that's when Angelica pulled up."

Frank could see her behind the wheel, her blonde hair streaming over her shoulders. "What did she say?" he asked.

"Well, she'd been a little nervous all night. I don't know why. Maybe it was the opening night jitters."

"What did she say, Stan?" Caleb asked insistently.

"She had this look in her eye. Like she was mad at me or something. I thought she was going to say something bad, but she didn't. I mean, she'd been really sharp to people all night. Everybody was waiting for Mr. Jameson to chew her out, but he didn't. He just stayed clear of her, like he was afraid of her or something."

Frank could see her face, the hard blue eyes, the tight strained mouth, the cool, lean words that came from it when she spoke.

" 'Get in,' she said," Stan told him. "It was in this hard voice. She just said 'Get in.' "

Frank wrote it down quickly.

"Is that all she said?" Caleb asked.

"That's all she said."

"So you got in, right?"

"Yes, sir," Stan said. "I got in and I really didn't know what was going on with her. So I just said, 'What's up, Angelica?' or something like that. And she just laughed this little laugh and she said, 'You'll find out, if you keep your mouth shut.' Then she pulled out of the lot. And I mean she really pulled out, squealing her tires, you know?"

Frank could hear the echoes of the tires as they resounded through the summer night, a high, thready wail.

"Where'd you go?" he asked.

"We headed downtown," Stan said. "I remember it very well. It was a clear night, and the dogwoods were blooming, and I said something about how beautiful they were, and she said, 'Yeah, beautiful.' "

"So you went downtown," Caleb said. "Whereabouts?"

"We ended up on the Southside," Stan said, "Grant Park, around in there."

"Did you just end up there, or did she look as if she was headed there in particular?"

"Well, now that you mention it, she seemed to know where she was going from the first."

"And she went directly to the Southside?"

"Yes, sir, directly," Stan said. "She went right to Grant Park. Then we circled the park a couple of times, maybe more. She was always looking out the window. I got the feeling she was looking for somebody."

"Did she mention drugs?" Caleb asked.

"No."

"Because a lot of dealers hang around the park."

"She didn't say anything about drugs."

"But she did circle the park?" Frank asked.

"Yes, sir. She circled it at least twice, maybe more."

"Then what?"

"She drove into the park itself," Stan said. "She went down to where they're doing the restoration on that historical diorama thing, you know, the battle of Atlanta?"

"The Cyclorama?" Frank asked.

"Yes, sir."

Frank wrote it down.

"And that's where she parked," Stan added.

Frank looked up from his notebook. "She parked at the Cyclorama?"

"That's right. She pulled over to this storm fence they have there, and she parked."

"How long did you stay there?"

Stan thought about it. "Maybe ten minutes. Maybe less, maybe more. I'm not really sure. To tell you the truth, I didn't exactly know what I was doing at that point. I mean, she hadn't said a word to me all the way downtown. I figured since we'd parked, maybe she'd start to talk. But she didn't. She just sat where she was, smoked a cigarette and stared into the rearview mirror."

"The rearview mirror?"

"Yes, sir."

"Not straight ahead?"

"Well, there was nothing but a fence in front of us," Stan said, "and the Cyclorama sign." He shrugged. "Once in a while she'd glance up at the sign, then back in the mirror."

"Did you get the idea she was waiting for someone?" Frank asked.

"I don't know," Stan said. "I couldn't figure out what was going on with her. She'd smoke one cigarette, then another one. I'd never seen her smoke before."

"She didn't say anything at all?" Caleb asked unbelievingly.

"Not until just before we left," Stan told him. "Then she just looked over at me with this real hard look in her eye, and she said, 'Well, this is your lucky night,' and that's when she started the car again, and we drove out of the park."

Frank could hear the engine as he wrote in his notebook and could smell the smoke of her cigarette, see its white garlands in the air around him.

Caleb leaned forward slightly. "Did she drive through the park some more?"

"No, not through it," Stan said. "We went around it once. I was getting sort of bored. She was so weird. She wasn't talking or anything, and when she did say something, it was something you couldn't understand."

"Why couldn't you understand it?"

"It was under her breath," Stan explained. "She was sort of muttering under her breath." He looked at Frank. "I just wanted to go home."

"Then why didn't you tell her to take you?" Frank asked.

Stan shook his head. "I don't know. I guess because she was so beautiful. Just being near her, it was like a thrill, or something. It was like something was coming off her body. It just swept around you. You couldn't pull away from it. At least, I couldn't."

As he listened, Frank tried to recall the intensity of such youthful desire. He remembered long nights when he'd been unable to sleep because of it. Everything became moist, swollen, infinitely sweet. He knew that that was how Stan must have felt as he sat beside Angelica Devereaux. Frank had felt that way for Sheila, and it struck him that the slow decline of such passion, the way time wore its sharpness down to a flat, featureless nub, was one of life's great losses.

"I had had some experience before," Stan said, quietly. "I mean, before that night. But nothing like Angelica."

"Where did you go after you left the park?" Frank asked.

"We drove around that same area," Stan said. "We just went all around that part of town." He shrugged. "I'd never been over there much before. But Angelica, she seemed to know it pretty well."

"How do you know that?"

"She just acted like she knew it, like she'd been around there a lot."

"Did she ever mention any names? People she might have known who lived in the area?"

Stan shook his head. "No."

"Did she concentrate on any particular streets?"

"Well, there was one that she went up and down a couple of times."

"Do you remember the name?"

"No, sir," Stan said.

"Are you sure?"

"I didn't notice a name. I'm sorry."

"Think hard," Caleb said.

"I've been trying to remember everything," Stan said, "I really have. But it was at night, and I'd never really been around that part of town much." He looked at Frank. "It's sort of seedy over there, you know. I got sort of nervous. I mean, I locked my door. I remember that. And I even told Angelica to lock hers."

"Did she?" Frank asked.

"No."

Frank jotted a few notes into his notebook then looked back up at the boy. "So you drove around the Grant Park area for a while, then what?"

"We ended up in this back alley," Stan said. "It was behind some buildings. I don't know exactly where it was."

"Did you notice any signs in the alley?" Caleb asked. "Any particular kinds of trucks, like a beer truck or a TV repair truck, anything like that?"

"It was empty," Stan said. "I think that's why she stopped."

"Because it was empty?"

"Yes."

"Why?"

"Because of what we did," Stan said. "I mean she picked it because she knew what she was going to do."

"Which was?"

"Well, have sex," Stan said hesitantly. "She stopped the car and just sat there for a while. She didn't say anything. She just stared out the window. I don't know how long. I didn't say anything to her. Angelica had a way of making people keep their mouths shut. When she wanted you to be quiet, she could make you, just with a look. And that's what she wanted, just to sit for a while and be quiet. Finally though, I just mentioned that we could go over to the Varsity and have a hamburger and onion rings."

"What did she say?" Frank asked.

"She gave this little laugh of hers," Stan said. "Very cold laugh, almost nasty. And she said, 'Hamburger? Is that what you want?' Then she laughed again. Then she said, 'Don't you want me, Stan? Isn't that what you want?' " He glanced nervously to Frank, to

Caleb, then back to Frank. "Then she just started to unbutton her blouse. She laughed again, that same laugh. 'Me,' she said, 'everybody wants me.' "

Frank could almost hear Angelica's voice, almost see the flinty look in her eyes. There was something in both that was wounded beyond repair. He could sense that some part of her was either already dead or swelling with the wish to die.

He wrote "everybody wants me" in his notebook, then looked up at the boy. "She started to unbutton her blouse," he said. "Then what happened?"

"I really didn't know what to do exactly," Stan said. "I mean, I'm not stupid or anything; I knew what she was getting at. But I couldn't figure out why she was doing this with me. She could have had anybody. Some hotshot college man or something. That's who I figured she'd end up doing it with. But not me." He shook his head. "And not like *that* with anybody. I mean, in the car, in a back alley. She didn't seem to be the type for a quick thing like that." His voice softened, and his eyes took on a look of tender wonderment. "She was so beautiful. I couldn't believe it." He stared out the front window as if he were looking for something in the trees. "Anyway, it was fast. And then she just got dressed and drove me back to Northfield."

"Did she say anything?" Frank asked.

"No," Stan told him. "Not one word. I tried to make a little conversation. Who wouldn't at a time like that? But she wasn't interested. Every time I tried to talk to her, she'd just glare at me like I was something terrible, something ugly, like she was disgusted with everything that had happened." He looked at Caleb. "And that's the way she looked at me from then on." He turned back to Frank. "Of course, I couldn't really blame her. I mean, when it's your first time, you want it to be special."

"First time?" Frank asked.

"Yes."

"For you?"

"For her," Stan said. "I mean, I haven't been around a lot, or anything. I'm not saying that. But I wasn't a . . . virgin."

"But Angelica was?" Frank asked.

170

"Yes."

"You're sure about that?"

Stan smiled. "I'm not that stupid," he said. "I know the difference."

"What was Angelica like when you saw her after this?" Frank asked.

"She acted just like she had before. Before that night, she barely knew I existed, and that's the way she acted after it."

Frank wrote it down, then closed his notebook. "Thanks for your help," he said.

Caleb stood up. "Yeah, thanks," he said. "And we'll stay in touch." He handed him a card. "You keep in touch, too. Especially if you think of something that could give us some help."

Stan got to his feet. "Listen," he said cautiously, "I know it's not exactly right to bring this up, but this pregnancy thing, my father doesn't know anything about that. I mean, I didn't know about it before you told me."

"And you'd just as soon keep the slate clean as far as your daddy is concerned, right?" Caleb asked him.

"If it's possible."

"It's possible," Caleb assured him. He looked at Frank. "Think we could keep this just between the menfolk?" he asked.

"Maybe," Frank said. He got to his feet slowly. "We'll probably talk to you again, Stan," he said. "We may have to go over everything several times."

"I understand."

Within a few minutes the three of them were standing together on the front lawn.

"Must be interesting, being a policeman," Stan said casually.

"Sometimes," Caleb answered dryly.

"I thought about law enforcement as a career," the boy added, "but my father wants me to go into something else . . . something more . . . more . . ."

"Well, he's probably right," Caleb said. "The flatfoots, they walk a ragged way, don't they, Frank?"

Frank nodded quickly. He could see Angelica in her muted frenzy, hear the sharp pain in her voice. What had caused it? He wondered if Sarah's silent agony had been like this, dark, sullen, edged in a rage he could neither see nor hear in his own daughter. A sudden wave of depression swept over him.

"Well, we'd better be going, Stan," Caleb said heartily. "Nice meeting you, son." He walked to the passenger side of the car and got in.

For a moment, Frank stood frozen, staring lifelessly at the neatly kept yard.

"Hey, Frank," Caleb called.

Frank turned to him. "I don't want to drive, Caleb," he said.

Caleb's eyes narrowed slowly. "You don't? Well, okay." He slid over behind the wheel, and waited as Frank took the now empty passenger seat.

"Nice boy," Caleb said, after he'd backed the car out of the driveway.

"Yeah," Frank said dully.

"No killer in Ansley Park, that's for sure."

"No."

" 'Course he could be lying," Caleb added, as he pulled the car into Piedmont Avenue and headed back toward downtown, "but I don't think so."

Frank fixed his eyes on the angular gray wall of the city as it rose before him.

"Hey, Frank, you okay?" Caleb said after a moment.

"Yeah, fine."

"You look like you ate something that didn't agree with you."

"I'm okay."

Caleb stared at him closely. "No, you're not," he said. "Do you need a drink?" He smiled softly. "All you got to do is tell me you can handle it."

"I can," Frank said firmly.

"Good enough," Caleb said. He pulled into the next bar he came to, a little plaster imitation of a Mexican tavern.

There was an empty booth in the back, and they walked directly to it.

"Give me one of them Tequila Sunrises," Caleb said when the waitress arrived. "What about you, Frank?"

172

"Scotch."

They drank silently when the drinks finally came, and Frank allowed his eyes to drift idly over the grain of the wood of his table, then up along the rough, exposed beams toward the plaster ceiling, and beyond that to where the sky could be seen, blue and vacant, through a small skylight at the very crest of the ceiling.

After about a half-hour, Caleb glanced at his watch. "Want another round?"

"No."

"You look like you're coming down with something, Frank."

"I got tired all of a sudden," Frank said. "Got very tired. That ever happen to you?"

"Yeah. It's the sign of a bad ticker, the doctor told me."

Frank nodded slowly. "Could be."

"That's what the doctor told me, anyway," Caleb added. "So I said to the doctor, 'If you got a bad ticker, what can you do about it?' He said you couldn't do very much. So I said, 'Well, there must be something I can do, for Christsake.' And that bastard just smiles at me and says, 'Just one thing, Caleb. Live like hell.' " He gulped down the last of his drink with a laugh and grabbed his wallet. "This one's on me, Frank," he said. "With a bad heart, you don't ever know, it might be your last one."

It took almost another half-hour to make it back to headquarters. Alvin was standing beside Frank's desk as the two of them entered the bullpen. His face looked as stricken as Frank had ever seen it. He looked as if everything he'd ever cared about had been tossed over a cliff.

"What is it, Alvin?" Frank asked immediately. He thought of Alvin's wife, of Sheila, even, illogically, of Karen, but he could not guess what dreadful thing had happened.

"What is it?" he repeated.

Alvin shook his head slowly. "Daddy died about an hour ago," he said quietly, as he drew his only brother gently into his arms.

17

It was almost midnight two days later before Alvin pulled over to the curb at Waldo Street to let Frank out.

"Well, I thought the funeral went about as well as could be expected," Alvin said.

Frank glanced toward the backseat. Alvin's wife and Sheila were both dead asleep. "Give them my best when they wake up," he said.

"I will," Alvin said. "Hey, listen. Maybe I could drop them off and come on back over here."

Frank shook his head. "I don't think so, Alvin."

Alvin leaned toward him. "Don't go on a drunk over this, Frank," he said.

"I won't," Frank assured him.

"You got a good case. Don't mess it up."

"Good night, Alvin," Frank said. He closed the door and headed up the stairs to his apartment.

The single lamp he'd left burning days before was still on in the living room, and the light, as it passed through the red shade, colored

175

the air like a spray of blood. He wanted to turn it off, but he didn't have enough energy to do it. It was as if he had returned to a different planet, one whose greater density and more rapid spin held things down with an enormous, insurmountable force.

He lit a cigarette, and watched helplessly as his mind went back over the last few days. He saw his father in the coffin, his face rouged and powdered, in his makeup for God. He could hear the preacher at the funeral, his voice flowing over the congregation: *His life was goodness. His reward is glory.* There was no doubt that his father had believed all that, and for a moment Frank felt himself all but captured in the mystery of such belief. And yet he knew such faith was lost to him, lost entirely.

He took a long drag on the cigarette and tried to think of something he believed in. Only the most negative ideas emerged. He believed that if you hit a man very hard in the face, he would pay attention to you after that. Everything else seemed soft and inconsequential when compared to the finality of sudden violence. "If I was God," Caleb had said, "I'd keep one hand on everybody's balls." Caleb had said it more or less as a joke, but to Frank it was the one true reality of life, the hard bedrock of everything else. But it was without comfort. It had no place for love or hope or mercy, but only raw and dreadful force, and the aching need for vengeance which it left behind.

He glanced about the apartment, taking in its usual disarray. He thought of Karen's house, then of Angelica's room, its immaculate walls, perfectly made bed, polished mirror. It seemed as little a part of the real world as his own, and he wondered if a balanced life did not have to be lived somewhere in between order and disarray, in a borderland of neither too many rules nor too few.

The smoke from the cigarette gathered in the far corner of the room. The light from the lamp gave it a distant, lavender hue. It was graceful in the way it moved, and for a time he watched as it coiled and spun in the reddish light. Slowly, his mind drifted to Karen, and he saw her as she had appeared to him on the day they met, a woman in an artist's smock. He wanted to see her, more powerfully than anything else he could think of.

Within a few minutes he was in his car, heading toward West

Paces Ferry Road. It was past midnight and the city seemed to sleep peacefully in a dark cocoon. The air was still warm with the day's heat, but he could feel a coolness in it now, a comforting relief, and he hung his arm out the window, as if dipping it into a mountain stream.

For a time, he hesitated at her door. The house was dark, but he felt certain she was not asleep. Finally, he knocked gently, and when she opened the door, she did not seem surprised to see him.

"I heard about your father," she said. "Mr. Stone at the police station told me. I'm sorry."

"I wanted you to know that it won't have any effect on how I handle your case."

"You could have told me that in the morning."

"I know," Frank said weakly. "But I didn't want to wait until then."

She stepped back from the door. "Come in."

Frank followed her into a small study toward the back of the house. It was not like the rest of the house. It was more cluttered. A few paintings lay scattered about, and there was a battered wooden desk and a few metal filing cabinets. A single bookshelf rose almost to the ceiling and, beside it, an ancient manual typewriter rested on a paint-spattered metal stand.

"This is my room," Karen said. "This is where I work." She smiled slightly. "I even sleep here sometimes. There's an old mattress in that closet."

"Are you going to stay in this house now?" Frank asked.

"No," Karen told him, "I'm not even going to stay in Atlanta."

Frank felt something very small break inside him. "You're not?"

"No."

"Where are you going?"

"New York."

"Why?"

"I just can't stand Atlanta anymore."

"I see," Frank said quietly. "Well, I'll be sorry to see you go." Because there seemed nothing else to do, he took out his notebook. "I wanted to let you know that we found out a few things about Angelica."

Karen pointed to a small wooden rocking chair. "Sit down."

Frank sat down, and watched as Karen pulled up another chair and took a seat opposite him. She took in a slow breath as if in preparation for more bad news.

"You remember that I took down the number of Angelica's phone?" Frank asked.

"Yes."

"She hardly ever used it."

"That doesn't surprise me," Karen said. "She never seemed to have any friends."

"Since April first, she made only three calls," Frank said. "And all of them were on the fifteenth of May."

"May fifteenth," Karen repeated softly.

"That's right," Frank said. "We found out that Angelica had gone to a doctor on May eleventh, an obstetrician named Herman Clark. Have you ever heard of him?"

Karen shook her head.

"She'd suspected that she was pregnant," Frank said. "She just wanted to make sure."

"I see."

"Well, Clark confirmed that she was pregnant. He told her on the fifteenth of May."

"So the calls were to him?"

"No," Frank said. "They were made to a young boy from North-field Academy. He lives over in Ansley Park. His name is Stanford Doyle, Junior. Have you ever heard of him?"

"No."

"Angelica never mentioned him?"

"She never mentioned anyone from Northfield," Karen said flatly. "Why did she call him in particular?"

"Because he is probably the father of her baby," Frank said.

Karen narrowed her eyes. "Did he kill my sister?"

"I don't think so," Frank said. "And according to the boy, they were only together one time. He says they hardly knew each other."

"Do you believe him?"

"Yes."

"Then so do I," Karen said. She stood up and pressed her back against the bookshelf. "So you're not any further along than you were at the beginning?"

"No, I think we've made some progress," Frank said.

"In what way?"

"Well, the night they were together, Angelica was acting very oddly."

Karen looked at Frank pointedly. "Of course, for Angelica, acting oddly would not be unusual."

"Well, she more or less picked him up at random," Frank explained. "She seemed angry, according to the boy. They went for a drive in her car. She appeared to know where she was taking him."

"Where did she take him?"

"Straight downtown. Not too far from where her body was found a few weeks later."

"I see."

Frank looked at his notes. "She didn't talk much that night. She circled Grant Park a few times, then drove down to the Cyclorama and parked."

Karen's eyes shot away from him. "Is that where they made love?"

"No," Frank told her. "They only stopped there awhile. The boy doesn't remember for how long. It seems they didn't talk much then, either."

"Well, she must have said something to him," Karen said fiercely.

"Not according to the boy."

"Are you telling me that Angelica just picked this boy up and . . . fucked him?"

"Yes," Frank said bluntly.

"And you believe that, too?"

"Yes, I do," Frank said. "But I believe she had some kind of reason for doing it."

"What reason?" Karen asked crisply.

"I don't know."

Karen shook her head despairingly. "I don't know if I can go on with this."

For a moment Frank let her rest in silence. Then, after a moment, he continued.

"They only parked at the Cyclorama for a few minutes," he began cautiously. "Then Angelica told the kid that this was his lucky night."

"Oh, God," Karen whispered.

"They drove around a little more after that," Frank went on. "The kid doesn't know exactly for how long. He doesn't know exactly where they went, either. He doesn't know the south side of town."

"Of course not."

"But Angelica did," Frank said. "That's the strange thing. She seemed to know exactly where she was and where she was going."

Karen looked at him wonderingly. "The area around Grant Park?"

"Yes."

"How would she know that part of town?"

"I don't know."

"She didn't say anything to this Stanford Doyle about it?"

"No," Frank said. "Had she ever mentioned anything about it to you?"

"No."

"Do you know if she had any friends out that way?"

"No."

"Any reason at all for her to be familiar with that part of the city?"

"She never mentioned anything about any place," Karen said firmly. "And she certainly never mentioned anything about Grant Park or the Cyclorama, or anything downtown for that matter." She shook her head wearily. "As far as I knew, she lived her whole life between this house and Northfield Academy."

Frank flipped a page of his notebook. "How about Stanford Doyle? Have you ever heard her mention his name?"

"No."

"People call him Stan."

"Nothing."

"He said she was very angry that night," Frank went on. "That was on the night of April first. Can you think of anything that might have made her angry?"

"No."

"Some little argument. Anything."

Karen began to pace slowly back and forth across the room. "No," she said. "Nothing."

"A bad grade," Frank pressed her. "A disappointment of some kind."

Karen whirled around. "Nothing, nothing, nothing," she said loudly. "I didn't know my sister! Can't you understand that!"

Frank stood up. "Something was happening to her, Karen," he said hotly. "Something very bad."

She turned away from him and drew in a long, deep breath. "I know," she said softly. "I could feel that something was going wrong. But I didn't know what it was." Her eyes closed slowly, as if searching for something inside herself. "I would have saved her if I could have." She looked at Frank. "I knew that something needed to be done, but I didn't know what it was. All I had was a feeling."

Frank thought of Sarah, of all the little hints she'd given, a sudden break in the middle of a sentence, a little gasp of fear when there was nothing threatening around her.

"I always thought that something was waiting for Angelica," Karen said. "It was as if some shadow was always gathered around her." She glanced away for a moment, then her eyes returned to him, very firm and determined. "I want to see where you found her."

"It's a vacant lot," Frank said. "Weedy. There's an old car in it, rusting away."

"I don't care what it looks like," Karen said.

"There's nothing to see," Frank said insistently. "We didn't even find footprints. The ground was too hard from the drought. A little brush was broken, where he dragged her. That's all."

"I don't care," Karen said. "I want to go there."

"All right."

"When can you take me?"

"We could go now, if you like," Frank told her.

Karen nodded thoughtfully. "Yes, I think I would."

During the long ride downtown, Karen sat silently beside him. Her face, as he glanced at it from time to time, appeared almost blue in the light, and just beneath it, he could see the same features, muted and less radiant, but clearly visible nonetheless, which others had seen, and probably adored, in her younger sister. And yet, to

Frank, Karen's beauty seemed deeper and more completed. There were faint creases about her eyes, and here and there in the deep black of her hair, he could see a strand or two of gray twining upward like a flower, which gave her a beauty that was beyond the scope of youth, larger, richer, more to be desired.

"I went out to the lot myself one night," Frank said, as he turned the car onto Peachtree.

She looked at him. "Alone?"

"Yes."

"To do what?"

"I don't know. To take it in, I guess."

"Take it in?"

"To see if I could feel something."

She turned back toward the street, her eyes fixed on the road ahead. "But you seem so meticulous. That little notebook. You're always writing in it."

"Yes, I am."

"So what did you expect to 'feel'?" Karen asked.

"Her death. Maybe her life. Something."

"And did you feel anything?"

"No."

"Then I probably won't feel anything either," Karen told him.

"No, with you it may be different," Frank said. "You were her sister. In one way or another, you've always been together. Something might be jarred loose. I've seen it happen. People suddenly remember some little fact or incident they hadn't thought of before. It happens all the time."

He turned off Peachtree and headed toward Glenwood. The glitter of the city fell behind them and the other world of squat brick buildings swept in around them like a wave.

"The day Angelica died," Frank said after a moment, "did you notice any change in her?"

"No."

"A sudden coldness or harshness, anything like that?"

"Nothing at all."

Frank turned the car onto Glenwood and edged it over toward the vacant lot.

"There it is," he said. He stopped the car at the edge of the field.

182

The lot rested to the left, its shrubs and weeds utterly motionless in the summer air.

"Oh, God," Karen whispered.

Frank pointed toward the middle of the field. "We found her over there. She was lying on her back." He looked at Karen. "We have a witness who saw someone carry a large bundle to the same area. Right now, we think it was a carpet, and that Angelica's body was rolled up in it."

Karen bowed her head slightly. "It's still so hard to believe."

"Do you want to get out?"

"Yes."

They got out of the car and walked to the edge of the field. The air was thick with the day's lingering heat, and in the streetlight, Frank could see a thin line of perspiration as it beaded on Karen's upper lip.

"Follow me," he said. "I'll show you exactly where I found her."

Together they waded slowly out through the thick brush. The surrounding streets were quiet, except for Glenwood, where the night traffic continued in a steady stream.

Finally, they reached the place where Angelica's body had been left.

"Here," Frank said. "She was on her back. And her hair was spread out around her head. I believe her killer arranged it that way."

"Why do you think that?"

"Because if he'd just laid the body down, her hair would have been beneath her head," Frank said. He stooped down to the ground and moved his hand in a circular motion. "Instead, it was all spread out around her."

"What kind of night was it?" Karen asked.

"Like this one."

"No wind?"

"No wind."

"Then we can find out for sure."

"How?"

"My hair is like Angelica's," Karen said, "so all you have to do is lay me down and see how my hair falls."

Frank walked over and very slowly lifted her into his arms. Then he bent forward and lowered her softly onto the ground. Her hair fell beneath her head and gathered there like a pillow.

"Like you thought," Karen said.

Frank nodded. "Yes." He could still feel the weight of her body in his arms, and for an instant he thought it came from his desire, but then, suddenly, it faded, and he could feel the moment of Angelica's death moving through him like a steady, electric charge. He stiffened.

"What's wrong?" Karen asked as she got to her feet.

"Nothing," Frank said, "nothing at all. Let's go."

18

"Sorry to hear about your father, Frank," Caleb said as Frank returned to the office the next morning.

Frank nodded quickly and sat down at his desk. He could feel his energy building again, and he wanted to take it at its peak. "Fill me in on everything."

"Well, the department didn't exactly let things go stale while you were gone."

"I didn't expect them to."

"And Gibbons, he was hot to trot the whole time. I figure that if you hadn't got back today, they'd of turned it all over to him."

"What did they do?" Frank asked.

"Well, the first thing they wanted to do was arrest Stan," Caleb said.

"Based on what?"

"They'd blood-typed the fetus Angelica was carrying," Caleb said, "and it was the same as Stan's. Gibbons was hot to move on that."

"What happened?"

"Brickman wouldn't buy it," Caleb said. "Too circumstantial.

Gibbons said they could use it to break a confession out of the kid. But Brickman said no."

"Good for him."

"Brickman thinks the daddy theory is all wrong," Caleb said. "He thinks it's a drug thing. Maybe a burn that went real bad."

"Any evidence of that come up?"

"No."

"What about Davon Little?"

"Nothing to connect him but that car."

"Anything in that?"

"Not a hair. Lab said they'd never seen a car that clean. Little did everything but vacuum the exhaust pipe. After the lab boys got back to me, I asked Little if he'd scrubbed the car. He said yes."

"So there was nothing in it at all?" Frank asked unbelievingly.

"Frank, if all we had to go on was what we found in that car, we'd have to swear that nobody but Davon Little had ever been in it."

"Anything else?"

"I checked out the kid."

"Clean?"

"As a whistle," Caleb said. "Good grades, fair athlete, all-around nice boy."

"So we're back at square one."

"Not exactly," Caleb said. "Because that kid did give us a little something to go on."

"What?"

"The fact that Angelica seemed to know the Southside."

"Yeah," Frank said. "I talked to Karen about that."

"Karen?"

"Karen Devereaux."

"When did you talk to her?"

"Last night," Frank said, as matter-of-factly as he could.

Caleb smiled slightly. "Oh." He cleared his throat softly. "And what did . . . uh, Miss Devereaux have to say?"

"She had no idea that Angelica knew about any part of town other than around West Paces Ferry."

"Which makes it not one bit less odd that she did, right, Frank?"

"Yeah."

"Why would Angelica know her way around Grant Park?"

"Caleb, if we knew that, I think we'd know a lot more."

"Me, too," Caleb said. "And the only thing I can figure is maybe drugs."

"And where would you go with that?"

"I already took it a little ways," Caleb said. "While you were back home, I went over to Northfield and talked to a few of the kids around there. They were a little jumpy at first, but after a while they started talking. Pot came up, then other things, like cocaine."

"What'd they say?"

"Well, practically everybody does a little pot," Caleb said, "and a few do more than that."

"And Angelica?"

"What I hear is that she was clean, at least at the time she died," Caleb said. "That's the funny part."

"What is?"

"Well, Angelica was like a lot of these kids at Northfield. She had the money and she had the cravings. Put those two together and it means she got the stuff."

"Pot?"

"And coke, a little."

Frank took out his notebook. "Go on."

"Well, at first I figured I was close to something," Caleb said. "I had it all mapped out. Angelica was a junkie, and that meant she had to have a connection. I mean, she wasn't muling it in with that BMW, you know?"

Frank nodded.

"So I figured her connection was in Grant Park, and that's why she knew the area."

"Sounds good," Frank said.

"To me, too," Caleb said, "but as the talk kept going, things fell apart."

"What do you mean?"

"Well, there's no doubt that Angelica had done a few drugs in her time," Caleb told him. "About three months before she died, this one kid spots her at one of these fast-food drive-ins. He goes over to her, and smoke just about keels him over."

"Three months ago?"

"That's right, and that's about the last time anybody saw Angelica with drugs."

"She just stopped?"

"Dead in the road, Frank," Caleb said. "Went totally off everything, as far as they know. Everybody agrees on that one."

Frank wrote it down.

"And that's not all," Caleb added. "She cleaned up her diet, too." He pulled a chair over to Frank's desk and sat down.

"Diet?"

"Angelica was a junk-food freak, the kids say. Always with the Fat Freddies and potato chips."

"She stopped that, too?"

"Dead in the water," Caleb said.

"And at the same time?"

"On the button. And this was *before* she found out she was pregnant."

Frank leaned forward slightly. "What was happening to her, Caleb?"

"She acts like somebody who all of a sudden got religion."

"So what was it? A change of heart?"

Caleb looked at Frank doubtfully. "When have you ever seen a case of that?"

Frank smiled.

"No, you were right the first time," Caleb said. "Something was happening to her."

"Yeah."

"It's the Grant Park stuff I can't figure," Caleb said after a moment. "I mean, everything is backwards. She should have met Grant Park on the way down. But it's like she met it on the way up. You know what I mean, Frank? She met it when she was going off drugs, not when she was going on them."

Frank shook his head wearily. "I have the strangest feeling about this one, Caleb."

"That's because nothing fits."

"Something goes very deep down in this one," Frank said. "You can't follow blood. You can't follow money." He shook his head despairingly. "So where do you go?" He flipped to the first page of his notebook. "Just back over everything, I guess."

He began reading his notebook.

"You're a slow healer, Frank," Caleb said after he'd watched him for a while.

Frank looked up. "What?"

"Your face," Caleb explained. "It don't look much better than it did a few days ago. You're a slow healer."

"Always have been," Frank said indifferently, as he returned to the notebook.

It was more like a sketchbook than anything else, and as Frank began the tortuous task of deciphering the minute, broken scrawl of his handwriting, it seemed to him that his notes contained little more than the basic facts of the case as he had meticulously gathered them. Aside from these, there was only an assortment of random thoughts and asides, intimations about character, impressions concerning how a particular person looked or spoke or gestured. He had noted that Arthur Cummings "appeared confident in his wealth and his innocence," and that Davon Little had talked in a loud voice, as if he knew that what he said was true.

"What are you looking for, Frank?" Caleb asked finally.

"I don't know," Frank admitted, but he continued to flip the pages of his notebook. He had noted that Albert Morrison was "very controlled," and that Jameson, the drama teacher, "had something sick in his eyes."

He turned another page, then another, until he was at Karen's house again. He had written that James Theodore "wanted to say something," and now those four words struck him as the only important ones he had come across so far.

He closed the notebook and looked up at Caleb. "Maybe we should turn up the burner a little," he said.

"How do you want to do it?"

"You take the park," Frank said.

"Anybody in particular?"

"Dealers, mostly," Frank said. "It's still possible that Angelica had a connection around there. Maybe it's old, but it still might be worth something."

"Okay."

"And do me a favor," Frank added. "Go light at first. Just show them the pictures of Angelica, and see if anybody's seen her in the area."

"Good enough," Caleb said. "See you this afternoon."

When Caleb had left, Frank pulled the telephone book from his desk drawer and looked up the address of the Nouveau Gallery. It was located in one of the vast, sprawling malls on the city's Northside.

He arrived at the mall quite early, and most of the shops were still closed. The mall was almost entirely deserted, but as he neared the brightly lit windows of the Nouveau Gallery, he could see Theodore at the back wall, struggling to hang an enormous picture. He tapped at the glass door, and Theodore turned immediately, lowered the picture carefully to the floor, and came to the door.

"Hello, Mr. Clemons," he said coolly as he opened it.

"I wonder if I could talk to you for a few minutes," Frank said.

"Of course," Theodore said. He opened the door more widely. "Come in."

"Thanks."

Theodore locked the door once again, then turned to Frank. "I don't suppose you're here to buy a painting," he said.

"No."

"Angelica?"

Frank nodded.

"Yes, of course," Theodore said. He glanced at his watch. "My assistant will be here in a few minutes, but we should have a little privacy before then." He pointed to a door at the back of the shop. "We can talk in my office."

Frank followed him into a small, cramped office whose walls were lined with stacks of paintings.

"Do you like paintings, Mr. Clemons?" Theodore asked as he sat down behind his desk.

"I don't know much about them," Frank told him.

"You don't have to," Theodore said. He nodded toward a large painting of a woman standing beside a lake. "Something like that is either beautiful or not." He tapped the side of his head with a single index finger. "And whether one finds it beautiful or not depends upon how one sees it, what one thinks about it." He smiled. "It requires no expertise."

Frank took out his notebook. "Do you remember when we were at Karen's together?"

"Yes."

"I made a note as I talked to you." Frank flipped through the notebook until he found the right page. "We only talked for a few minutes, and then Karen came down the stairs. Do you remember?"

"Yes."

"I made the note just then." He handed Theodore the notebook. "See?"

Theodore glanced at the page. " 'Wanted to say something,' " he repeated. He looked up at Frank. "You mean me?"

"Yes."

Theodore handed the notebook back to Frank. "What gave you that idea?"

"I don't know," Frank admitted. "It could have been anything."

"It hardly matters in any event," Theodore said.

"What do you mean?"

"It's true," Theodore said, "I did want to say something."

Frank flipped through his notebook until he found a blank page. "What?"

"Well," Theodore began, "I didn't want to talk to you that afternoon. At least, I didn't want to talk to you in front of Karen."

"Why not?"

"Because what I had to say would hardly have helped her situation."

"Something about Angelica, you mean?"

"Yes," Theodore said.

"Then why didn't you talk to me later?"

Theodore shook his head. "I don't know. I really don't. It's very easy to avoid unpleasantness." He smiled thinly. "That's what most of the people around me spend most of their lives doing, after all."

Frank said nothing.

"Well," Theodore added, "as a few more days passed, I simply did nothing. I suppose I would have come to you eventually."

"Well, now I've come to you," Frank said pointedly.

"Yes," Theodore said. He folded his hands together and placed them quietly on his desk. "You've already gathered that Angelica was basically friendless, isolated."

"So far, that's the picture."

"Well, it may not be a completely accurate one," Theodore said.

"In what way?"

"Well, in what it suggests," Theodore explained. "I mean, the image of Angelica it suggests. We have this somewhat shy, melancholy, perhaps tragic young girl who lives in a large house and has practically no life of her own at all." He smiled. "Is that what you're turning up, that image, the one I've just described?"

"Yes, something like that," Frank said. "At least at first."

Theodore pulled back slightly. "You mean, you've found something else?"

Frank did not answer.

Theodore looked at him knowingly. "You have, haven't you? My congratulations, Mr. Clemons. I'm surprised, because Angelica must have been very careful. I mean, it was by sheer accident that I came to see her . . . as you might say . . . out of character."

Frank lowered his pencil to the page. "What do you mean, 'out of character'?"

"The shy, aloof, breathtakingly beautiful young girl who appears hardly even to know how beautiful she is."

Frank wrote it down. "Go on," he said.

"Well, I never quite bought that, if you want to know the truth," Theodore said.

"Why not?"

"Because I don't believe that anyone that beautiful can be oblivious to her beauty."

"So you had your own ideas about her?"

"Yes."

"What were they?"

"That she was into something," Theodore said bluntly. "I didn't know what. I thought it might be drugs. All I knew is that it had to be something. I just didn't buy the notion that someone like Angelica could have absolutely no social life. Instead, I assumed she had one that had certain characteristics which made secrecy necessary." He smiled. "For a time, I thought she was probably gay." He pulled a bottle of brandy from his desk and opened it. "Care for a drink, Mr. Clemons?"

"No, thanks."

An odd sadness suddenly flooded Theodore's face. "Really? Why?"
"It's a little early."

"For me, it's already a little late," Theodore said quietly. "As you can see, Angelica is not the only human being who ever had her secrets." He poured himself a drink. "It gives me strength," he said. "Nothing else does." He took it all down with one quick gulp. "I drink because if I don't, time stops for me. Completely stops." He poured himself another round. "Even if I were happy, that would be unbearable." He glanced at his watch. "Ah, see, time is moving again." He laughed. "All quite simple, when you put it together, don't you think?"

"What about Angelica?" Frank asked insistently. He already knew that each man had his own individual reason for the bottle.

"Well, as I said," Theodore replied, "I always assumed that something was going on in Angelica's life, although I never knew what it was. Still, during the last few months before her death, I could see something in her."

"What?"

"She grew even more aloof," Theodore said. "She would hardly speak to me when I came over to talk to Karen, and she never came into the gallery anymore. There was a time when I would sometimes see her in the mall. That all ended, too." He shrugged. "Of course, one can always assume that it's some strange stage or something. But I never felt that was the case with Angelica."

"Why not?"

"Because she was not a person for stages," Theodore said. "Some people are somewhat eccentric from the beginning. Angelica was like that."

"What was her eccentricity?" Frank asked.

Theodore poured himself another drink. "Her beauty," he said. "That was the thing that distorted her." He smiled. "For some people it's money; for some, it's power. Whatever it is, it takes you out of the world's common experience. And whatever does that, Mr. Clemons, cripples and perverts you." He glanced at the bottle on his desk. "And so you have to find some other way to make contact with real life. With me, it's this." He smiled knowingly. "With Angelica, it must have been something else."

"A secret life," Frank said suddenly.

"Yes."

"What kind of life?"

"I'm not sure of that," Theodore said. "But I am sure that she had some sort of life outside that pristine little existence she lived at home and at school."

"How do you know?"

"I came across it," Theodore said. "And it was all quite by accident." He took another drink, and then carefully put the bottle away. "As you can see from the gallery," Theodore began, "my taste in art is quite varied. Because of that, I keep in touch with all sorts of little art movements here and there. I visit small, out-of-the-way galleries in Atlanta and in a great many other places." He drew in a long, slow breath. "And that's what I was doing around three months ago."

"Going to galleries," Frank said as he wrote it down in his notebook.

"One in particular," Theodore said. "A place called the Knife Point Gallery. It's an awful place, actually, and it has a sort of sadomasochistic air about it. I mean, there were chains coiled on the floor, and a little collection of whips in a gold frame." His lips curled downward. "It was all quite ridiculous, really. And it certainly had nothing to do with art."

"Where is this place?" Frank asked.

"Over on Piedmont," Theodore said. "Near where it runs into Peachtree."

Frank noted it in his book.

"It's really a dreadful place," Theodore repeated. "Quite unappetizing. It looks rather like a combination dungeon-whorehouse. Dark little rooms with all these little artifacts of . . . well . . . pain." He poured himself another drink. "I knew this morning that it would be like this for me today. I hope you don't mind." He emptied his glass in a quick gulp. "Anyway, among all these disgusting implements of torture, there was Angelica." He smiled. "Shining Angelica. So beautiful."

"What was she doing?" Frank asked.

"She appeared at first to be touring the gallery," Theodore said. "I was amazed to see her there. I mean, she'd never had much

194

interest in art. I certainly hadn't expected her to have an interest in the sort of trash that was hanging in the Knife Point."

"Was she alone?"

"I think so," Theodore said. "There were a few other people in the gallery. The sort you would expect. A rumpled painter in one corner, a drooling sadist in the other."

"Did you speak to her?"

Theodore shook his head. "No, I didn't. I rather shrank away, actually. I had an odd feeling, like I'd come upon someone doing something that she didn't want me to know about."

"So after you saw Angelica, you left the gallery?" Frank asked.

"Yes, I did," Theodore said. He leaned forward slightly. "And I would appreciate it if you would keep all this to yourself. I mean, Angelica's dead. It hardly matters at this point how she lived."

Frank said nothing.

"And besides, what could she do about it?" Theodore asked. "I've learned enough about the world to know that people do the things they do because they can't do anything else." He glanced toward the drawer where he'd put the bottle. "That's the great lesson of life," he said. "Helplessness."

"Did you see Angelica leave the gallery?" Frank asked.

"No."

"And you're sure she was alone?"

"I think she was."

"Does the gallery have a parking lot?"

"Yes."

"Did you see Angelica's car in it?"

Something seemed to catch in Theodore's mind. "That was before she got the BMW, wasn't it? You know, I don't even know if she had a car before then."

Frank wrote it down.

"Which means someone must have brought her to the gallery," Theodore said, almost to himself.

"The other people in the gallery that day, did any of them look like kids from Northfield?"

Theodore laughed. "Hardly. Even Angelica didn't look like a kid from Northfield."

"What do you mean?"

"The way she was dressed," Theodore explained. "It wasn't exactly Northfield prep."

"How was she dressed?"

"It's hard to explain," Theodore said. "Except that she seemed dressed for a purpose. It was almost as if she were in costume."

"Can you describe it?"

"Well, a black blouse, very low-cut," Theodore said. "I mean, for maximum exposure. And she had on a black leather skirt, quite short."

Frank wrote it down. "Anything else?"

"She'd changed her hair."

"In what way?"

"It wasn't down. She'd piled it up on top of her head. And there were little curls everywhere. Sort of baby-doll curls, you know?"

"Baby-doll curls?"

"That's what really finished the effect."

"What effect?"

"The, well, seductive effect," Theodore said, as if it had all just come together for him. "That's what it looked like she was aiming for. Seduction." He glanced about the room. "And there was something else. She wasn't really looking at the stuff on the walls. She didn't pay any attention to it at all."

"Then what was she doing?" Frank asked.

"Well, she just wandered from room to room," Theodore said. "She'd hang out in one for a while, then move onto another one. She was sort of slinking around."

Frank looked up from his notebook. "So, you didn't leave the gallery immediately?"

Theodore's face gave the appearance of someone who had just discovered an odd but incontrovertible fact. "I guess I didn't," he said slowly. He looked at Frank. "I guess I must have followed her."

"Do you think she saw you?" Frank asked.

"No, I don't think so," Theodore said. "But I'm not sure if that would have mattered to her."

"To be followed, you mean?"

"Yes," Theodore said. His eyes dulled; their light turned inward.

Then they suddenly snapped back toward Frank. "Because I think that may have been exactly what she wanted, to be followed, to be admired."

"By you?" Frank asked.

"Not me in particular, no," Theodore said.

"By everyone?"

"She was the thing that was on display in that sordid little gallery, Mr. Clemons," Theodore said with an odd certainty. "It was as if she had decided to be her own dark work of art."

19

As soon as Frank pulled into the small gravel driveway of the Knife Point Gallery, he realized that Theodore's description of it could hardly have been more accurate. If anything, it appeared even more dilapidated than he had described. The unpainted wooden porch slumped to the right, and even from a distance Frank could see where wind and rain had all but eaten through one of its supporting columns. A single noose of thick brown rope hung from one of its sagging beams.

Frank touched it lightly as he stepped up to the door. It swung languidly in the thick summer air, its dark gray shadow passing almost the full width of the narrow porch.

As Frank walked into the front room, he felt himself engulfed by the odd, disquieting atmosphere. The air seemed to hold a sense of barely controlled violence. He could feel it like a small, hissing breeze, and for an instant he felt the impulse to button his coat and lift his collar against the chill.

"Welcome to the Knife Point."

Frank turned and saw a large man in a black suit and white,

open-collared shirt. He was very tall, his head almost touching the low ceiling, and when he smiled, Frank saw the glint of metal in the back of his mouth.

"This is what we call a gallery of the Alternative," the man said quietly. "Have you ever been here before?"

"No."

The man nodded slowly. "Then you are in for a treat." He smiled thinly. "This is the front exhibition room," he said, as he swept one arm out gracefully. "It's not very large, as you can see, but we manage to use the space well."

Frank followed the swing of the man's arm. The room was dimly lit by a scattering of freestanding lamps. Their orange shades turned the air faintly yellow, and yet oddly luminous.

"Light is an atmosphere," the man said. "Because of that, we at the Knife Point think of it differently than the more established galleries. We do not seek to illuminate. We seek to shade." He nodded toward the opposite wall. "Our first exhibit."

The entire wall had been painted red, and a great black feather seemed to swirl out at its center. It created a strange, willowy maelstrom, and for an instant Frank felt himself drawn toward its center.

"It is called *The Fall of Satan*," the man explained, "and I think it captures a certain tragic grandeur." He looked calmly at Frank. "But please, don't think that the Knife Point is some sort of satanic enclave. We have nothing to do with that sort of idiocy. We are an alternative gallery, as I said. We are dedicated to nothing but alternatives." He swung around slowly and faced the wall to his left. "And so, we have works like this."

It was a large canvas, painted white, then streaked with blue. Oval drops of blood fell from the strips of white, then gathered in scarlet pools at various places along the green base of the canvas.

"Do you find this disturbing?" the man asked.

Frank continued to look at the painting. "No."

"Some do," the man said. "It's called *Lifeblood*."

Frank felt himself quite unexpectedly moved by the image before him. It seemed to speak more deeply of the world he knew than anything he'd seen in Theodore's gallery or Karen's living room.

"Who painted this?" he asked.

"Derek Linton. Ever heard of him?"

"No."

"He's a local artist," the man said. "Perhaps the best there is."
He watched as Frank returned his gaze to the picture. "We have a
few more of his works in the other rooms."

Frank continued to look at the painting. The rain of blood seemed
to fall silently and without melodrama, then gather in small lakes
of quiet grief.

"Who sent you here?" the man asked, after a moment.

Frank turned to him. "Sent me?"

"Well, you don't exactly look like an art collector."

"I'm not."

"Then how did you find out about the Knife Point? It's hardly
on the tourist itinerary."

"James Theodore told me about it."

The man looked surprised. "Theodore?"

"Yes."

The man laughed derisively. "Then I'm surprised you came at
all."

"Why?"

"Well, Theodore is hardly supportive of our work," the man said.
"Have you ever seen *his* gallery?"

"Yes."

"Paintings for the rich and oblivious," the man said. "Works of
art that are just placid enough so as not to disturb your guests while
they sip their champagne." He smiled proudly. "As you can see,
we are not interested in such things."

"Yes, I can see that," Frank said.

"So, Theodore sent you over here. Why? To scoff? To have a
laugh?"

"No," Frank said. He pulled out his badge. "Frank Clemons."

The man glanced at the badge, then back up at Frank. "Funny,
I didn't take you for a member of the Gestapo."

Frank pocketed the badge. "What do you mean?"

"A spy for Theodore and his crowd," the man said. "Are they
still looking for some way to close us down?"

"Not that I know of."

"Then what's your connection with him?"

"He owns his gallery with Karen Devereaux."

"Yes, I know."

"And Karen's sister, Angelica, was murdered a few days ago."

"Ah, so you're investigating her death?"

"Yes. Could I ask you your name?"

"It's Leland Cartier," the man said. "I own the Knife Point." He looked at Frank closely. "Of course, that still doesn't explain why Theodore sent you over here." He laughed quietly. "I mean, does he think I killed his partner's sister in order to get even?"

"Get even for what, Mr. Cartier?"

"For the way he's been deriding everything we do here," Cartier said. "It's a campaign to destroy us. He hates what we do. He believes that art should be gentle. He's even written that somewhere, that art should be 'life-affirming.' " He smiled sarcastically. "An odd attitude, don't you think, for an alcoholic?"

Frank took out his picture of Angelica. "Have you ever seen her?"

Cartier looked at the picture. "Is this Karen Devereaux's sister?"

"Yes."

Cartier continued to gaze at the photograph. "Yes, I've seen her," he said slowly. "But I had no idea who she was."

"Did you know that she was dead?"

Cartier handed the picture back to Frank. "No, I didn't."

"This same photograph was in the paper only a few days ago," Frank told him.

"I don't read the papers," Cartier said. "I don't find anything in them to be of use to me. I suppose you find that a strange attitude."

"A little."

"Life is short," Cartier said. "That's the only real law of life, that it very quickly comes to an end. Since that is so, it requires certain choices. One of them is to distinguish the things you can do something about from the things you can't." He shrugged. "The things in the paper are beyond my effort. I can't do anything about them, so I don't bother to learn about them." He smiled coolly. "It makes a certain amount of sense, don't you think?"

Frank took out his notebook. "You said that Angelica had been in the gallery, that you'd seen her here?"

"Yes."

"But you didn't know who she was?"

"That's right."

Frank wrote it down. "But you do recognize her from the photograph?"

"It took me a moment but, yes, I recognize her."

"Why did it take you a while?"

"Because she was dressed quite differently when she came in here."

"How was she dressed?"

Cartier thought about it for a moment. "Some sort of black outfit," he said. "I don't notice clothing that much, but I notice the mood it gives off."

"Mood?"

"Yes," Cartier said, "and Angelica's clothing gave off a sort of blackness. Of course, that's not unusual for the people who come in here. They're sometimes looking for anything but a work of art. They see the noose on the door, and something about it attracts them."

"Was Angelica looking for art?" Frank asked.

"I don't know what anyone's looking for, Mr. Clemons," Cartier said. "Do you?"

"When was she here?"

"About three months ago, I'd say," Cartier told him. "But come, you seem interested in some of the works we have. Let's walk through the gallery while we talk." He turned and headed into the adjoining room. He walked to the center of it, then stopped and looked back at Frank. "What do you think?" he asked.

Frank looked around the room. It was even more dimly lit than the first, and the mood it gave off was more sinister. A pair of silver handcuffs hung from a gold tack, and a black whip had been coiled up tightly and then nailed to the wall with a silver stake.

"Did Angelica come back here?" he asked.

"Yes," Cartier said. "As I recall, she lingered in this particular room. This one, and the last one, in the very back. Do you want to see it?"

"Yes."

"Follow me."

The paintings in the back room of the Knife Point seemed to drip, rather than hang, from the walls. The bright red and yellow canvases looked like gashes in the plain white plaster, their three-dimensional insides spilling out onto the floor. A kind of thick, acrid smoke seemed to fill the room, and as Frank moved through it, it was as if he could feel his own fires burning within him.

"I think she liked this room best," Cartier said.

Frank turned toward him. "Why?"

"Perhaps because it seems so raw," Cartier said. "So primitive."

"And Angelica seemed that way?"

"She had a certain look," Cartier said. "Like a creature stalking something." He looked at Frank. "That's the irony now, isn't it? I mean, apparently she was the one being stalked."

"Was she alone?"

"Yes."

"You're sure?"

"Absolutely."

"What did she do while she was here?"

"Not what you'd expect."

"What do you mean?"

"Well, she really didn't look at paintings," Cartier said. "It was like they were only there to serve as her own personal background."

"Background for what?"

"I don't know, whatever it was that she was trying to be."

"Which was?"

Cartier smiled helplessly. "I'm afraid I can't read minds, Mr. Clemons."

"Well, if she didn't look at the paintings, what did she do?"

"She would slink about the gallery," Cartier said.

"Slink?"

"Yes."

Frank wrote it down. "Did she act as if she were trying to pick someone up?"

"Not exactly," Cartier said. "It was more like she wanted to be seen. Only seen. Not touched, or even approached, for that matter."

"Did anyone ever try to approach her?"

"A few brave souls," Cartier said, "but she gave them a look, and they left her alone."

"How many times was she here?" Frank asked.

"Three or four," Cartier said.

"And she was always alone?"

"Yes."

"And she never talked to anyone?"

"No."

"Did anyone ever follow her out?"

"Not that I noticed," Cartier said. "But that's not surprising. She created a very distant sort of mood." He smiled. "Derek called her 'The Queen of Ice.' "

"Derek?"

"Derek Linton," Cartier said, "the painter I mentioned out front."

"He knew Angelica?"

"Only slightly," Cartier said. "They met here at the Knife Point."

"When?"

"I think it was the last time I saw her," Cartier said. "Yes, it was. They met the last time she came here."

"He talked to her?"

"It was more as if she talked to him," Cartier said. "Derek wouldn't have been interested in Angelica."

"But she was interested in him?"

"Yes," Cartier said.

"How do you know?"

"Because she did something I'd never seen her do," Cartier said. "She walked over to Derek and started to talk to him."

"About what?"

"About his painting," Cartier said. "*Lifeblood*. Derek was hanging it that day, and Angelica was in the front room. She looked at the painting for a long time, then she asked me who the artist was. I told her it was Derek, and then she went over and talked to him."

"How long did they talk?"

"Just a few minutes," Cartier said. "As I told you, Derek would not have been interested in Angelica." He thought about it for a moment. "But Angelica was quite persistent," he said. "She actually followed him out to his truck. I was quite surprised. As a matter of fact, I must have been quite taken with it, because I walked out on the porch and watched them for a while."

"What did they do?"

"Just talked," Cartier said. "Derek was in the cab of the truck and Angelica was standing beside it."

"Could you hear what they were saying?"

"No."

"Then what happened?"

"Well, as you can see, we don't have much of a parking lot," Cartier said. "So after a while, another car tried to get in, and Derek pulled out to give it his space."

"About how long did they talk?" Frank asked.

"It couldn't have been more than three or four minutes," Cartier said. "At least that time."

"Did they meet again?"

"Yes, they must have," Cartier said. "I know because Derek complained about it."

"About Angelica?"

"That she had come over to his house and imposed upon him a bit."

Frank quickly wrote it down. "What did he say exactly?"

"That he had no time for this sort of thing," Cartier said. "I remember his exact words. I started to joke with him about being chased by a beautiful young girl, and he said, 'In my faded condition, I don't need a Queen of Ice.' "

Frank scratched the words into his notebook. He looked at Cartier. "Do you have this man's address?"

"Yes," Cartier said. Then he gave it to him.

"That's in the Grant Park area, isn't it?" Frank asked.

"Yes, it is," Cartier said. "Derek's lived there almost all his life."

Frank continued to look at the address, 124 Bergen Street, staring at it so hard that his eyes seemed to bleach the blue ink into a blazing white.

20

Even over the phone, he realized suddenly, Karen's voice drew him toward her like an invisible wire.

"Hello," she said.

"Karen, it's Frank."

He waited for her to respond in some intimate way, with a sudden caught breath, a sigh, a whisper.

"Frank Clemons," he added.

"Yes, I know, Frank," Karen said with a small laugh. "You're such a formal man."

He wanted to stop right there and ask her what she meant, but he knew he couldn't.

"Listen," he said quickly. "Have you ever heard of a place called the Knife Point?"

"A gallery?"

"Yes."

"I've heard of it," Karen said. "James has mentioned it a couple of times."

"But you've never been there?"

"No."

"What do you know about it?"

"Not much," Karen said. "James has always treated it as a joke, but that doesn't mean anything. He's very rigid when it comes to art."

"So you don't know anyone who is connected to the gallery?" Frank asked.

"No."

"Did Angelica ever mention it?"

"No. Why?"

"How about Derek Linton? Have you ever heard of him?"

"Yes," Karen said. "He's a painter. He's very good."

"Did Angelica ever mention him?"

"No," Karen said. Her voice tightened. "What's this all about, Frank?"

"I've found out that Angelica sometimes hung around the Knife Point."

"Hung around? Why?"

"I don't know," Frank told her. "But I also found out that she knew Derek Linton."

"And they met at the Knife Point?"

"Yes."

"But what would Angelica be doing at a place like that?"

"She's been there a few times," Frank said. "The owner recognized her."

There was another silence, and in his mind, Frank could see Karen's eyes as they grew softer and more somber.

"Frank," he heard her say finally. "Be careful."

There was a strange, insistent quality in her voice, and Frank could still hear it echoing faintly in his mind as he pulled the car up to 124 Bergen Street. It was a small woodframe house, but it was well-kept-up compared to the rest of the neighborhood. It had been recently painted a gently muted white, and the bright green shutters shone cheerfully in the hard afternoon light.

But there was still something sad about the house, and as he got out of the car and headed up the cement walk, Frank could feel that sadness gathering around him. It was in the soft sway of the flowers that bordered the walkway, and the gentle, lonely tinkle of the stained-glass wind chimes that hung on the front porch. It was in the huge wall of shrubbery that all but blocked the end of the walkway, and which turned the porch into a lush green cavern, one whose moist leaves seemed already to be fading toward a crackling brown.

The door opened not long after Frank knocked, and he saw a tall, very lean man staring at him from behind the screen.

"If you've come to collect some bill or other," he said, "you can forget it."

Frank pulled out his badge.

The man squinted at the gold shield. "There's no possible reason why the police would be interested in me."

"Are you Derek Linton?" Frank asked.

"Yes."

"Frank Clemons. I'm investigating a murder."

"Murder?"

"That's right," Frank said. "I understand you're a painter, Mr. Linton."

"Is that a crime now?"

Frank returned the badge to his pocket. "I need to talk to you for a few minutes. It's important."

"You don't mind a mess, do you?"

"No."

"All right then," Linton said. He swung open the door. "Come in."

The front room looked as if it had never been straightened, and yet, Frank noticed, it did not have the same sense of hopeless confusion which he found in his own apartment. There were spots of paint on the floor, walls and furniture. Stacks of frames leaned haphazardly against the walls, and assorted canvases were gathered together in jagged piles in all four corners of the room. A rickety, paint-splattered easel stood near a large open window as if it were the still-surviving testament of an undefeated heart.

"I do love this place," Linton said as he eased himself into a light blue overstuffed chair. He took a bottle of red wine from beside the chair and poured himself a glass. Then he lifted the bottle to Frank. "Would you like a drink?"

"No, thanks."

"Because you're on duty?"

"Because I don't want one," Frank said.

Linton smiled. "Sit down, Mr. Clemons."

Frank sat down in a small wooden rocker and took out his notebook.

"Very thorough," Linton said. He picked up a single plastic bottle from an array of medicines which covered the top of the small table beside his chair. "Just a moment, please," he said, "it's time for this one." He placed a large white pill in his mouth and washed it down with the wine. "They're not supposed to go together," he said, "but I do what I like." He replaced the bottle on the table. "Quite a collection of medicines, don't you think?"

Frank nodded.

"Dying," Linton said, as he gazed at the assorted drugs. "And don't want to." He motioned toward the collection of medicines. "These are all parts of the resistance," he said, "and they are as far as I will go." He ran his fingers through his great mane of white hair. "Don't want to lose this. I'm too vain. Cancer has a way of taking your dignity before it takes your life."

It had once been a beautiful face, Frank thought, as he gazed at Derek Linton, and although it had now grown slack and terribly pale, it still retained a certain heroic loveliness.

Linton reached for a framed photograph and handed it to Frank. It showed a tall, robust man with beautiful white hair and wild, blue eyes. "That's the way I looked just a year ago," he said. He took another sip of wine. "But that's not what you're here to talk about." He leaned back in his chair. "Now, you said something about a murder?"

"Yes," Frank said. He opened his notebook to the first blank page.

"Do you take everything down?" Linton asked.

"Most everything."

"Whatever can be said in words, right?"

"I have a bad memory," Frank explained. "I don't always trust it with the facts."

Linton's face suddenly stiffened. "Forgive me," he said, "the pain."

210

"Can I get you something?"

"No," Linton said quickly. "Please, it will pass." He took a deep breath. "I've always been very jealous of my dignity. That's what makes it so hard now. There's no dignity in pain. None at all." He shook his head resolutely. "But I don't want to get into that. Too much self-pity." He grabbed his wineglass and squeezed the stem. "Please, let's go on," he said in a high, strained voice. "The murder. You were talking about a murder."

Frank took a picture of Angelica from his coat pocket and handed it to Linton.

"Have you ever seen this girl?"

Linton nodded slowly. "Yes. That's Diana."

"Diana?"

Linton looked up from the photograph. "Isn't that her name?"

"No," Frank told him. "Her name is Angelica Devereaux and she was murdered a few days ago. Her body was dropped in a vacant lot over on Glenwood. It was in the papers. They published this picture."

Linton's eyes fell back toward the photograph. "I didn't know," he said with a kind of mild self-rebuke. "It's this damn disease. It isolates you. It's all you think about. I'm sorry."

"But you do recognize her?"

"Yes, absolutely," Linton said. "I met her about three months ago. I was hanging a painting at this gallery."

"The Knife Point," Frank said.

"You've been there?"

"Yes," Frank said. "I talked to the owner."

"Cartier told you everything, then," Linton said.

"Not quite."

"What do you mean?"

"He said she approached you that day," Frank said. "Can you tell me about that?"

"There's not much to tell," Linton said. "Of course, I wouldn't be interested in a . . . in Angelica, you said her name was?" He smiled. "But I suppose I have my vanity, and I must admit that to have such a beautiful young girl . . . it was pleasant."

"What did she say to you?"

"She said she liked my painting."

"*Lifeblood.*"

"Yes, that one," Linton told him. He shrugged. "I don't really think of it as anything special, myself. But this girl, Diana, or I should say, Angelica, kept talking about it."

"What did she say about it?"

"That it was beautiful," Linton said, "that she admired it. What else can you say?" He took another sip of wine. "I think she was somewhat drawn to me," he added after a moment. He looked at Frank questioningly. "Was she an orphan, by any chance?"

"Yes."

"Ah, so that's it."

"What?"

"Father figure, that's what she was after."

"Do you think it was that simple?"

"You never know, if you're an artist, exactly what it is that people see in you, or in your work," Linton told him. "It could be anything." He glanced wistfully toward the rickety old easel. "But it's a wonderful thing, to be an artist, to touch people in such odd and decent ways." He looked back at Frank. "I believe that this girl was sincere, that she had responded in some way to that painting. Perhaps that's just my vanity. I don't know. But I believe that something in that painting moved her."

Frank wrote it down.

Linton leaned forward slightly. "Why are you writing all this down?"

"Bad memory, like I said."

Linton shook his head. "No, it isn't. It has nothing to do with your memory, bad or good."

"I like to have all the facts at my fingertips," Frank told him.

Linton stared at him piercingly. "Bullshit, Mr. Clemons. I'll bet that you have all those notebooks somewhere. I'll bet you've saved them all."

For a moment, Frank could see them piled in a box in one of his disordered closets, stacks of little green books, one on top of the other. He had kept them all, as if something in them was worth preserving, the accumulated knowledge of his life.

"Was that all you talked about, your painting?" he asked Linton.

"More or less," Linton said. "Except for what I noticed about her."

"What was that?"

"That she was different from the way she looked," Linton said. "Did Cartier tell you about how she looked that day, Mr. Clemons?"

"I have an idea," Frank said. "Not everybody's description was the same."

"Like a cheap little S&M whore," Linton said bluntly. "That's what she looked like. I actually thought she was one of those prostitutes who specialize in that sort of thing." His eyes narrowed. "She wasn't a prostitute, was she?"

"I don't know what she was," Frank said. "That's what I'm still trying to find out."

"Perhaps she didn't know what she was either," Linton said. "It's not easy to know, especially in this world." He took another photograph from the table beside him and handed it to Frank. It showed Linton in infantry uniform, a young man with a cigarette dangling from his mouth and an M1 strapped to his shoulder.

"World War Two," Linton said. "I was at Anzio."

"So was my father," Frank said. "Or at least not far from there."

"On that day, when we hit the beaches, I knew exactly what I was made of," Linton said. "Since then, it's been anybody's guess." He tugged the photograph from Frank's hand and placed it back on the table. "When your life is flat, when nothing is ever at risk, you have to create your own identity. Maybe that was Angelica's problem. She told me she was rich. Was she?"

"Yes."

"Sheltered?"

"I think so."

Linton nodded. "Maybe she had no idea who she was, and so she dressed up as something she wasn't. You know, just decided to be something in particular for a day." He nodded toward Frank's pocket. "Show me that photograph again."

Frank gave it to him.

"Ah yes," Linton said. "The face is the same, but her hair was different, and her makeup." He handed the picture back to Frank.

"She did look like that when I saw her the first time. And the second time I saw her, she looked completely different from the first."

"Cartier said that he thought you saw her at least one more time."

"He was right."

"Where did you see her?"

"Here, at my house."

"She knew where you lived?"

"She could have looked me up in the phone book," Derek said. "I guess that's what she did, because I know I didn't tell her where I lived when we were at the Knife Point. I mean, there was no time for that. She followed me out, and this other car wanted to come in, so I backed out very quickly and made a space." He smiled. "An artist must always give way to a customer."

"So she just showed up at your house?" Frank asked.

"Yes."

"When?"

"About two days later," Linton told him. "And as I said, she looked completely different. None of that S&M black. Just the opposite, in fact. She wore a lovely, frilly sort of light blue dress, and her hair fell over her shoulders. She looked very, very beautiful."

"How long did she stay here?"

"About an hour," Linton said.

"What did you talk about?"

"I showed her my paintings. She seemed to like them. She had no education in art, no experience in it. But she seemed genuinely interested. She asked to see my studio, and so I took her into the back room and showed it to her."

"May I see it?"

"My studio? Why?"

"Just to get a feel for the place."

"All right," Linton said with no further question. He pulled himself up and led Frank slowly into the back room.

A rush of bright sunlight swept the room, and Linton's white hair gleamed brightly in its rays.

"This is it," he said, "my life's work."

It was like a world of half-created things, canvases of ill-formed landscapes, half-colored faces, sketches, drawings, splotches of color that seemed little more than random, careless splatterings of red and yellow. It was as if Linton had spent his life in random, sporadic attempts to capture something that continued to elude him.

"This is where you took her that afternoon?" Frank asked.

"Yes."

Frank peered about the room. There was something beautiful about it. The canvases were bound evenly, the frames neatly stacked. But it was not order which made it beautiful, it was the struggle to bring some order to everything outside the room, to all that was less tractable than mere frames and brushes.

"It's a nice place," Frank said.

"I've seen worse."

Frank glanced toward a vase of freshly cut flowers which rested on one of the tables near the easel.

"A friend of mine brings them here occasionally," Linton said. "As a matter of fact, she brought them the day Diana came. We were in the studio when Miriam came in. She looked a little surprised to see the girl. She said, 'Oh, it's you.' "

"She knew her?"

"I guess she did."

"Did she say anything else?"

"No," Linton said. "She just smiled and dropped off the flowers."

"And the woman. What is her name?"

"Miriam Castle," Linton said. "And if you're looking for the closest thing this city has to a real art patron, that's Miriam."

"Where does she live?"

"She spends her summers in La Grange," Linton said. "She's very rich. She has one of those huge plantations out there."

"And the address?"

Linton laughed. "You won't need an address. Everybody in La Grange knows where the Castle plantation is." He looked slowly around the room. "God, I will miss this place." He nodded toward the corner. "The girl stood in that area right over there. I gave her a quick tour of the place. I showed her some paintings, some sketches, the usual stuff. It was like giving a lesson to a kindergarten kid."

"Did she seem that young?"

"She seemed hardly to exist at all," Linton said.

215

"Did you ever mention her to . . . is it Miss or Mrs. Castle?"

"Miss."

"Did you ever mention her to Miss Castle?"

"No."

"It never came up?"

"Never," Linton said. "And that's not unusual for the two of us. We never talk about mutual acquaintances or anything having to do with each other's personal lives."

"Why not?"

"We've had a certain division of feeling over the years," Linton said. "She wanted something that I couldn't give her." He stepped back toward the door. "I'd rather not stay too long in here."

"Of course," Frank said.

A few minutes later, Frank was on the porch again, staring at Linton through the gray screen.

"Thanks for your time," he said.

Linton looked at him closely, his eyes still fixed on Frank's slowly healing face.

21

E ven in his dreams, Frank could not have imagined the splendor that greeted him as he passed through the large gate and entered the grounds of the Castle plantation. It had taken him almost two hours to get to La Grange, but the beauty of the estate suddenly relieved much of the long drive's accumulated weariness and tension. Huge magnolias spread their great leaves in a rising tower of gently swaying green. To the left, weeping willows hung motionlessly over a blue lake, and beyond the water, almost like a phantom, he could see the great white portico that looked out over everything.

A small woman in a black dress and white apron greeted Frank at the door.

Frank took out his badge. "I called earlier. Miss Castle agreed to see me this afternoon."

"You must be Mr. Clemons."

"That's right."

"Please come in, Miss Castle will be with you in a moment."

The luxuriance of Karen's house was muted when compared to the sweeping foyer he entered now. An enormous staircase unfolded from the second floor and down along walls covered with paintings and brightly colored tapestries.

"May I take your hat, sir?" the woman asked.

"No, thanks," Frank said. "I'll hold on to it."

"Miss Castle has asked that you wait here," the woman said. "She'll be down in a minute."

"That'll be fine," Frank said.

A few minutes later, Miriam Castle arrived. She walked down the long, winding staircase, and even from a distance, Frank could see that she was an elegant, graceful woman with silver hair and a remarkably unlined face.

She offered her hand gently as she stepped over to Frank.

"I'm pleased to meet you," she said. She smiled politely. "I was just going out for my evening walk. I was hoping that you might join me."

"Yes, fine."

"Good," Miss Castle said. "Come."

A few minutes later, the two of them were strolling slowly amid the rich foliage of the grounds. Wisps of Spanish moss hung from the branches overhead, and in the distance a small clear stream meandered right and left through the oak and elm.

"We gained all this through slavery," Miss Castle said. "One of my distant relatives was in the slave trade almost from its beginnings. Family legend has it that he was a kind man. But then, what family legend ever contained a cruel one?" She laughed. "A fact which Derek never tires of pointing out."

"How long have you known him?"

"Forever," Miss Castle said. "Or at least it seems that long. Actually, it's been about forty years. I still bring him flowers, you know."

"Yes, I saw them."

She turned toward him. "I don't know, Mr. Clemons, perhaps it's just the light or the way the lake looks right now, but I feel quite full of things."

"Things?"

"Truths," Miss Castle said. "Even difficult ones sometimes seem quite beautiful." She walked to the edge of the lake and stopped. "What did Derek tell you about me?"

"Nothing."

She smiled. "Of course. He's always been like that."

"What should he have told me?"

"Well, for one thing, that I've been in love with him for all these many years."

Frank said nothing.

"Does that strike you as tragic?" she asked him.

"No."

She looked back at him. "Why not?"

"Because it lasted."

"But others have a quite different opinion," Miss Castle said. "They see me as a woman who's spent her life loving a man who . . . well . . . who cannot love women." She laughed. "It's really more a comedy, don't you think?"

"Neither one," Frank said.

Miss Castle looked at Frank sweetly. "Women of my class are attracted to two things, Mr. Clemons, money and character. Derek had character."

"He still does," Frank said.

"Yes, and he will maintain himself intact," Miss Castle said. She allowed her eyes to follow the flitting movement of a starling in the tall white oak. "How is he?"

"He's dying."

"Yes, I thought so," Miss Castle said, "of that awful disease." The bird took flight and she looked back at Frank. "I shall think of myself as a widow, even though he would not approve of that."

"Perhaps, he would."

"No, he wouldn't," she said determinedly. "I won't lie to myself about that. I have desired a man who does not and cannot desire me. Tragedy or comedy, in either case, it is the truth."

Frank took out his notebook. "Mr. Linton said that you met Angelica Devereaux at his house."

"Yes."

"And that you said, when you saw her, 'Oh, it's you.' "

"Possibly."

"So you recognized her?"

"Not as Angelica Devereaux," Miss Castle said, "but only as a young girl I'd seen in various out-of-the-way galleries in the city."

"Then you didn't know who she was?"

"No. I only knew that I had seen her before at such places. She was always dressed differently, but when you are that beautiful, dress cannot hide it."

"You said the galleries were 'out of the way'?"

"Yes."

"What do you mean?"

"I mean that they're not among those on the Northside, the more prestigious galleries," Miss Castle said. "They are smaller places, with cheaper rents, that sort of thing."

"Places like the Knife Point Gallery?" Frank asked.

"Yes, that's the sort of gallery I mean."

"And you saw Angelica at places like the Knife Point from time to time?"

"Yes," Miss Castle said. "I had no idea who she was. And she was always dressed somewhat differently. But she was very beautiful. Quite striking. If you saw her once, you weren't likely to forget it."

"Did you see her often?"

"Not often, but on occasion."

"How many times?"

"I didn't make a note of it."

"Give me your best guess, then."

"Five, maybe six."

"Over how long a period?"

"I started running into her about four months ago," Miss Castle said.

"Was she always alone?"

"Yes, and that struck me as very strange. After all, she is, as I've said, very beautiful, and that sort of girl is rarely alone. It would have been natural for her to have had some sort of escort."

"But she never had one?"

"Not as I recall."

Frank wrote it down. When he looked back up, he saw that Miss Castle had been eyeing him cautiously.

"I have a confession to make, Mr. Clemons," she said.

"Confession?"

"Yes. I'm afraid that I had an ulterior motive for asking you up here this evening."

"Which was?"

"To find out about Derek," Miss Castle said. "Beyond that, I must tell you that I know practically nothing about your young girl. I never spoke to her or had anything at all to do with her."

"I understand," Frank said, "but you did at least see her from time to time, and that's important."

"Is it?"

"Yes," Frank said. "Now, about these places where you met Angelica, these galleries, where are they?"

"Actually, I never saw her at the Knife Point," Miss Castle said. "No, she was always somewhere else." She thought about it for a moment. "Yes, I remember now. She was always at one of those galleries on the Southside. There's a street of them. Not too far from Grant Park."

"Grant Park?"

"Yes, there's a street of them. Three or four in a row. It's all pretty run-down for the most part, but once in a while I've been able to find some interesting work."

"These galleries," Frank said. "What are their names?"

Miss Castle ticked them off one by one, as Frank wrote them down in his notebook.

"And you said they're all on one street?" he asked.

"Yes. Hugo Street," Miss Castle said.

Frank wrote the street name under the names of the galleries and underlined it.

"This girl," Miss Castle said after a moment. "Was she in love with Derek?"

"I don't think so."

"Where did they meet?"

"The Knife Point," Frank said, "then she dropped by his house."

"And that's all?"

"As far as I know."

Miss Castle smiled. "Old as I am, still jealous." She laughed sadly. "And of a woman, of all things."

221

Frank walked over to her, and for a moment the two of them watched a small flotilla of ducks as it skirted effortlessly across the placid surface of the lake.

"I still find life quite mysterious, Mr. Clemons," Miss Castle said at last. She looked at him. "Do you?"

"Yes."

She smiled, and drew a long thin strand of Spanish moss from one of the limbs that hung low above her. "This particular species always looks dead," she said. "It's always gray and dusty." She laughed faintly. "My father used to take me to the window at night. He'd point to this moss and he'd say, 'Look, Miriam, there in the moonlight, the ghosts are hanging in the trees tonight.' " She coiled the strand delicately around her finger. "How long does Derek have?"

"I don't know."

"Does he look . . . frail?"

"You haven't seen him?"

"No, not for a few weeks."

"But the flowers."

"He finally gave me a time when I could bring them and he wouldn't be there," Miss Castle said. "He doesn't want me to see him."

She began to walk slowly along the edge of the lake. "I've seen others, of course. They look dead before they die." She turned abruptly to Frank. "Does he?"

"He looks thin, that's all," Frank said. "He doesn't really look like he's dying."

"He had so much energy," Miss Castle said.

"He still does."

She looked surprised. "Does he?"

"Yes," Frank told her.

She shook her head. "Such a stubborn man. I've offered him all sorts of help. I've done that for forty years. It wouldn't only have been him. I'm a patron, as they say, of the arts. I buy their works, and sometimes I get them jobs that won't destroy them. Restorations, touch-ups, museum work, that sort of thing. I could have done that for Derek." She laughed. "God knows I've done it for artists far less

222

gifted than he is." She shook her head despairingly. "But he would never take anything. He would never even sell me one of his paintings. He would give me one from time to time, but money never passed between us." She stopped again, her eyes drifting over to the lake. The water was turning red in the twilight. "So, you see, I wouldn't have found it unusual if that girl had loved Derek."

"When you saw her in those galleries, did you have an impression at all?" Frank asked.

"Yes, I did."

"What was it?"

"That she was a seductress," Miss Castle said. "It was the way she might slink from one room to another, or stand in a corner somewhere, sucking a fingernail."

"Did you ever see her talk to anyone?"

"No. Never. I saw people approach her from time to time, but she would always turn them away. That's why I found it so odd that she was at Derek's house that day."

"Why odd?"

"Because she was obviously using her beauty as blatantly as she could," Miss Castle said. "And, as you must have guessed, for Derek, a woman's beauty remains pretty much a matter of abstraction. I don't think he's capable of feeling anything beyond that."

"Are you saying that Angelica was a tease, Miss Castle?" Frank asked.

"That would be the vulgar term, yes," she replied. She turned toward him and touched the large, purplish circle beneath his eye. "Does that still hurt?" she asked.

"Yes."

She drew her hand away. "Beauty is not always a soothing thing, Mr. Clemons."

"And what about Angelica's beauty?"

"Not soothing. Not soothing at all. At least, she didn't seem to use it in that way. Just the opposite, in fact."

"Which would be?"

"Well, to inflame people, if you're looking for the most dramatic term."

"And you think she liked to do that on purpose?"

"Yes," Miss Castle said firmly. "That was my impression. And the fact that she is dead does not surprise me." She stared at Frank pointedly. "There's a danger to inspiring too much flame. You may become engulfed by it."

Frank had seen that happen before, but in every case, the rage had been obvious in what it left behind, bodies mauled beyond recognition, flayed open or beaten flat, sprawled across rumpled beds, or still dangling from the ropes that had been used to restrain them while the rage swept over them again and again until they couldn't feel it anymore.

"Did you notice anyone who might have felt that way about Angelica?" he asked.

"No," Miss Castle admitted. "But then it wouldn't always be obvious, would it?"

"No."

"It might build slowly, day by day. And while it built, it might be invisible."

"Yes."

"Do you know what Derek says? He says that we are 'junglehearts.' Do you know what he means by that?"

"No."

"That we react to things, rather than create them," Miss Castle explained. "Do you think that's true?"

"Sometimes," Frank said.

"It would work like this," Miss Castle added. "A group of cells arrange themselves into a body that is beautiful. That would be Angelica Devereaux. This creature would then create certain reactions in the other creatures it encountered. One reaction might be to adore her, one might be to love her, one might be to hate her, and one might be . . ."

"To kill her," Frank said.

"Yes," Miss Castle said. A single white eyebrow arched upward suddenly. "And now you, Mr. Clemons, are called upon to react to *that*." She drew her collar more tightly around her neck, as if to ward off a sudden chill. "We are all hopeless. You, me, Angelica. All of us. We don't know what we are. We don't know what we

do. And we can't even begin to calculate the effects of what we do."
She smiled very briefly, then offered him her hand.

"And so good-bye, Mr. Clemons," she said. "Let us part gracefully, one stranger to another."

She turned briskly and headed back toward the great house. Its immense white facade seemed to stare down at her with a sightless eye.

22

During the long ride back to Atlanta, Frank tried to bring all the details he had discovered into some kind of order. The portrait of Angelica Devereaux had now changed radically, but it was no less confused. The remote, private, obsessively solitary girl who slept in a room full of dolls had become something else entirely, a girl who dressed in different clothes, wandered through seedy art galleries, and, in her own way, tried to attract as much attention as she could.

But even this was too simple, Frank thought, as he continued to consider it. For this was the same girl who'd suddenly approached an old man with what appeared to be genuine affection, the same girl who, a few weeks later, had driven a boy she hardly knew to a littered alleyway and taken him angrily in the cramped space of a red BMW. It was as if she had lived many lives, or wanted to, and that none of them had ever satisfied her.

It was already past nine at night when Frank made it back to headquarters. Most of the detectives had cleared out long ago, with only the sullen graveyard shift to occupy the empty desks of the bullpen. They sat around, staring vacantly at newspapers and magazines or roaming idly from one desk to another as if still searching wearily for the final key to things.

Only Gibbons retained his energy, and as he sat down at his desk, Frank could see him scrambling through the last stack of memos from the FBI. It was a sad, despairing sight, but Frank could not figure out exactly why it struck him that way. It was as if something were missing in Gibbons, missing in the way he hunted down his prey with that relentless, deadly professionalism that had served him so well. His busts were always clean. He lived by the letter of the law, and left its spirit as shallow and untended as an abandoned grave.

"Hello, Frank," Caleb said as he walked up to the desk. "Eyeing the competition?"

"What?"

"I saw Brickman talking to our friend Gibbons this afternoon," Caleb said. "Thought they might have shifted the case over to him."

"Not that I know of."

"Good," Caleb said. He pulled a chair over to the desk and sat down. "Score one for our side." He leaned back leisurely and pulled out his pipe. "By the way, where you been? Alvin's been worrying about you."

"La Grange."

"For the sights?"

"I got a lead, someone who's seen Angelica in various places."

"What places?"

"A few galleries," Frank told him. "There's a street of them near Grant Park."

"Grant Park again," Caleb said thoughtfully.

"Yeah."

"You know, Frank, I've been thinking she was maybe a hooker."

"Who was also a virgin?" Frank replied doubtfully.

"That kid might not know the difference, Frank," Caleb said. "What I was thinking is, you've got a bored rich kid who has a taste for slumming. Things get stranger and stranger. She ends up taking a few bucks. The idea appeals to her. She does it a few more times, and then she picks up this john and before she can even think about it, she's dead."

Frank shook his head. "I don't think so, Caleb."

"It's happened more than once."

"Yeah, I know. Tell me, Caleb, how many cases of murdered prostitutes have you handled?"

"More than I can remember."

"How'd they look after it was over?"

"Like hell."

"Like Angelica?"

"Bummed up more."

"Exactly," Frank said. "If you want to kill a whore, you use a gun or a knife or a hammer."

Caleb thought about it for a moment. "All right, I could be wrong. But how do you make it, Frank?"

"I don't know," Frank said. He stood up. "Want to go for a ride?"

"Where?"

"Around the park."

Caleb pulled himself wearily to his feet. "You driving?"

They walked down to the garage together, then drove directly through midtown until they reached Cherokee Avenue and the northern end of Grant Park.

"According to the kid," Frank said, "Angelica took him around the park a few times." He pulled over to the curb and stared out into the park. The lights had been turned on, and they gave off a silvery haze.

"Like she was looking for somebody," Caleb said.

"Right."

"But not a connection."

"Not if what you found out is true," Frank said, "that she was off drugs."

"But what about action, Frank?" Caleb said. "What if she was just out cruising for a little action?"

"With Stanford Doyle, Junior, sitting right next to her?" Frank asked.

"Maybe she wanted to shock him," Caleb said. "Maybe that was part of the thrill."

Frank shook his head.

"Why not?" Caleb asked. "The fact is, Frank, we don't know what was going through that girl's mind. She was young, real young,

229

and you must remember what that was like." He smiled knowingly. "Young blood, Frank. It craves action. For God's sake, you know what I'm talking about."

For a moment, Frank remembered his own young blood, how it too had craved action, how it still leaped toward something raw and immediate, how, even now, so much of life seemed like a lazy doze compared to what his blood desired.

"I remember it," Caleb said quietly. "I remember it real well. And you know what? When I saw that girl all laid out in that goddamn lot, I thought to myself, 'I know your story, darling.' "

"What do you think her story is, Caleb?" Frank asked very seriously.

Caleb considered it for a moment, as if trying to find the right words. "That she bit down too hard on life. She wouldn't be the first, you know." His eyes seemed to withdraw into their sockets. "Sometimes you pay a price, when you want too much, too fast. That's what I figure happened to Angelica Devereaux. She wanted what we all want in our hearts, Frank, something interesting, something that's got a fever to it."

Frank nodded. "Yeah."

Caleb's eyes drifted over to the park. The silvery light appeared to thicken as the night deepened around them, turning into a summer fog.

"It always was a shithole, Grant Park," he said, in a tone that struck Frank as oddly sad and even a little bitter. "Used to be whiskey more than dope. Used to be fucking more than killing. But it was always rough. And it was always interesting." He looked over at Frank. "Know why? Because it was always full of life." He scratched the side of his face with a huge hand. "Maybe that's what she came for. Just life. The real thing." He smiled knowingly. "And if that's true, then busting dopers and pimps won't get us anywhere."

"Maybe not," Frank said.

"You came over here to roust the park, didn't you?"

"Yes."

"Turn it upside down, screw it around, see what drops. Am I right?"

Frank nodded. "The only thing I've been able to figure out about

Angelica is that she hung around this area, that she knew something about it." He looked out into the distance. The haze seemed to tumble in the heated summer air. "This is where she brought the kid that night. And she was spotted in a few of the galleries around here."

"And the galleries are closed for the night," Caleb said.

"That's right."

"So that just leaves the park."

"Yeah."

"Okay," Caleb said reluctantly, "but you'd better watch yourself." He nodded gloomily toward the park. "There's nothing out there this time of night that don't already have a problem." He pulled on the door latch and swung open the door. "You ready?"

"Yeah."

"Let's go then."

The thick haze seemed to hold greedily to the day's exhausted heat, and by the time Frank had walked only a few yards into the park, he could feel his shirt becoming soaked in the armpits and down the back. Great droplets of sweat poured down Caleb's face as he walked beside him, and in the odd, diffused light of the street-lamps, they appeared to glisten like flecks of ice.

"Keep an eye to what's behind you," Caleb said softly as they continued through the stifling haze, "and an ear to what's on either side."

Within a few minutes, they were deep into the park. Far away they could hear the low moan of creatures in the zoo, lost and plaintive, bewailing their odd imprisonment. The light faded more and more around them until, after a while, it simply died away and they were covered in the deep summer darkness.

"Hear that?" Caleb said after a moment.

Frank listened. He could hear faint groans at a great distance.

"You got to want it real bad to do it here," Caleb said with a sad smile. "We could go over and throw a few questions, but I don't think they'd be able to help us much right now." He nodded straight ahead. "Let's just let them be. What do you say, Frank?"

They continued to move deeper into the park. The brush thickened slowly around them, wrapping them in warm, leafy arms. To the right, they passed a derelict sleeping soundly, his naked arms wrapped lovingly around a bottle of cheap wine, and to the left, a wiry young woman in a flowered dress who was muttering madly to a stone.

"After a while," Caleb said, almost to himself, "it's what you see that kills you."

They were almost halfway through the park before they heard the first coherent voices. Two voices. A man and a woman. The woman's voice was high, thready, the man's was low, gruff, threatening.

"You gone tell the kids 'bout it?" the woman demanded. "You gone tell them how you back in the joint again?"

"Just shut the fuck up, nigger," the man said angrily.

Caleb stopped and patted the pistol beneath his coat. "Careful, Frank. You know how it is. Nothing worse than a domestic."

They continued to walk forward together, and as the fog parted around them, Frank could see a man and woman as they faced each other beside an enormous oak tree. They were arguing frantically, their voices echoing lowly, despite the enveloping fog. They were entirely oblivious to everything but the fury of their struggle.

"Evening, folks," Caleb said gently.

The man whirled around instantly, his hand reaching for his belt.

"Easy now," Caleb said sternly. "Police. Don't move."

The man's hand continued to linger at his belt.

Frank stepped to the left and pulled out his revolver. "Put your hands up," he shouted. "Now!"

The man's hands leaped into the air.

"Turn around, and put your hands on that tree," Frank commanded.

The man did as he was told, standing motionlessly while Caleb frisked him.

"This a toy?" he asked with a laugh, and he pulled a twenty-two pistol from his belt.

"I knew they'd ketch you," the woman said mournfully. "You too dumb, Charlie. That's yo' problem."

Caleb shoved the pistol into his jacket pocket. "Turn around, Charlie," he said.

Frank put his pistol back in its holster.

Caleb eyed the woman's purse. "Got anything in there, ma'am?" he asked.

She shook her head slowly.

He eased the purse from her fingers. "Don't mind if I take a look, then." He opened the purse, searched it, then returned it to the woman. "Thank you," he said quietly.

"I just knowed they'd ketch you," the woman repeated sorrowfully. "Now it's me and the kids by ourselves again."

"He's not caught yet," Caleb told her.

She looked at him wide-eyed. "Whut?"

"We're just here to ask a few questions," Frank explained.

The man looked at him suspiciously. "Whut kind of questions, man?"

"Well, how's this?" Caleb asked as he dangled the pistol in the air. "You got a permit for this?"

"Nah."

"How about a record, Charlie, got one of those?"

The man turned away and grunted under his breath.

"Long as my arm, I bet," Caleb said. "Guy like you probably shouldn't have a piece." He looked at Frank. "What do you bet our friend here is out on parole?"

The man stared lethally at Caleb. "Fuck you, man."

Suddenly, with furious speed, Caleb slapped him hard across the face. The man stumbled backward, his back slamming against the tree. Caleb leaped forward, grabbed him by the collar and pulled him up into his own face.

"The woman said something about kids, you asshole," he shouted. "You got kids?"

The man nodded slowly.

"You ought to take care of them," Caleb said. "You hear me?"

"Caleb," Frank said gently, "back off."

Caleb drew in a long, deep breath to calm himself. He released the man's collar, then stepped back.

"Go ahead, Frank," he said.

Frank moved closer to the man and woman. "You folks live around here?" he asked.

"Yeah," the woman said.

"Where?"

"Over on Cherokee."

"So you're in the park a lot?"

"Sometimes," the woman said.

"With kids, you must be out here quite a bit."

"I'm out here some," the woman said cautiously.

Caleb stared at the man. "You do a little business in the park?" he asked coldly.

"I don't do nothing," the man said. He massaged his cheek. "You didn't have no right to hit me, man."

"Disarm a felon," Caleb said, "I didn't have a right to do that?"

"Wanted to sell me," the woman hissed angrily. "Wanted to sell my ass around here." She thumped her chest bitterly. "His ownself's wife, the motherfucker!" She shot him a withering look. "My mama didn't raise me to be no ho!" she screamed.

"So you decided to pimp for your wife?" Caleb asked, his eyes fixed on the man.

Frank quickly took the picture of Angelica from his pocket and handed it to the woman. "Have you ever seen this girl?"

The woman glanced at it halfheartedly. "She on the street?"

"Just tell me if you've seen her around," Frank said.

"Naw, I ain't seen her," the woman said.

Frank took the picture and handed it to the man. "How about you?"

The man glanced contemptuously at the photograph. "I don't deal with no white ass," he sneered.

Frank stepped over to him. "What did you say?"

The man's eyes narrowed into tiny, snakelike slits. "Like I done told you, I ain't seen that piece. I don't deal with no white ass."

Frank could see Angelica's body as it lay sprawled across the vacant lot. White ass. He could feel a terrible rage build slowly within him, and he knew that he wanted to take his pistol from his belt, press its cold black barrel into the man's face, and pull the trigger again and again until all his strength was gone.

"Dead white ass," the man said, as he leered at the photograph. "That's all you got there."

Frank could feel the nails of his fingers as they bit into his palms. "You'd better shut your fucking mouth," he said thinly.

The man smiled confidently. "You stop the fatman. The fatman stop you. That's the way it works."

Frank felt his hands release, felt one of them as it made a slow crawl toward his pistol. He knew what it would look like. The man's eyes would widen in one moment of frozen terror. For an instant he would believe that it was all an act: and then, for a single, shattering instant, as the sound swept over him and the bullet struck his skull, he would know that it was not, that a wild, passionate justice had finally overtaken him, and there would be no appeal.

"Not yet," Caleb said, and suddenly Frank could feel Caleb's fingers wrapped around his wrist.

"Get on out of here," Caleb said harshly to the man and woman.

Frank stood motionlessly and listened to the couple's footsteps as they rushed away from him. He could feel an immense exhaustion in his arms and legs, a heaviness in each cell of his body, as if he were being pulled downward by millions of tiny weights.

Caleb tugged gently at Frank's arm, urging him out of the park. "You know, when I was a kid . . . still in uniform, I mean. Well, I had a partner. His name was Ollie Quinn. He had come right out of the country, just like me. Atlanta was like the big time for him." He shook his head as he and Frank continued to move steadily out of the park. "He should never have left the farm. He should have spent his little life fishing in the river and picking muscadines. But no, Ollie came to the big city, got a job on the force, and ended up walking a beat with me, night after night, listening to my bullshit."

He glanced to the left, out into the park. "This was our beat, mine and Ollie's. And one night we got a call. It was a domestic. Neighbors had heard a woman screaming, kids, too. From what they could tell a guy was beating up on them." He turned to Frank. "Well, we headed over there, Ollie and me, and, sure enough, it was a domestic, all right. From way outside, we could hear that bastard tearing through the house, throwing people around. It scared the shit out of Ollie, and made him mad, too." He took out his pipe and began to fill the bowl. "Anyway, we busted in, and dear God, Frank, what we saw. A couple of little boys beat to shit, lying unconscious in one corner. And just a few feet from them, the wife, slumped against the window with an extension cord wrapped around her neck. The man was all on her, strangling her with that cord when we broke through the door."

He lit the pipe and the blue smoke sailed behind him as he walked. He looked like a locomotive cutting through the fog. "Well, we jumped this guy. Actually, I jumped him. I pulled him off the woman and threw him over to the other side of the room. Ollie went to the woman and started trying to untie the cord. That's when she bit him. She sunk her teeth into his hand and wouldn't let go. Ollie kept trying to get loose from her, but she kept bearing down on his hand, so he finally hit her." He pulled the pipe from his mouth. "That's when the man got loose from me. He just bolted right over me and slammed into Ollie full force. He started pounding on Ollie, and the woman started scratching at his face. I pulled the man off, but the woman kept at it, screaming at the top of her voice. Ollie finally got up, but the woman kept at him, screaming like you can't imagine, Frank, like a wild animal, and clawing at Ollie's face while he backed away from her. But she kept coming at him, with this scream, and clawing at him until his face was covered with blood, and he kept stepping back, trying to get away, but she wouldn't let him. Ollie pulled out his pistol and waved it in the air, but she just kept on him, clawing and screaming, until he leaped away from her, Frank, and lifted that goddamn pistol, and shot her right between the eyes."

He stopped dead and simply stared out toward the end of the park to where their car could be seen in the ghostly distance. Then he looked at Frank, his eyes glistening in the streetlight. "They sentenced Ollie Quinn to life for that, Frank," he said slowly. "There was a lot of politics and a shithead D.A., and Ollie Quinn got life." He glanced away, his eyes rolling upward to the phantom trees. "But he didn't serve much of it. He hanged himself two days after the trial." His eyes shot back to Frank. "And that husband? His name is Towers, Harry Towers. He still lives in that same fucking house. He's had a wife or two since then, and he's beat up on all of them, new wives and new kids. We still get domestics on him." He smiled coldly. "He lives at Two Sixty-five Boulevard, Frank,

236

and one day, after I'm retired, one day, Frank, when it feels just right, I'm going to go over to Two Sixty-five Boulevard, and I'm going to blow Harry Towers' head off." He looked at Frank pointedly. "But not yet, my friend, not yet."

A few minutes later they were in the car together. For a moment Caleb sat motionlessly behind the wheel. Then, suddenly, he hit the ignition and pressed his foot down hard on the accelerator, pumping the engine wildly until it filled the air with an angry roar.

23

Frank began calling the galleries early the next morning, but all of them were still closed. He wasn't sure when they opened, but he thought that Karen might know, so he called her instead. She sounded breathless when she answered the phone.

"I'm a little harried," she explained.

"Why?"

"I've been packing for New York."

"You're leaving right away?" Frank asked unbelievingly.

"Within a few days, I hope," Karen said.

Frank could feel all of his remaining strength drain out of him. "I'm sorry you're going so soon," he said quietly.

For a moment, she did not answer, and Frank could feel something in her as it reached out to him. He wanted to seize it like a bird out of the air and draw it gently into his arms. He loved her, he realized with astonishment, with the kind of feeling they sang about in those plaintive, heartbroken ballads Caleb sometimes listened to on the car radio.

"Listen, Karen," he said softly, "I need to see you."

"What about?"

He couldn't answer her as he wished, couldn't tell her that he wanted to be with her, talk to her and touch her until the bond between them had become so firm that nothing could draw them apart.

Instead, he stammered, "The galleries."

"Galleries?"

"There are a few of them in Grant Park," Frank said.

"Yes, I know. What about them?"

"Evidently Angelica sometimes hung around in them," Frank told her, his voice now under control again. "And so I was thinking that you might want to check them out with me."

"When?"

"Soon. This afternoon, if possible."

"Well, I have a few things to do this morning," Karen said, "but I could be free by noon. Would that be all right?"

"Yes," Frank said. "Should I pick you up?"

"No, I'll pick you up this time. Will you be at headquarters?"

"Yes," Frank said. "Do you know where that is?"

"Yes, I do," Karen said. "Unfortunately." Then she hung up.

Two hours later, Frank glanced up from his desk and saw Karen as she entered the detective bullpen. She was dressed in a summery, light blue dress, and every man in the room turned to look at her.

"Mighty fine," Gibbons whispered as he passed Frank's desk.

Frank glared at him. "Go to work, Charlie."

Gibbons smiled thinly. "You seem a little strung out, Frank. That's not a good image for a cop."

Frank turned away from him and watched as Karen came up to the desk.

"I made it a little early," she said.

"That's okay."

"Are you ready, or should I go somewhere and wait for a few minutes?"

"No," Frank said, "I'm ready."

It took them only a little while to reach Grant Park, and as Frank pulled the car onto Cherokee, he remembered the night before, the way his hand had inched to the pistol before Caleb could stop him. He had never done anything like that before, and it scared him that he might have killed without justice, out of some impulsive rage, like a blind serpent that strikes toward nothing but the nearest heat.

"It's odd to be here in the daylight," Karen said.

Her voice returned him to the present, the grim gray street, the parched edge of the park. He turned left off Boulevard and headed up Cherokee.

"According to the boy, Angelica knew this area pretty well," he said. "But I've already told you that."

"Yes."

"I've been trying to find out how she knew it," Frank added.

"Have you found out?"

"I'm not sure," Frank said. "But I do know that she's been seen in a few galleries around here. And she's been seen in them more than once."

"You mean the galleries on Hugo Street?" Karen asked.

Frank nodded.

"Then turn left on this street, then take the second right," she said. "It's the only street around here that I know how to get to." She paused a moment, her eyes lifted upward. The bright summer light had faded slightly as a wave of grayish clouds began to drift over the city. "Maybe we'll get some relief soon," she said.

Frank looked at her. "From what?"

"The heat," Karen said quietly. She turned to him. "You know, it doesn't surprise me that Angelica was up to something. Her life was too flat. It was too much like mine." She smiled softly. "But yours has action, doesn't it?"

"Some."

"It seems more real," Karen added. "And I think maybe that's what Angelica was after, something she could touch, something real."

"Is that what you're after, Karen?" Frank asked.

"Perhaps."

"And you think you'll find it in New York?"

"I think I will try to find it there," Karen said. "But this city, at least for me, is full of ghosts."

Frank took his second right and eased the car slowly up and over a small hill.

"There it is," Karen said, pointing to a narrow side street. "Gallery Row." She smiled derisively. "Like everything else in Atlanta, pretentious."

Frank pulled the car over to the curb. "I thought we'd just walk it together. Go into each gallery, see what we can see." He smiled. "I don't have a plan, Karen. I'm just trying to find my way out of a dead end."

She took his arm, and he felt a tremor run through him. He wanted to sweep her into his arms and carry her away to some place where they could be alone forever, where she could paint and he could think through the whole scattered landscape of the life he had seen through the battered golden screen of his badge.

"We'll just take them one at a time," he said.

"All right."

There were three galleries on the block. The first of them was called New Palette. It was in a large Victorian house which had been painted bright blue with white shutters.

"It's all mythological themes," Karen said a few minutes later, after they had walked through each of the gallery's brightly lighted rooms. "Nothing but paintings of Diana and Aphrodite." She glanced down at a small plaque beside one of the paintings. "Vincent Toffler," she said. "He must be interested in—what would you call this— erotic mythology?"

"Whatever it is, it doesn't sell," someone said from behind.

Frank turned to see a short man in jeans and sweatshirt. He peered at them through thin wire glasses.

"I don't suppose you'd want to buy any of this stuff," the man added. "Maybe for the barn, or some bathroom you don't use anymore?"

"If you don't like them, why do you sell them?" Frank asked.

The man shrugged. "I'm just the manager, not the owner," he said. "Ours is not to reason why. Now, what can I do for you?"

Frank took out his badge.

The man looked surprised. "Police?"

Frank handed him a picture of Angelica. "Have you ever seen this girl?"

"Very pretty," the man said, "but I'm afraid I've never seen her." He laughed. "And believe me, if something like this came in, I'd notice."

"She's dead," Frank said.

The laugh died away. "Oh, sorry." He handed the picture back to Frank. "I didn't mean to be disrespectful."

"Are you sure you've never seen her?"

"Absolutely. Why?"

"She's been seen in this area before, in the galleries on this street."

"Not in this gallery," the man said. "I don't mean to be crude, but she does have a certain look a man is liable to notice."

Frank put Angelica's picture back in his pocket. "Okay, thanks." He took Karen by the arm. "Let's go."

The next gallery was called the Hidden Agenda, and it was small and considerably more modest than the first.

"I've always liked this one," Karen said as they walked through the front door. "It has a little bit of everything. It's not as rigid as the one James and I own. But then, we have a rigid clientele." She seemed to brighten as she glanced from here to there in the front room. "Look, that one's by Edgar Benton," she said. She walked over to it. "He's very good." She walked to the next painting. "And this one's by Stirling Fox."

"You know these people?" Frank asked.

"Slightly," Karen said. "Stirling has a tendency to be reclusive. One hardly ever gets him to a party." She shrugged. "It's part of his persona."

"And the other one?"

"Edgar's more social. He's been over to our house a few times."

"Did he know Angelica?"

"Not that I know of," Karen said. She stared at the painting. "He's very intense in what he does."

Frank looked at the painting. It was of a brilliant streak of light passing through a dark cloud. It was entitled *Consummation*.

"Does that look like it was painted by a very intense person?" Karen asked, as she continued to gaze at it.

"Yes," Frank said.

"Well, that's the way Edgar is," Karen said casually. She turned quickly and walked into the adjoining room. A tall man in a brown double-breasted suit stood near the center of the room. Karen walked up to him immediately. "Hello, Philip," she said.

"Hello, Karen," the man said effusively. "So good to see you." His eyes softened. "I heard about Angelica. So sorry."

"You knew Angelica?" Frank asked.

"Yes," Philip said. "I saw her off and on before she died."

"Where?"

"Here in the gallery," Philip told him. "She would come in and walk around for a while. I hadn't seen her since she was a very little girl, and I'm sure she didn't recognize me. I could tell she was going through a stage, so I didn't introduce myself."

"What do you mean?" Frank asked, as he showed the man his badge.

"Well, by the way she was dressed," Philip explained. "Always something different. It was like she was in costume." He looked back at Karen. "I really can't tell you how sorry I am about what happened to her."

"Did she come alone?" Frank asked.

"Yes."

"And left alone?"

"Always left alone, as far as I can remember," Philip said. "Are you making any progress in the investigation?"

"Some."

Philip shook his head despairingly. "It's terrible what can happen in this world, isn't it?"

"Yes," Frank said, then suddenly realized that Karen had left the room.

He found her standing alone on the front porch of the gallery. She was staring up at the steadily darkening sky. "I'd like to believe that Angelica was up there somewhere, but I don't."

Frank draped his arm gently over her shoulder. "There's only one more gallery, Karen. Then you can go to New York. You won't hear from me again until I've found the man who killed her."

Karen nodded slowly. "All right," she said.

It was called the Broken Frame, and it was a small, neatly painted building, white with lavender shutters. Inside, the rooms were bright and well-lighted. A young woman in a wildly colored peasant dress greeted them at the door.

"Hi," she said.

"Hello," Frank said. He glanced about the room. The paintings were carefully arranged on the wall so as not to be crowded together. The colors were pastels, and they added their own delicate light to the interior of the room.

"Just browse all you want," the woman said. "No pressure at the Broken Frame."

Frank drew out his badge, then a picture of Angelica Devereaux. "Have you ever seen this girl?" he asked.

"Yes," the woman said. "This is the girl who was found dead not far from here."

"Her name was Angelica," Frank said.

The woman continued to gaze at the photograph. "She never mentioned her name. She would just stand around. She never spoke to anyone."

"Did she ever talk to you?"

"No," the woman said. She looked at Karen. "You must be her sister. I can see the resemblance."

Frank pointed to the picture. "Did she look like this in the picture?"

"Yes, just like this," the woman told him. "Very fresh and beautiful. She wore lots of lace. High collars. She sometimes looked as if she'd walked right out of *Gone With the Wind*."

"Did you ever see her with anyone?"

"No."

"She was always alone?"

"Yes."

"Did she ever leave with anyone?"

The woman smiled. "Lots of people tried to get her to leave with them. And, you know, sometimes, I think she liked that. She would sometimes throw one of those 'come hither' looks. But only at other women."

"Other women?"

"Yes," the woman said. "She didn't seem interested in men at all."

Frank took out his notebook. "Did you ever see her talking to other women in the gallery?"

"No," the woman said determinedly. "As I told you, she never talked to anyone."

"But she seemed to concentrate on women?" Frank asked again.

"Absolutely," the woman said. "It was strange. She would look at them with this odd glance, shy, but not really shy, if you know what I mean."

Frank wrote it down. "How many times did you see her in here?"

"Three, maybe, four," the woman said. She turned suddenly to Karen. "It's just hit me, you must be Karen Devereaux."

"Yes," Karen said.

"We have two of your paintings," the woman said happily. "I liked them so much, I bought them from another gallery." She tugged Karen cheerfully into the adjoining room. "See," she said. She pointed to a small, delicately rendered portrait of a man sitting in a wing chair, his hands folded neatly in his lap, a look of terrible, wounded concentration in his eyes.

"My father," Karen said, almost in a whisper.

"And that one," the woman added. She turned Karen slowly around to face the opposite wall.

"Oh, yes," Karen said. A smile suddenly struggled to her lips.

The painting was of a vase of flowers. It was done in muted colors with a light, feathery brushstroke, and as Frank looked at it he could feel a kind of solemn pleasure flourishing in it, rising, against all odds, to claim its own bright space.

"I'll take it," he said, before he could stop himself.

Karen turned to him. "Don't be silly, Frank," she said. "I'll give you a painting."

He looked at her somberly. "But I want this one," he said.

The woman wrapped the painting while Frank asked her a few remaining questions. Then he picked it up carefully and took it to the car.

"Where are you going to hang it?" Karen asked.

"My apartment," Frank told her, "it could use a touch of something nice."

"Is it one of those drab, broken-down, private-eye sort of places?" Karen asked with a light smile.

"That's about right."

"How long have you lived there?"

"It feels like my whole life."

She looked at him tenderly. "Take me there, and I'll help you hang the painting."

The dinginess of his apartment seemed even greater with Karen standing in the middle of it, but she didn't seem to mind.

"It really is one of those private-eye places," she said with a laugh.

"I told you."

She walked to the middle of the room, then turned slowly, examining the walls. "Over there," she said at last, "that would be the best place for it."

Frank rifled through several cabinets before he found a nail. Then he hammered it into the wall, and together he and Karen lifted the painting onto it, then stepped back to take in the effect.

"Very nice," Karen said. She looked at him. "It brightens the room."

"Yes, it does."

Karen continued to look at it for a moment, then walked over to the window, parted the blinds and peered out. "I was happy when I painted that," she said.

Frank walked over to her. "You can tell you were," he said.

The first wave of rain suddenly swept down over the city, and a gust blew it forcefully against the window pane.

"I want a storm," Karen said, "I want a wild, booming storm."

"Maybe you should paint one," Frank said.

She turned toward him. "Do you think a single afternoon can make a difference?"

"For that afternoon, yes," Frank said. And then he drew her into his arms.

24

I t was late in the evening before Karen left, and as Frank sat on
his sofa, staring at her painting, he could still feel the warmth
of her body as it had clung to him hungrily hour after hour. She
had talked once again of leaving this city full of ghosts, and as he
continued to gaze at the painting, it struck him that she had not
painted the flowers themselves, or the almost translucent blue vase
that held them, but the airy ghosts of these things. It was as if she
had been able to feel the slowly fading pulse of each leaf and petal,
and it was this overall sense of steadily departing life which she had
captured.

He had bought the painting because it was hers, and because he
thought it might brighten the space around him. But now he could
see nothing but its sorrowfulness, its mournful sense of departure
and farewell.

He walked into the kitchen and fixed himself a quick meal of
beans and nearly burnt bacon. He ate it with a single slice of white
bread. It was a joyless, bachelor's fare, he realized, and each mouth-
ful tasted of a life that had itself turned utterly flavorless.

He returned to the living room and once again sat down on the sofa. He felt the need to view his life as some kind of whole, as if it could be captured in a single tone or color. But nothing held firm. Nothing but his work, his pursuit—however blind and full of error—of something which could be called justice, or at least, retribution. People had to pay for what they did, and he was one of the ones who made them pay. It was the badge which gave him the right to do that, and he suddenly found that he wanted to cling to it with all his remaining strength. Nothing could bring back Sarah or Angelica or Ollie Quinn, or any of the scores of others whose bodies lay torn and broken in his memory, but whose spirits still moved sleeplessly through him. They were more real to him than all the living who crowded the streets and buses. They lived more fully in his mind, and their flesh was warmer and more tangible. It bled and bled, as if the one great heart of all the unjustly dead still beat on through the ages, their cries still ringing out through time, heard like a low moan in the ground, or like a scream echoing above it.

He took a bottle from the cupboard, returned to the sofa and took a long, slow drink. Its warmth moved down into him, and he could feel its comfort settling in. He started to take another, but stopped himself. He knew that if he took another, then he'd take another after that and still another, until the world grew hazy around him, and he would find himself on the floor in the morning, the stink of his own breath in his nose, and feeling so tightly wrapped in his own skin that he could hardly breathe without splitting open and spilling his insides across the plain wooden floor.

He put the bottle down on the little table beside the sofa and glanced up at the painting. The afternoon had stretched into the night, but nothing that had happened had convinced her not to go. She was leaving, like everything else, and so it seemed that only his work mattered. Everything else went away. Children and wives, and women who loved for a few sweet hours and then took planes to distant cities. The painting was right; everything lived in a certain stage of fading. What lasted was what you did, your work. Everything else was a phantom.

He reached for his notebook and started to go through it. He flipped one page, then another, his eyes combing each line intently, as if something might be drawn from even the most routine details. He noted the abandoned lot, the rusting car, the beautiful body laid out in its shallow grave. He read about guardians and trust funds, private schools and plays, dreams of acting and plans to leave for New York. One by one, the pages fell away. He read and read and read about a little girl's room, a telephone that was used only once, a date, May 15. He read about pregnancy and a late-night ride through Grant Park. He parked with her again at the Cyclorama, then left with her and drove up and down some obscure street. Then he went with her to an alley and made love to her joylessly, and with a frantic anger. He searched her closet again, and found none of the clothes she'd been seen wearing at various places in the city. His finger moved through the neatly arranged skirts and blouses, still looking for the frilly laces and black velvets that were the costumes of her secret life. He talked to a dying painter once again, and then to the woman who had loved him futilely all her life. He listened to her song of art, to her efforts to find her artists certain dignified forms of work, touch-ups, restorations. He read again and again, until the words dissolved into one black line, and, at last, he fell asleep.

———————

Thunder awakened him. It came from far away and lingered in the air, rolling heavily over the city in a deep baritone groan.

He walked to the window and looked out. It had stopped raining, but he could tell by the thick feel of the air that it was about to begin again, hard and heavy, a jungle torrent. He thought of the animals in the zoo at Grant Park, soaked in their thick fur, their eyes staring vacantly at the deserted grounds. He could feel his mind wandering through the zoo, then over the grassy knoll that bordered it, and across the wet swamp to where the Cyclorama rested with immense heaviness on the bare earth. He could see the rain-soaked area around the building, the sea of mud which no doubt now encircled the great granite edifice. That was the only place she had stopped that night, the only place she had lingered. She had pulled up to the storm fence, glancing occasionally into her rearview mirror, and then straight ahead again, her eyes fixed on the far corner of the building.

He released the blind and it clattered shut. Then he walked out onto his porch and peered out toward the park. He couldn't see it from where he was, but he knew it was there, swept with rain, deserted except for the few homeless souls who clung to shelter beneath the enormous trees. Some of those same trees rose gracefully around the Cyclorama, and he could see Angelica as she sat beneath them, thinking of her next move. It had been to leave the park and ride up and down a particular street a few times and then drive directly to the alley. He tried to put all these things in their proper, sequential order: stopped at the Cyclorama, waited for a few minutes, then drove to a street and went back and forth along it for a few minutes, and then, after that, headed for the alley. It seemed to Frank that Angelica had made her decision to go to the alley only after she had not been able to find what she was looking for on that street. But which street was it? He flipped through his notes, found Stan Doyle, Jr.'s phone number, and called him immediately.

"Hello?"

"Stan, this is Frank Clemons."

"Oh," the boy sputtered. "Yeah, right."

"I need a little help."

"Like what?"

"I want to drive you around the Grant Park area for a few minutes."

"But I told you everything I knew."

"I want you to show me exactly where you and Angelica went that night."

The boy seemed to consider it for a moment. "Well, okay," he said at last.

"I'll pick you up in half an hour," Frank said. He walked to his car, glancing back toward the house as he pulled himself in. Something stirred in him suddenly, and as he continued to look back at the old house, he realized that he had always sensed a strange grief all around it, as if some ancient wrong had seeped into it and was still there, absorbed into the woodwork, held there forever like a deep, abiding stain.

Stan ran hurriedly out to the car as Frank pulled into the driveway.

"My daddy's due back tomorrow morning," he said breathlessly. "I've been trying to clean up all the mess."

"I'll get you back pretty quick," Frank said, as he steered the car back out into the street.

"I hope so. I've got a hell of a lot to do."

"I just want to take you back over the route you went with Angelica that night," Frank explained. "Maybe something will come together in your mind."

"Yeah, okay," Stan said. "No problem."

It took nearly half an hour to get back to Grant Park. The long rains had cooled the air considerably, and the moisture on the leaves seemed almost icy beneath the streetlamps.

"I just want to retrace your movements that night," Frank said, as he pulled the car over at the corner of Sydney and Boulevard. "She turned right at this corner, isn't that what you said?"

"Yes."

"You're sure?"

"This is where she turned," Stan said confidently. "I'm positive about that."

"Then what?"

"She headed up this street until she got to the end of the park," Stan told him, "then she turned left."

"Did she turn off anywhere?" Frank asked.

Stan shook his head emphatically. "No, she went all the way down the length of the park."

"Then what?"

"She circled the park."

"How many times?"

"Three, I think, maybe four. I don't know for sure."

Frank pressed his foot slowly down on the accelerator. "All right, let's do it," he said.

The car veered left off Cherokee and headed down the park. At the end, Frank turned left, then at the far corner made another left.

"Now this is what she did, right?" he asked at each turn.

"That's right."

Frank headed down Boulevard, this time from the opposite direction, circling the park entirely.

"That's what she did," Stan said, as Frank eased the car onto Cherokee again.

"And she did it about three times?" Frank asked.

"That's right."

"Did she act like she was looking for someone?"

"No."

"She was staring around, glancing left and right?"

"No. She kept her eyes on the road."

"Okay," Frank said. "What happened next?"

"She drove down into the park."

"Where?"

"Wherever it is, if you're trying to get down to the Cyclorama," Stan said.

Frank drove around the park once again, then turned left down the winding road that led to the Cyclorama.

"Where did she park exactly?" he asked.

Stan pointed to the left. "Over there, by that fence," he said.

"Facing it?"

"Yes."

"Show me exactly."

"Where that sign is," Stan said. "She parked right in front of it."

Frank eased the car into position. A huge sign all but blocked his vision. It was white with red lettering:

CYCLORAMA RESTORATION
DEPARTMENT OF PARKS
CITY OF ATLANTA

"I must have read that sign a hundred times that night," Stan said, as Frank brought the car to a halt.

"How long did she stay here?" Frank asked.

"It's hard to say. Maybe ten minutes. Maybe a little more."

"You said she kept looking out her rearview mirror, is that right?"

"Yes."

Frank glanced at his own rearview mirror. The curving road which led down to the Cyclorama was clearly visible within it.

"Did any other cars come down the road while you were here?" he asked.

"No," Stan replied. "It was just Angelica and me."

"You didn't see any other light?"

"No. Nothing."

Frank drew his eyes from the mirror and looked straight ahead. Behind the sign there was nothing but a muddy field. He could see the discarded materials used in the restoration, piles of cement blocks, wood slats, yards of torn and rain-soaked cloth. He could see the north side of the building, blank and white, with nothing but a small door at the rear. A large pile of torn and paint-splattered drop cloths lay outside the door. Various crates and empty paint cans were scattered about the grounds, along with the jagged, broken parts of metal scaffolding. It looked like a place that had been pillaged of every scrap of value and then left to the rain.

"So you two sat here for about ten minutes," Frank said.

"Yes."

"Then what happened?"

"We left," Stan said. "She floored it. I mean she peeled out of here. I remember seeing a spray of gravel thrown up behind us."

"Peeled out?"

"Yeah, and really loud, too," Stan said, "enough to wake the whole town up." He motioned to the right. "She whirled around this lot and just highballed it out of the park."

Frank hit the ignition and drove the car back up to the main road.

"Which way did she turn?" he asked.

"Left."

Frank made the turn. "Did you circle the park again?"

"No," Stan said. "She drove to the end of it, then she turned left and headed straight down that road."

"Good," Frank said. "It's coming back."

255

"I just remember going straight," Stan said.

Frank drove on, heading the car in the way Stan had indicated. He turned left at the edge of the park, then went almost its full length, passing under a single traffic light.

"She turned here," Stan said, pointing to the right.

Frank made a right onto Ormewood Avenue.

"She went straight, like we are now," Stan said excitedly. "This is getting to be interesting. Is this what it's like to be a cop?"

Frank kept his eyes locked on the road ahead. "No," he said. He continued to move forward, passing under one traffic light, then another, until the car nosed up a small hill, and then over it.

"I remember this," Stan said suddenly.

Frank eased his foot off the accelerator. "What?"

"We went over this hill."

"How do you know?"

"It has a little dip at the bottom," Stan said. "That's where we turned."

Frank let the car cruise slowly down the hill. He felt the dip, like something hard and blunt pressed against his belly.

"Next right! Next right!" Stan cried. He looked at Frank excitedly. "That's the street. The one she went up and down a couple of times."

Frank made the right turn, then stopped and looked at the street sign: Mercer Place. When he turned back to Stan, the boy's face was pale.

"I know this is it," he said, slowly. "She took me up and down it a couple of times. Then we went to the alley." He shivered slightly. "It gives me the creeps."

Frank made a slow turn onto Mercer Place and then headed down it.

"Did she seem interested in any particular house?" he asked.

Stan shook his head. "No. She just looked straight ahead. But she did get a look in her eye, like she was forcing herself not to look one way or the other."

"Did she say anything?"

"No."

Frank glanced left and right as he continued to cruise slowly down the street. Small, dilapidated houses lined it. Some leaned in one direction, some in another. But all of them looked as if they were trying to let some unbearable burden slide from their shoulders at last.

———————

It was almost midnight by the time Frank returned to his apartment. He'd gone back to the Bottom Rail for a while, just to see if it still had any appeal to him. He found that it didn't, but he didn't know of anything to replace it with, except a solitary drink on a soiled sofa, with his eyes locked helplessly on a square of painted flowers.

His green notebook still rested where he had left it earlier in the evening, curled up next to the bottle on the little table by the sofa. He reached for it immediately and went through it once again. Facts and suppositions swarmed in and out of his mind. He saw people and places that were real enough: Cummings and Morrison and Jameson and Theodore; offices and great halls and small, spattered studios. Karen's portrait of Angelica came back to him, and then dissolved will-lessly into her vase of flowers. Ghosts. A city of ghosts. He thought of Linton, then of Miriam Castle, then of the little paved street that wound down from the edges of the park. He could see the storm fence, the muddy ground, the small door and mound of speckled drop cloths.

Something caught like a hook in his flesh. He sat up slowly, and all the great, teeming chaos suddenly came together in a dead and frozen order.

25

By nine o'clock the next morning, Frank was at the Cyclorama. He pulled the badge from his coat and dropped it on the desk. It gleamed like pure gold beneath the lamp.

"I'd like to see David Curtis," he said.

"Mr. Curtis is busy at the moment," the man said. He was wearing a blue uniform with a badge emblazoned on the front, a large tin one that carried the name of the security firm he worked for in bold letters.

"Where is he?" Frank asked.

"The rotunda."

"Go get him," Frank said.

"Mr. Curtis don't like to be disturbed when he's working," the man said.

Frank snapped his hand up to the badge and ripped it off the coat.

"Hey, man!" the guard cried.

Frank tossed the badge onto the floor. "Don't get the idea that little piece of tin means anything. You can buy them at a toy store."

The guard fingered the rip in his coat. "They're going to shit when they see this, man."

Frank grabbed one of the large buttons on the guard's coat and tugged down on it. "How do I get to the rotunda?" he asked.

The man glared at him helplessly. "Just go through the room behind me, and then through them double doors."

Frank let go of the button, then stepped around the desk and walked through the double doors of the rotunda.

It was very large and very dark. He could see the terrible fury of the battle of Atlanta as it spread out in miniature before him, a vision of desperate struggle in the smoking ruin of the South's premier city. He could almost feel the heat of the flames, hear the roar of the cannon. An air of pain and terror hung over the display, loss and grief like a black shroud in the tiny trees.

"May I help you, sir?"

The voice came from a tall, slightly stooped man who stood next to one of the models, a Union soldier almost half his size.

"I'm looking for David Curtis," Frank said.

"I am David Curtis," the man replied.

"On the sign outside, it says that you're in charge of the Cyclorama restoration."

"Yes, I am," Curtis said. "But if you're looking for work, I'm afraid that all of our positions are filled."

"I'm not looking for work," Frank told him. He pulled out his badge.

Curtis leaned forward slightly. "What's that you're holding?" he said. "In this light, and with my eyes . . ."

Frank stepped over to him. "Frank Clemons. Police."

The man squinted at the badge. "Oh, yes." He walked a few feet away and hit a switch. A steely gray light suddenly flooded the rotunda. "That's better, don't you think?"

Frank nodded.

Curtis walked back over to him. "Now, what is all this about the police?"

"I'm investigating a murder," Frank said. As he glanced around, he realized that he was standing almost in the dead center of the battle. It seemed to rage ferociously below him, a world of smoking air and exploded buildings, horrifying even in miniature.

"Odd, isn't it?" Curtis said quietly.

"What?"

"This place."

"Yes, a little."

"Sometimes I feel like ducking quickly, to avoid a musket ball that's hurtling toward me."

It was a landscape of hellish misery, and as Frank's eyes lingered on it, the misery itself seemed to gather around him in a cloud. It was as if every streak of pain and cry of grief had been collected in this room, all the folly of a million years suddenly rolled into one heartbreaking ball.

"My God," he whispered.

Curtis looked at him curiously. "You've never been here, have you?"

"No."

"Most people see it from up in the stands," Curtis said. "It's quite different when you're down here." He tugged Frank gently by the arm. "Come, we'll go to my office now."

Frank followed him slowly into a small room at the rear of the rotunda. It was cluttered with tiny figures of soldiers and military equipment, tiny flags fluttering in an invisible wind, patches of smoldering earth, stands of burning trees.

Curtis sat down behind his desk. "Now, you said something about a murder?"

"Yes," Frank said. "A young woman." He handed Curtis the picture of Angelica. "Her."

Curtis brought the photograph very close to his eyes. "I broke my glasses yesterday," he explained. "I'll have a new pair by this afternoon. But for now, I'm a bit handicapped."

"Do you recognize her?" Frank asked.

Curtis shook his head. "No. Who is she?"

"Angelica Devereaux."

"Oh, yes, it was in the paper a few days ago."

"That's right," Frank said. "Her body was found not too far from here."

"Really? I thought the paper said that it was found off Glenwood."

"You have a very good memory," Frank said.

"Yes, I do." Curtis handed the picture back to Frank. "Was the paper wrong?"

"No," Frank told him, "but I've been tracing her movements in the days before her death. One night, she came here."

Curtis looked surprised. "Here? But the Cyclorama is closed until the restoration is finished. She wouldn't have been able to get in."

"She didn't come into the building," Frank said. "She parked in the lot outside."

Curtis smiled quietly. "Oh, I see. Well, that's not unusual. The park is open to everyone. That's the way it should be." He looked at Frank pointedly. "You, of all people, should know that recently the parks have been taken over by the less wholesome element of the city." He smiled cheerfully. "But now we're taking them back. It's happening all over. New York City. Boston. Everywhere. And in Atlanta, part of that effort involves the restoration of the Cyclorama."

"But she seems to have come here for a reason," Frank said.

"What reason?"

"I don't know," Frank said. He pulled out his notebook. "Are you here at night, Mr. Curtis?"

"Sometimes," Curtis said. "I love this work. It moves back into history."

"How about other people?"

"What other people?"

"The ones you work with?"

"Well, a maintenance crew comes in at around seven, but they're usually gone by nine."

"How about security?"

"Only during the day."

"Why?"

"It's for personal security," Curtis explained, "in case some derelict might try to get in."

"But you're not worried about break-ins at night?" Frank asked.

Curtis smiled. "There's nothing to steal here," he said calmly, "except a vision of human history. And of course, that's not something that can be stolen."

"How about other workers, do they come in at night, the artists you use on your restoration?"

"Sometimes," Curtis said. "They have a key to the rear entrance."

"But all the workers use it?"

"Of course."

Frank wrote it down, then looked up. "She knew this area very well," he said. "And we don't know how she came to know it."

Curtis looked at him closely. "So you don't think the body was simply dumped?" he asked.

"It was dumped," Frank said, "but that doesn't change the fact that she knew this area."

Curtis shook his head slowly. "I wish I could help you, Mr. Clemons."

"Did you ever see a red BMW parked in the lot outside?"

"No," Curtis said, "but that doesn't mean much. I wouldn't have noticed it. I would notice a vintage automobile, something old and with a lot of character. But these new sports cars? No, I wouldn't notice them." His eyes fell back toward Angelica's picture. "Beautiful face," he said softly.

"She didn't always look the way she does in that photograph," Frank told him.

Curtis looked up, puzzled. "What do you mean?"

"She sometimes dressed differently. Sometimes fixed her hair in a completely different way."

"Why?"

"We don't know," Frank said.

Curtis looked at the photograph again. "So sad. One life." He glanced up at Frank. "That's the tragedy. That we have only one life, and it's so short." He smiled solemnly. "That's what I think when I walk through the diorama. All those people, dying." He shook his head mournfully. "When you think of them as a group, the death gets lost. But when you think that each one is losing his or her one and only life, that, Mr. Clemons, is almost too much to bear." He picked up one of the small figurines on his desk and turned it slowly in his hand. It was a Confederate soldier, his gray uniform torn by musket fire, his arms thrust back and frozen in an attitude of sudden and astonished death. "Who was this man? And why did he die like this? That's the real mystery." His eyes shifted over to Frank. "This is my dead body, and I think of it just as you think of that girl's." He placed the figure back on his desk. "I wish

263

I could help you, but I never saw her. That's the hard, dull fact."
He stood up. "I've a lot of work to do now, Mr. Clemons, so, if
you'll—"

"One more thing," Frank said. "Do you know a woman named
Miriam Castle?"

Curtis looked surprised to hear her name. "Yes. Why?"

"She mentioned to me that she sometimes gets work for local
artists."

"Yes, she does."

"Did she get any from you?"

"You mean to work on the restoration?"

"Yes."

"She tried to get some work for Derek Linton," Curtis said, "but
he wouldn't work on the project. It was some objection, something
about how it glorifies war."

"Anyone else?"

"Well, we have about three local artists who are working on the
Cyclorama," Curtis said. "By local, do you mean artists who live
in Atlanta?"

"Yes."

"That would narrow it down to two," Curtis said. "All the rest
are imported."

"But you have two from the city?"

"Yes."

"And did Miriam Castle recommend them?"

Curtis thought about it. "No, I don't think so. She was very keen
on Linton, but I don't think she brought up anyone else for this
particular project."

"These two," Frank said, "who are they?"

Curtis pulled a sheet of paper from his desk. "Everyone who
works on the project is listed here." He handed Frank the paper.
"I hope this helps you."

Frank's eyes moved down the column of names and addresses.
Many were from out of state, specialists brought in from Washington, Boston and New York. Only six were local artists. One lived
in Doraville, one in Marietta, and yet another in Hapeville, a
southern suburb of Atlanta. Two of them lived in the city itself.
And one of these lived on Mercer Place.

Frank looked up from the paper. "Who is Vincent Toffler?"

"He worked mostly on touch-ups," Curtis said.

"Worked? He's not here anymore?"

"His part of the project was finished about a week ago," Curtis said.

"Is this Mercer Place address where he still lives?"

"As far as I know."

Frank wrote the address down in his notebook. "How well do you know him?"

"Not well at all."

"Do you have a picture of him?"

"In his personnel file."

"Would you mind if I took it with me?"

"Not at all," Curtis said. "He's finished here, anyway." He walked to a single, freestanding file cabinet and pulled out a picture of Toffler. It showed a tall, lean young man with curly blond hair. He was dressed in jeans and a flannel shirt. There was a paintbrush in his hand.

"Thanks," Frank said as he pocketed the photograph.

"My pleasure, Mr. Clemons," Curtis said. "Here, let me show you out."

Frank turned his head out toward the front of the building.

"No, no," Curtis said quickly. "We'll use the rear entrance." He took Frank's elbow and tugged him gently to the right.

They went out the side door on the north side of the building. The drop cloths were still piled by the single cement step, and as Frank glanced toward the parking area, he realized that Angelica had parked in an almost direct line of vision from the door.

"If one of your artists were working late," he said to Curtis, "would he use this door to go in and out?"

"Yes," Curtis said, "the front is locked after five." He glanced about the park, then up at the high gray wall of the Cyclorama. "This restoration is going to benefit this whole area of the city," he said.

"It could use it," Frank said, as he started walking toward his car.

"This neighborhood has quite a history, did you know that?" Curtis asked.

Frank shook his head as he walked on.

"Much of it was a burial ground," Curtis said. "We learned that during the excavations."

"What excavations?"

"When the first piping was put in," Curtis said. "That's when certain areas were uncovered. Workmen found a great many bones." He nodded in the general vicinity of Waldo Street. "Especially over there, in the area beyond Boulevard." Curtis' eyes darkened. "The workmen reported it to the police. They weren't archeologists and anthropologists, after all. It was an odd find. So many bones. Human bones." His eyes shifted back to Frank. "All female. All from teenage girls."

Frank began to feel dizzy.

"So rather than an ordinary burial ground," Curtis went on, "we think it was probably a place of sacrifice. There was no evidence of trauma, no fractured skulls, for example. We think their throats were cut."

In his mind, Frank could see the young girls as they flailed about on the ground, bleeding slowly to death. He could feel the blade as it sliced through their long brown throats, and the wave of warm blood as it washed down their naked chests. The high wail that came from them seemed to struggle upward into the air around him.

26

Frank dropped the photograph on Caleb's desk. "His name is Vincent Toffler."

Caleb glanced at the photograph. "Okay." He looked up. "Want to tell me the rest?"

"The night Angelica went for that ride with the Doyle kid, she stopped at the Cyclorama. I always thought she was waiting to see somebody, but I was wrong. I think she was waiting to *be seen* by somebody."

Caleb tapped the picture with his finger. "By this guy?"

"Yes."

"Go ahead."

"After she left the Cyclorama, she headed for this particular street, Mercer Place. She drove up and down it a few times. Again, like she was trying to be seen."

"And this guy lives on Mercer?" Caleb asked.

"Yes," Frank said. "He works at the Cyclorama and he lives on Mercer Place. From where Angelica parked, she could see a little door at the back of the building."

"Slow down, Frank," Caleb said. "Which building?"

"The Cyclorama," Frank went on methodically. "This door is the artists' entrance to the building, the one Toffler would have used either to go in or come out of the building."

Caleb nodded slowly. "So we've got him at Cyclorama and on Mercer Place." He smiled indulgently. "It's good, Frank, but it's circumstantial."

"And one other thing," Frank added, "those galleries Angelica went to near Grant Park, there are three of them on the street. She was seen in two of the three. The one she wasn't seen in has Toffler's work hanging in it."

Caleb scratched his cheek thoughtfully. "It's still circumstantial, but it's worth checking out." He stood up. "It'll be a treat. I haven't seen the Cyclorama in years."

"He's not there anymore," Frank said. "He finished his job there a week ago."

"So it's Mercer Place then," Caleb said wearily.

"Yeah."

Caleb drew in a slow, despairing breath. "Dear God, I hate to go get a guy at home."

They pulled up to the house on Mercer Place a few minutes later. It was a small, wood frame structure that looked as if it had been fully restored. The white, freshly painted exterior gleamed brightly in the late-morning sun, but the interior was utterly dark, and the adjoining driveway was empty.

"I don't see any movement in there," Caleb said as he eyed the front of the house. "Looks like nobody's home."

"We don't have enough for a warrant," Frank said.

Caleb looked at him. "Can you dig up anything else right quick?"

"No."

"Just have to wait till he comes home then."

"We could look around outside," Frank said.

"Okay," Caleb said. "But let's make sure nobody's there before we go poking around in the yard."

The new wooden steps did not creak at all as the two of them walked up on the front porch.

"This guy's really fixed this place up," Caleb said as he took up his position at the left side of the door. He paused a moment, then knocked.

No answer.

He waited a moment, then knocked again.

No one came to the door, and no sounds came from inside the house.

"I think he's gone," Caleb said.

"Yeah."

They walked down the stairs together, then split up, Frank heading around the left side of the house, Caleb around the right. The foundation was low, and as he moved along the side of the house, Frank could easily look through the windows as he passed. The front room was sparsely furnished, but everything was arranged with an eye to neatness, order, a sense of well-used space. There was a plain blue sofa and matching chair, a knotted rug, and a slender wooden rocking chair. Through the dark air of the interior, Frank could see Caleb's large face as it stared into the same room from the other side of the house. He smiled quickly, then pointed to the rear, and the two of them made their way toward the back of the house.

The next window was much smaller and the shade was drawn halfway. It was the bathroom, and Frank moved past it quickly and on to the third window. It was a bit higher from the ground, but he had no trouble seeing over the ledge. It was a neatly arranged kitchen, larger than he had expected, with shelves along the front wall, facing a polished white stove and refrigerator. Again, he could see Caleb's face as it stared at him from the other side of the room. For a moment it seemed to fade slowly, then break apart like a piece of crumbling statuary, and Frank squinted hard to bring it back together.

"Nothing strange around here," Caleb said, as the two rejoined each other in the back yard.

"No," Frank said. "Nothing at all."

"Bedroom's on the other side of the bathroom," Caleb added. "Just a bed, all made up, and a closet with the door open."

"Anything in it?"

"Only what you'd expect. A bunch of clothes."

"So he probably still lives here," Frank said.

"Yeah. That's the one good thing about it."

Frank glanced around the back yard. There was a small building near the back fence. It looked as if it had once been a garage.

"Let's check that out," he said.

It was a small wooden structure and one side had been peeled of its paint, as if someone were stripping it for a new paint job. Shades had been drawn down over the two small windows along either side.

"Shades are open at the house," Caleb said quietly. "Why not here?"

Frank stepped over to the door. He looked at Caleb. "What do you want to do?"

"Step back, Frank," Caleb said without hesitation. Then he raised his leg and slammed it against the door. The whole building shook as the door banged open and slammed against the inner wall.

It was utterly dark inside, and for an instant Frank hesitated to go in. He could feel death like a thick smoke in the air around him, and as he finally stepped into the interior darkness, he felt as if life itself were cracking like dry earth beneath his feet, dissolving into dust.

"Find the light," Caleb said.

Frank moved quickly to one of the small windows and threw open the shade. A shaft of silver light swept into the room.

Caleb opened a second shade, and the air brightened around them, revealing a neatly ordered artist's studio. Several large canvases leaned against the far wall. A sculptor's bench stood in the center of the room, and a plaster model of a naked woman rose from it like a small, half-finished monument. And to the right, blocking one window, but showered with light from another, was an enormous painting. It was of a young woman dressed in a willowy veil. Her sleek white legs were vaguely visible through her clothes, and as Frank's eyes slowly rose, he could see her pale white thighs, then her small rounded breasts, and up along the tapered neck to a face rendered so beautifully that he suddenly realized that he had never seen its true radiance before.

"Angelica," he said wonderingly.

Caleb turned toward the painting. His lips parted softly, but he said nothing.

"She was here," Frank said, almost to himself. "She came here many times."

"Yes," Caleb said.

Frank drew his eyes from the painting. There was a tall wooden armoire next to it. He walked to it and pulled open its double doors. It was full of clothes, the frilly lace and soft velvet, the red satin blouse and the black leather skirt. He could smell the fragrance of Angelica's body on the cloth. It was a soft, subtle musk that struck him as the last sad remnant of her life on earth. He felt his hand reach out to caress the cloth tenderly, then stopped himself and turned to Caleb.

"I'm going to wait for him," he said. "I don't care how long it takes."

"Me, too," Caleb said. He shrugged. "I ain't going no place but the grave."

They walked out of the shed and carefully closed the door behind them. Then they returned to the car and drove it a few yards away, turned around and headed back up the street. There was a narrow alleyway not too far from the house, and they backed just far enough into it so that they could watch the house without being seen.

The bright light of midday slowly turned to gray as the afternoon deepened into night. Far in the distance, they could see a band of storm clouds moving slowly toward the city.

"Going to be another toad-stringer," Caleb said. He looked at his watch. "Been here five hours."

"You can go home if you want to," Frank said.

Caleb shook his head. "Nah, not yet." He shifted uncomfortably in his seat. "It's my ass that's complaining," he said with a smile, "not my old bulldog heart."

An hour later the first sounds of thunder rolled over the city. Jagged streaks of lightning blazed out of the darkness, and a few minutes after that, the rain swept down upon them in thick, wind-blown sheets.

Caleb leaned toward the dashboard and peered toward the house. "Well, we still won't have no trouble seeing him."

"No, we won't."

Caleb leaned back in his seat, and released a long slow sigh. "Retiring next year, Frank, did you know that?"

"No."

"Life's funny. You get too much of one thing, and not enough of something else. Now this stakeout shit, that's something I've had too much of."

Frank's eyes drifted over to the house. "I sometimes think of quitting."

Caleb looked surprised. "You do? How come?"

"Just tired, I guess."

"Of too much blood?"

Frank shook his head. "No, not that. But just that people should live better than they do, Caleb." He looked at his partner. "I don't know what keeps them from it. I'd like to find that out, sometime. I'd like to really *know*."

Suddenly two shafts of yellow light swept down from the small hill at the end of the street. They moved slowly down Mercer, two bars of glowing light that finally came to rest and then flashed off in front of Toffler's house.

Frank pulled out the photograph Curtis had given him and looked at it. Then he handed it to Caleb. "Check it out again, let's don't roust the wrong guy."

Caleb glanced at the picture then back up toward the car. "Get out of the fucking car," he whispered.

Frank pressed his eyes near the windshield and stared out toward the house. The car stood motionlessly in front of it. Then the door opened on the driver's side, and as it did so a flash of bright lightning broke over the street.

"That's him," Frank said.

The man was now standing by the car, the door still open. He looked behind him, then toward the dark house.

Caleb squinted hard. "Yeah, you're right," he said.

The man quickly strode into the front yard, then veered to the left and headed behind the house. For a moment, he disappeared into the covering darkness. Then a light flashed on in the shed out back.

"Good," Caleb said. "No place to hide in that little shack." He picked up the radio. "This is A one zero four. We're checking out a murder suspect. Extent of danger, unknown. Would appreciate backup at one two one Mercer Place. No siren, please. Just be there if we need you." He put down the mike, and smiled. "That puts a lid on it, Frank." He opened the car door. "Let's go."

The door of the shed was wide open, and a wide slant of light swept out of it. From time to time a shadow would flit between the lamp and the sheeting rain, and each time Frank saw it, he felt his breath catch in his throat. As he walked toward the open door, he felt the lightness of his flesh, the weak, uncertain web that held his life. He glanced at Caleb and felt a sudden overwhelming urge to touch his arm and warn him to take care.

Instead, it was Caleb who turned. "Be careful, Frank," he whispered. Then he smiled and walked on.

They stopped at the edge of light, paused for just an instant, then knocked lightly at the door.

"Who's there?"

Frank pulled out his badge and went through the door.

"Police," he said.

The man looked up. He was tall, slender, with blond hair and light blue eyes that gave his face a startling beauty. He was standing by the sculptor's bench, his thumb poised at the statue's throat.

"What do you want?" he asked.

Caleb came up beside Frank. "Just a few questions."

"About what?"

"Are you Vincent Toffler?"

"Yes. Why?"

Frank returned his badge to his coat. "We have a few questions for you." He took out the picture of Angelica Devereaux and held it up. "Do you know this girl?"

The man nodded. "Yes."

Frank took a small, cautious step toward him as he pocketed the photograph. "How did you happen to know her?" he asked.

"She was my subject," the man said matter-of-factly. He pointed to the large painting to his left. "That's her, as you can see."

"How well did you know her, Mr. Toffler?" Frank asked, almost amiably.

"She was my subject."

"You said that."

"Well, that means that I painted her," Toffler said. "She was my model. You can't paint what you don't know."

"So you got to know her fairly well?" Frank asked.

"Yes," Toffler said. He looked at the sculpture. "Do you mind if I continue with this while we talk?"

"Not at all," Frank said. He took another step. "So she was your model."

"Yes," Toffler said indifferently. He pressed his thumb into the statue's upper arm and drew it down smoothly.

"Where did you meet her?" Caleb asked. He walked over to the opposite wall and leaned heavily against it. "From the look of that painting you did, you got to know her better than fairly well."

Toffler glared at Caleb. "That's offensive," he said.

"Why don't you just answer his question?" Frank replied.

"Well, it wasn't exactly that I painted her," he said. "It was more like I painted what she inspired."

"Which was?"

"Desire," Toffler said. "She was the central figure, the creature who made it possible."

"Made what possible?" Frank asked.

"My study."

"Of Angelica?"

Toffler laughed. "Angelica did not merit a study," he said. "No, my portrait of human desire. That's what I wanted to capture. Desire in men and women of all ages. Angelica inspired it in people." He smiled slightly. "She could walk into a room and make everyone in it want her, more than anything they had ever wanted in their lives. That was her gift, that kind of beauty. They wanted to touch her, all of them."

"How do you know that?" Frank asked.

"I could see it in their eyes," Toffler said. He returned to the sculpture, carefully rubbing his thumb across the woman's throat. "It wasn't exactly subtle."

"Where would you see these people?"

"Wherever I sent her," Toffler said. "It was the same kind of

274

reaction no matter where she was. It could be a poolroom or theater, it didn't matter."

"How about an art gallery?" Frank asked.

"Even more," Toffler said. "Even more."

"So you would take her to various places, is that it?" Frank asked.

"Yes."

"And watch the way people reacted to her?"

"Watch their desire, watch the way they hid it," Toffler said. His thumb dug into the clay. "She was made to be watched. That's what I explained to her." He drew his thumb from the clay, then tried to smooth over the wound. "And she understood it, at least for a while. She did it well. People yearned for her. It was more than lust. Angelica inspired a deep, deep longing. That's what I wanted to capture."

"And so you used her?" Frank asked.

"The way I might use a brush, yes," Toffler said. "What's wrong with that?" He looked at Frank evenly. "Nothing should ever come before one's work." He returned his attention to the sculpture. "Besides, she did it all quite willingly."

"All of it?"

Toffler hesitated. "Well, at first."

"But then she stopped?"

"She met this ridiculous old man, a painter."

"Derek Linton?"

"Yes," Toffler said. He didn't seem surprised they knew. "She met him at a gallery. I saw them standing together in front of one of the galleries, so I know it was Linton who did it."

"Did what?"

"Killed her."

Frank took another step toward him. "Derek Linton killed Angelica?"

"Killed her reason for being," Toffler said impatiently. "She was on assignment one day, at one of the galleries. That's when she bumped into Linton. She looked at that mindless idiocy he paints, and was . . . seduced by it." His voice grew thin. "Faded old romantic. Lost in the mists of Innisfree. Ridiculous." He dug his thumbnail into the statue's shoulder and peeled away a small bit of clay. "I saw them together. I knew what she was trying to do."

"And what was that?" Caleb asked, as he edged away from the wall.

"To fuck him, I guess," Toffler said. He turned toward Frank. "What happened to your face?"

"You dressed her up in various ways," Frank said. "And then you set her up in a gallery or some place else, so that people would see her."

"Yes."

"And then you watched the people who watched her?"

Toffler nodded. "It was living art, fantastically successful, perhaps the best work I've ever done." He shook his head. "But then Angelica vulgarized it. She became a disgusting little tease in front of that old man."

"I guess you guys went a few rounds over that, didn't you?" Caleb asked.

Toffler's eyes flashed toward him. "What?"

"You fought," Frank said.

"I fought for my art," Toffler said.

"But Angelica wouldn't give in," Frank said.

"I tried to make her understand," Toffler said, "but she had lost it. Even then, I think I still could have been able to work with her, but then she ruined herself, ruined the whole project."

"By getting pregnant," Frank said.

Toffler nodded. "That was unbearable. She was going to be just another fat, flabby, pregnant teenager." He stared at the portrait of Angelica. "What good would she be after that?"

Frank eased himself forward cautiously, his feet hardly leaving the floor. "And so you killed her," he said.

"No," Toffler said. "Of course not. That would have been ridiculous. In fact, she even had a change of heart. She came back to me. She said she'd gotten a lot of money by telling her guardian that she was pregnant and was going to keep the baby."

"But she wasn't going to do that?" Frank asked.

"Of course not," Toffler said. "She was going to get rid of it. She was going to move to New York and then she was going to get rid of it. I told her that by then it would be too late, if she wanted an abortion, it had to be done now."

"So what did she do?" Frank asked.

"I told her to get rid of the baby," Toffler repeated. "It was as simple as that."

"Did you tell her to use lye?"

"I told her nothing," Toffler said vehemently.

Frank pointed to the small stool which rested at the back of the room. "Did you tell her to sit on that stool? Did you tell her to expose herself? Did you tell her that it wouldn't hurt?"

"No!" Toffler nearly shouted. "That's enough. I've told you everything I know, so will you please just get out!"

Frank braced himself as Caleb stepped over and took Toffler by the arm. "We're not through yet, Mr. Toffler. I think you'll have to come with us."

Toffler glared furiously, as if he was going to resist. Instantly, Frank stepped toward him, and as he did so, Toffler seemed to regain control of himself. "All right," he sighed.

Frank felt himself begin to breathe again. The air seemed to flow around him, warm and infinitely soothing. He heard the rain on the roof again, and he felt that it was over, that Angelica's death would be avenged, that righteousness sometimes did flow down, as his father had always proclaimed, like a mighty, mighty stream.

Then suddenly his eyes flashed down and he saw Toffler's hand as it grabbed the chisel, then flew up into the air and plummeted downward into Caleb's back.

Caleb bolted forward, but the hand pursued him, slamming down again as Frank grabbed for it. He could feel himself stumbling forward, reaching for the hand, but it plunged through his grasp again and he saw it bury itself into Caleb's throat.

"No," Frank shouted, but his voice died in the low, gurgling moan that came from Caleb's mouth as he slumped backward and the chisel fell through the air and slashed his face. Frank could see his own bloody fingers as they grasped desperately for the chisel, but it fell again, this time into Caleb's one open, staring eye, and the groan rose to a high, animal wail, then died away in slow degrees while Frank wrapped his arm around Toffler's neck and squeezed until his arm went numb. The only thing he could feel was Toffler's life flowing out of his body, and he squeezed harder, squeezing it out and out, until someone pulled him backward, and he saw the badge on the patrolman's coat, then the steel blue barrel of the pistol as he pressed it into Toffler's bright, blonde hair, and he could feel his breath again, and hear the rain, but the only voice that came to him was Caleb's, half a moan, half a whisper, *You're safe, Frank*, his last words.

27

Caleb was buried on a bright, sun-drenched day. The heat settled into the small gray stones of the crowded municipal cemetery, and as Frank stood silently beside the open grave, he could feel the thick, stifling air like a pillow pushed down upon his face.

Karen stood beside him, her eyes on the plain brown coffin, her lips tightly sealed. She remained in that same motionless position until the police honor guard had fired its salute, and the last of the mourners had made their way out of the cemetery.

"I can't tell you how sorry I am, Frank," she said finally.

Frank looked at her. "He deserved better than this."

"Yes."

"When something this wrong happens, you ought to be able to appeal it somehow, take it to a higher court."

Karen curled her hand around his and gently tugged him away from the grave.

"I'm leaving tonight," she said.

"I thought so."

"Why?"

"I don't know. A look."

"I'll come back for the trial," Karen said. "I promise you that."

Frank shook his head wearily. "That's between you and the district attorney."

Karen stopped cold and stared at him piercingly. "No, it's between *us*."

"You know how I feel about that."

"I can't stay here, Frank," Karen told him. "There's just no way I could endure it."

"I know," Frank said with a slight smile. "Believe me, I understand." He started to drape his arm over her shoulder, but suddenly Toffler's face rose in his mind, and for an instant he was back in the interrogation room, the two of them facing each other over a splintered brown table.

"Frank?"

"Do you know what Toffler said, Karen?" he asked her. "He said that if we found dirt in her mouth, it was because she was dirt." He shook his head wonderingly. "He is alive to say a thing like that."

Karen pulled herself under his arm. "Don't, Frank. It's over. Everything is over."

But it seemed to Frank that just the opposite was true, that nothing was over. He could still see Toffler's face in his mind, his long hair nearly white under the lamp, his translucent blue eyes, at times languid, at times blazing, but always open, terrible and sleepless, staring out forever.

"They'll get him off on insanity," Frank said, almost to himself. "He'll end up in a state hospital. But he isn't insane. He's just rotten at the very core of himself." He looked at Karen. "The air is always cold around him. He has no appetites. He doesn't care about food or sex, or anything like that. He says he never touched Angelica, never wanted to. I believe him."

"No more, Frank," Karen said pleadingly. "Please, enough of this."

Frank looked at her pointedly. "A person is lost, isn't he, Karen, when he no longer cares about anything pleasurable?"

Karen stepped away from him. "I won't talk about him anymore, Frank," she said firmly. She walked quickly over to her car and got in. "I wanted you to take me to the airport tonight," she said. "But now, I'm not so sure."

Frank tried to smile. "When's your flight?"

"Two in the morning. Everything else was booked up."

"I'll pick you up at home," Frank told her. "Be ready at mid-night."

But first he had some more questions to ask.

"You must be drawn to me," Toffler said quietly, as he took his seat across the table.

Frank peered into his eyes. "Why do you say that?"

Toffler shrugged. "Second day in a row you've come to see me." He folded his arms on the table and leaned forward. "What do you see when you look at me like that?"

"I don't know."

Toffler smiled confidently. "And you never will."

Frank took out his notebook and flipped to the last pages. "It must have taken her a long time to die. Did you enjoy that?"

"I didn't enjoy it. I wasn't there to enjoy it. A thing lives. A thing dies. No one has to be there."

"Thing? Angelica?"

"Whatever she was."

"You never felt anything for her?" Frank asked.

"Felt?" He laughed. "You mean love?"

"I mean anything."

Toffler sat back slightly, and the blue of his eyes suddenly deep-ened to the shade of the gray prison uniform he was wearing. "She could be used. That's what a thing is for." He nodded toward Frank's notebook. "Like that thing there, that little notebook, and that little yellow pencil. Used. Like that." He shrugged. "I wasn't jealous. She could have fucked that old queer until he died, and I wouldn't have cared." His eyes drew together into two small slits. "But she had lost her use. And when you can't use something anymore, then you throw it away."

"And so you just threw her away?" Frank asked.

Toffler shook his head despairingly. "This girl, she means every-thing to you." He smiled. "She liked old men, though. Sick old men. He's probably the only guy she ever fucked."

"You mean Linton?"

"Him, yes."

"They weren't lovers," Frank told him.

Toffler looked at him. "Of course they were."

"You think Derek Linton was the father of Angelica's baby?" Frank asked.

"Who else could it have been?"

"It was a boy she knew. We blood-typed the fetus."

Toffler's eyes drew in, and his lips parted slowly. "So she was wrong," he murmured.

Frank leaned forward. "Angelica?"

Toffler's face stiffened. Nothing Frank could do would get him to say another word.

For two hours after he left Toffler, Frank sat alone in one of the remote corners of Piedmont Park. Something was missing. He had missed something. He could see Toffler's lips as they parted in surprise. *So she was wrong.*

Who? Who was wrong? Angelica was wrong about who the father was? But she'd called Doyle three times on May 15. No, she knew who'd gotten her pregnant. Then what?

He remembered what he'd always been told about a murder. Follow blood or follow money.

He saw the old man in the portrait which hung from the white walls of Karen's foyer. Blood. There was so little left for the Dev-ereauxs. Both parents gone, and after that, Angelica. Devereaux blood had been reduced to a single set of veins.

He set his mind adrift, let blood flow in a steady red stream. Arthur Cummings' face swam into his mind. It was a calm, rea-sonable face. His voice was the same, stable, solid, matter-of-fact. Frank could hear it very clearly: *She's all alone now, Karen. An-gelica's money will go to her, of course.*

Of course it would, Frank thought, for there was no other Devereaux. There was only Karen. Angelica was dead, along with her baby. But Karen? He could not see Karen having anything to do with Angelica's death. He could not. There must be something else.

Desperately, he took out his notebook and went over the details of the case yet another time. There were hundreds of them, separate, isolated. Blood or money, he whispered to himself, as he turned one page after another.

Then suddenly he stopped, his eyes staring at a single note. It was blood, yes. And it was money. But they were both arranged in a different configuration. Money might be gained by murder, but it could also be spent for it. And though blood usually meant kinship, it might also mean passion—sudden, fiery, beyond explanation, and yet to all mankind still the one lost clue.

He was surprised that she answered the door herself.

"Good afternoon, Miss Castle," Frank said.

"Edna has the afternoon off," she explained.

She looked at him solemnly, then closed the door behind her.

"Let's stay out here, if you don't mind," she said. "Did you have any more questions, Mr. Clemons?"

"Yes," Frank said. He took out his notebook. "I suppose you read about the arrest."

"And the man who murdered Angelica?" Miss Castle asked. "Yes, of course."

"Did you know him?"

"What?"

"His name is Toffler. Vincent Toffler. Did you know him?"

Miss Castle sighed. "Yes, I know him. The Atlanta art world is small, Mr. Clemons, you can't help running into such people. A disagreeable person, I always thought, and a bad artist."

Frank glanced down at his notebook. "Yet I've done a little research tonight," he said. "Toffler hung a lot of his paintings in one of the galleries on Hugo Street. It was the only gallery that hung his works."

Miss Castle looked at him steadily.

"You own that gallery, Miss Castle."

Miss Castle said nothing.

Once again, Frank drew his eyes down to his notebook. "I was looking through all my notes," he said. "All the interviews, that sort of thing. Something struck me."

Miss Castle turned away slightly, resting her eyes on the distant stream.

"When we went for that walk, you said something about truth," Frank said. He flipped a page of his notebook. "Right here it is. You said that you were feeling like you were 'full of things.' Then I asked you 'what things?' And you said, 'Truths.' " He looked up at her. "Then you said that even difficult truths could be beautiful."

"Yes," Miss Castle said, without looking at him.

"Something else, too," Frank said. He flipped to another page. "You said that Angelica was trying to inflame people, and that there was a danger in that. You said that a person might get engulfed by the flames."

Miss Castle nodded quickly. "You are very thorough in your notes, Mr. Clemons."

Frank closed the notebook and put it in his pocket. "You believed that they were lovers, Angelica and Derek Linton."

Miss Castle's eyes lowered slightly. "Yes."

"You were close enough to Toffler to know that he knew Angelica," Frank added.

Her eyes stayed closed.

"The gallery on Hugo Street," Frank said. "The one you own. It hung all of Toffler's paintings the morning after Angelica died."

She looked at him now. "That was the greatest pain, I think, having to hang that dreadful man's work on my walls." She turned to Frank. "I have loved Derek Linton all my life. I could endure his lifestyle. I could endure that. His men did not betray me."

"But when you thought it was another woman," Frank said.

"That was unendurable," Miss Castle said. "And I knew that she would destroy him, rob him, in the end, of what little he had left. I couldn't let that happen." She stepped off the porch and walked a little way out toward the stream. For a moment she stopped, stood very still, then turned back toward Frank. "You don't have to worry about my leaving," she said quietly. "I'll be there when you come for me. I've spent my whole life waiting."

It was close to midnight when he pulled up to the house. He'd sent a car for Miss Castle, but had refused to stick around for Brickman's questions. There was one thing left to do, one piece of unfinished business. Standing at Caleb's graveside that day, he had promised he would take care of it, but now, sitting in the car outside the man's house, he wondered if he could go through with it.

And then he thought of Caleb again, of the chisel rising and falling into his neck, his face, of Angelica's abused body lying in its shallow grave, of all the bodies he had seen for so many years and all the faces, battered, bruised, of those not quite dead. And he knew he owed it to them all.

He could see a single light shining in the front room, but he could not see any movement inside. He took a deep breath and, when he thought he'd achieved a certain, vague calm, he got out of the car and walked quickly up to the front door.

It opened just enough from him to see a single, brown eye.

"Yeah?" the man said harshly. "What do you want?"

"Are you Harry Towers?" Frank asked.

"Who wants to know?" the man asked coldly.

"Ollie Quinn," Frank said. He stepped back slightly, then slammed into the door. "And Caleb Stone." Towers' body crashed backward and tumbled over a small wooden table. He scrambled to his feet, and reached for the pistol in his belt.

Frank hit him in the stomach, then jerked him up and punched him twice in the face. Towers staggered backward and fell on his back, moaning loudly. He tried to rise, but Frank fell upon him, grabbed his head in his hands, and pounded it twice against the floor.

Towers groaned again, as his eyes closed, then fluttered open.

Frank tossed the pistol across the room, then grabbed his own.

For a moment, he wanted to press the barrel into Towers' gaping, toothless mouth and pull the trigger. He wanted to see Towers' head explode beneath him, but he saw Karen in the darkness, the rose still in her hand, and heard her voice over his shoulder, whispering Caleb's words: *Not yet*.

Instead, he put the gun beside Towers' head, the barrel pointing toward the floor, and fired. The house shook with the reverberating roar.

"If I ever come here again," he said, "you won't hear a thing."

"You're late," Karen said, as she walked quickly out of the house.

"Sorry," Frank said.

"That's all right. We'll make it. There won't be much traffic at this time of night."

"No," Frank said. He glanced down at the single suitcase she carried in her hand. "That's all you're bringing?"

"I'm having other things shipped up," Karen said.

Frank took the suitcase and tossed it into the backseat of the car. "Well, let's go," he said.

It took a little over a half-hour to reach the airport, and for most of the ride, Frank said nothing. It was as if he had gone to the very brink of what he could feel, and now, there was only heat, night, silence. Perhaps there could be nothing more.

They were already boarding the plane when Frank and Karen reached the gate.

Karen took her suitcase from Frank's hand.

"I'll be back soon," she said.

Frank nodded silently.

"I really will," Karen insisted. "I promise."

"Good-bye, Karen," Frank said softly. Then he kissed her.

She disappeared into the crowd of passengers more quickly than he could have imagined, and he sat down in one of the bright red chairs and watched the lights of the plane as it waited for clearance beyond the enormous window. In his mind, he could see her as she settled into her seat, fastened on her seat belt, then lifted her eyes toward the front of the plane and thought, he knew, of him. He saw her once again as she had first appeared to him, somber in her artist's smock, her dark eyes full of things that were immense and unsayable, and it struck him that this deep, abiding gravity was the badge she carried with her all the time, and that others possessed it, too, a way of looking into the heart of the general misfortune. He drew out his gold shield and stared at it for a moment. It belonged to Atlanta, but he knew now that he could take it anywhere.

The ticket agent looked up slowly as Frank approached the booth.

"May I help you, sir?"

"Is it too late to get on the flight to New York?"

"No."

"Then I'd like to go," Frank said. "One way."

The agent made out the ticket and handed it to him, glancing curiously at Frank's face. "What happened to you?" he asked.

For once, Frank realized, he had an answer that seemed right.

"A woman," he said. Then he walked onto the plane.